MW01716361

THE STARLING

Wings of the West Book 8

KRISTY MCCAFFREY

The Starling

Cover: Earthly Charms

Editor: Grammar Chick

Proofreader: Diane Garland

Author Photo: Hannah McCaffrey

E-book ISBN-13: 978-1-952801-20-4

Print ISBN-13: 978-1-952801–21-1

https://kmccaffrey.com/

kristy@kmccaffrey.com

BOOKS BY KRISTY MCCAFFREY

Wings of the West Series

The Wren

The Dove

The Sparrow

The Blackbird

The Bluebird

The Songbird (Novella)

Echo of the Plains (Short Story)

The Starling

The Canary

The Nighthawk

The Swan (Coming Soon)

Stand-Alone Novel

Into The Land Of Shadows

Short Story Collections

The Crow Brothers Collection

The West: A Romance Collection

Long Novellas

Alice: Bride of Rhode Island

Rosemary

Blue Sage

The Peppermint Tree

A Mirthful Wish

Contemporary Adventure Romances

Deep Blue

Cold Horizon

Ancient Winds

Sapphire Waves

Praise for the Wings of the West series

The Wren

"...McCaffrey's mastery of setting and historic details gives this western gritty realism." ~ Romantic Times BOOKclub

"I am a true historical western fan so this book was really an exceptional read for me. Don't miss...what is sure to be a great series to follow." ~ The Romance Studio

"Handsome, rugged heroes, strong heroines and a super storyline make THE WREN a keeper." ~ The Best Reviews

The Dove

"...glorious descriptions of the Sangre de Cristo Mountains, Las Vegas of the late 1800's, and the Ryan homestead. This reviewer felt herself transported to the very locales being described." ~ Love Romances

"Ms. McCaffrey writes from the heart...a definite must read." ~ The Romance Studio

"If you are a lover of western romances, I'd recommend reading this one." ~ Romance Junkies

The Sparrow

"Readers will love the story..." ~ RT BookReviews

"I...commend McCaffrey for the historical accuracy of her stories...a phenomenal read that I'd recommend to anyone who enjoys historical romance, with a hint of the other." ~ Jonel Boyko, Reviewer

"Ancient Hopi and Havasupai legends have a new voice in McCaffrey. Her inspired writing made her main character's mystical journey into another realm entirely believable and kept the pages turning long into the night." ~ City Sun Times

The Blackbird

"With dastardly villains, plenty of action, a strong heroine, surprising twists and turns, and a sexy cowboy, all underlined by a sensual love story, this historical western romance has something for everyone." ~ Janna Shay, InD'tale Magazine

"A steamy, intelligent historical fiction set in the Arizona desert where the harsh environment matches the characters who populate it. Can two wounded souls find each other and flourish? Find out in Kristy McCaffrey's hard to put down, fourth book in the *Wings of the West* series, *The Blackbird*." ~ Chanticleer Book Reviews

The Bluebird

"The reader will find themselves often sitting on the edge of their seats...a quick and exciting read!" ~ Belinda Wilson, InD'tale Magazine

"...a fast paced read with a depth to the characters and the story that kept my interest from the first page to the last..." ~ Jo, Romance Junkies

"...packed with adventure and action that left me breathless...quite unable to put it down!" ~ Maia, The Silver Dagger Scriptorium

To persevering,
especially during the hard times.

CHAPTER 1

Trinidad, Colorado
May 1899

Kate Ryan shifted on the hard seat of the buckboard as it rattled along the road. The setting sun cast rays of light from its western position, blossoming like a flower.

"Why didn't your husband pick you up and take you to this party?" The question broke the spell of her anxious anticipation. The driver, a burly older man the Pinkerton Agency had hired at the last minute, glanced at her.

"I've arrived a day early and didn't have the opportunity to send word to Hen—" She caught herself at the last second. "To Gilbert." *My husband's name is Gilbert.* She repeated the mantra a few more times, trying to drill it into her brain. Henry Maguire was the man playing her husband. She was getting the break of a lifetime—the ability to work as a full agent on a case at only nineteen years old—and she didn't want to spoil it by ruining the other agent's cover.

"It's a surprise," she added in a rush.

"Huh."

Kate frowned, uncertainty fluttering in her chest. "You don't think this is a good idea?" Her heart sped along with a steady rat-a-tat-tat, her palms clammy, and her mouth tasting like cotton balls, offering little help in wetting her dry lips.

Her nerves were stretched to the brink.

"He don't know you're coming, and he's at the Wingate's party without you? It's just ...." He pulled on the reins, guiding the team around a bend in the road, and cast a sympathetic look her way. "You seem like a nice young woman. I just don't want you to be disappointed ... or have your feelings hurt."

For a moment, Kate was at a loss as to what he meant, and then it walloped her over the head like her brother, Eli, sometimes did when the two of them argued. Not an actual wallop but a verbal harangue. Kate, however, had always held her ground with her older sibling. And she would need to do so now.

The man was implying her husband was a philanderer. Of all the circumstances she had anticipated dealing with, this one honestly hadn't crossed her mind. Mostly, she supposed, because this wasn't a real marriage. It probably was true that Henry had a woman somewhere, although she knew from the Pinkerton office that he wasn't married. Well, this driver wouldn't rattle her. She had a job to do. And part of that job was to be Henry's loving wife as well as his partner on the job. She could do it. She *would* do it.

"I'm sure it will be fine. I know my Gilbert, and he would never be anything but a gentleman. He was expecting me tomorrow. I'm just a day early. He left me a note at the house as to where he would be this evening," she added, warming to the prevarications spilling from her mouth.

"So he knew you were coming? But you said he didn't."

"Well, I, ah." She cleared her throat. "He wasn't certain when I was to arrive. I was visiting my mother. She's very ill, you see. I had told him I might arrive tonight, or tomorrow. I told him to go to the party and not to wait for me." *Stop talking, Kate.* She folded her gloved hands onto her lap and glanced at the countryside, dense pine trees standing vigil in the fading light. Lying was going to prove a challenge for her.

Her mentor at the agency, Louise Foster, who had single-handedly gotten Kate this assignment, had told her during her training to keep the mistruths to a minimum. It would make it easier to remember them.

"Well, then," the driver said. "I'm sure it will be fine. Your Gilbert will be mighty happy to see you."

They crossed beneath a large wrought iron arch and entered a massive ranch. It hadn't been a long journey from the cabin where she and Henry would be staying together as husband and wife, but her bottom was sore from the buckboard. She would have been much happier on her own horse, but Edgar Jones, her boss, had insisted she not enter the fray alone. He embraced working with female agents on his payroll, but he was careful with their safety as well.

Mr. Jones had sent word to Henry via a courier that she was arriving, but it hadn't been clear whether the message had been received. It had contained Louise's suggestion that Kate attend the party. Louise had argued with Jones from her hospital bed that Henry was sometimes too stubborn in wanting to work alone and that if they didn't force Kate upon him, he might keep her away from the investigation. Kate had been uncomfortably present for that exchange, leading her to wonder if Henry were a good agent after all, but underlying the discussion was a genuine tone of concern in both Jones and Louise's voices.

However, now that Kate was here, the bigger problem presented itself—Henry was expecting Louise as his "wife" partner, not Kate. In fact, Kate had never met Henry, so of course he wouldn't know who she was when she arrived.

Hence her anxiety.

In the distance, the lights of the main house blazed, growing brighter as they neared. The front area was crowded with buggies, horses, and carriages. Her driver was forced to stop some distance from the front porch.

He set the brake, climbed down, and came to Kate's side. She gathered the full folds of her royal blue gown, quite the fanciest thing she had ever worn. The Rocking Wren, her folks' ranch, rarely required this level of poshness. She clasped the driver's hand and stepped down.

She confirmed she had her reticule looped around a wrist and then patted her brown hair, pinned into a fancy upsweep. She had to trust she looked presentable considering that she'd had to dress behind the cabin because it had been locked and she hadn't had a key.

She turned to the driver. "I'm so sorry, but I didn't get your name."

"Francis, ma'am. It was a pleasure, Mrs. Gilbert ...." He raised a bushy brow in question.

"Holmes. And please, call me Sallie." She was immensely proud that she had gotten her alias correct, although she had no doubt that this was the smallest of tests she was about to endure. Still, she must take every victory she could get.

"Shall I wait for you, Sallie?" Francis asked, his gaze filled with genuine concern. Kate felt badly for having thought him a bit strange when she'd found him waiting for her in front of the cabin. He'd been inspecting the front steps and frowning, and for some reason she'd found his behavior peculiar.

"No, of course not. My husband will see me home." She hoped.

Francis donned his hat, giving a nod and a tug on the brim. "It was a pleasure to make your acquaintance."

"Perhaps I'll see you again, Mr. Francis ...." She leaned forward and raised a brow.

He chuckled. "O'Malley. I'm new to town, but I run the livery and the blacksmith. If you need a horse shod, you give me a holler. I'll do it for free. It's the least I can do."

As she started to turn to leave, he added, "And watch yourself in there."

She looked over her shoulder at him. He really was a nice man, and her first point of contact on this job. A tinge of embarrassment came over her from their awkward first meeting.

"Mrs. Wingate, she can be a little ... too much. Don't let her scare you. People like her sense fear and they pounce. Someone like you don't deserve that. If you ever have any trouble and your husband isn't doing his job, you come see me, you hear?"

Kate relaxed her shoulders, feeling the genuine concern emanating from Francis. "Thank you. I appreciate it. I truly do."

She left him and made her way to the entrance of the grand home, feeling as if every step were taking her into the lion's den. But she wouldn't be afraid. She had wanted to have a career in law enforcement since she had turned sixteen. It was why she had pursued employment with the Pinkerton National Detective Agency, one of the only places that allowed women—and especially young women—to have a chance to do important work.

The front entrance was open and attended by a butler. Kate took a deep breath and crossed the threshold.

HENRY SCANNED the bustling ballroom filled with partygoers chattering away—men in suits and women in gowns awash with color. Everyone loved a good Wingate extravaganza, or at least that's what Henry had learned in the past week of undercover work.

His gaze rested briefly on Arthur Wingate, his target in this investigation. The man was tall, making it easy to find him in a crowd, his gray-streaked black hair slicked back. He was holding court with three men. While he didn't recognize the two on the left, Henry knew the other one was William Phelps, a manager at the First National Bank of Trinidad.

And it was odd because it had been the bank that had contracted the Pinkertons for this job in the first place. They had hired the agency to investigate possible money counterfeiting and insurance fraud, and Henry was certain that Wingate was at the center. All he had to do was prove it. But he was also certain that Phelps wasn't included in any of the communications with Henry's boss, Edgar Jones, back at his temporary headquarters in Albuquerque. Jonesy would have told him.

But Henry also had a secondary reason for being here, one he hadn't shared with his boss, despite that he and Jonesy were more than employer and employee. They were friends, too. But Henry didn't want Jonesy and the agency implicated if things went south. Henry's father, Hugh Maguire, had died in Trinidad eight years ago. The official story: he'd fallen down a mine shaft, and it had been ruled an accident. But Henry had reason to believe that hadn't been the case.

And at the center of it all was Arthur Wingate.

Henry was here to prove that Wingate was not only a criminal, but a murderer as well.

His brother's voice echoed in Henry's head. "There was an investigation, Henry," Ian had said, "and no foul play was found." He and his older brother often failed to see eye-to-eye, hence Henry had told no one his true reason for being here, least of all Ian.

He took a sip of his brandy ... barely. He had no intention of clouding his judgment with alcohol this evening.

"Sir." A valet drew his attention.

Henry nodded his acknowledgement.

"Your wife has arrived, sir."

My wife ....

What the hell? Louise was here? Now?

Jonesy had agreed that Louise Foster would be summoned when Henry sent word. And he hadn't sent word. Dammit.

"Of course," Henry replied. "Thank you."

"Please follow me, sir."

Henry thought of abandoning the drink he'd been nursing for the last hour, but instead kept it as he followed the valet through clusters of people and the low din of talking and laughing. In fact, he took a large gulp as he walked to soothe his nerves. Sometimes his own rules needed to be amended. This wasn't a disaster, he reminded himself. Louise was a good field agent, one he'd worked with more than once, and he respected her abilities. She was also his friend, one of the very few along with Jonesy. If she were here now, there must be a good reason. While his cover had included a wife, Henry rather liked working alone, and he'd told Jonesy that Louise could join him when it seemed necessary. And it hadn't been necessary ... yet. But apparently Edgar Jones had pulled rank, thinking differently.

As Henry entered the foyer, his gaze landed on a young woman in a stunning blue gown, curls of dark brown hair accenting her oval face, her figure lithe and youthful. Her reserved countenance indicated her discomfort as she conversed with Arthur's wife, Lottie, near the front entrance, and Henry couldn't help but feel sympathy for her. Lottie Wingate had been mostly unwelcoming to him.

The young woman's poise drew his eye and for a moment, Henry considered what it would be like if he weren't working, if he could simply pursue a conversation with an attractive woman. He had purposely not set down roots. His work made it impossible. Well, not impossible. He'd simply never met a woman who could turn his attention from his job.

And hell if that didn't remind him that he was more like his old man every day.

He pushed aside the memories of the last time he'd seen his father, of the terrible fight they'd had, of the anger that had pulsed white hot within Henry.

Instead, he focused once more on the alluring distraction of the woman in blue, and then, reluctantly, he peeled his eyes from her and searched the foyer for Louise, but she was nowhere to be seen.

"She must have stepped into another room," Henry said to the valet.

"No, sir." The young man stopped and gave a nod toward Mrs. Wingate and the striking woman beside her.

Henry endured a brief state of confusion, an unnatural occurrence since he kept everything in his life compartmentalized and in order.

Recovering quickly, he said, "Of course, thank you. I must need my spectacles this evening." He left the valet before he was forced to converse further, giving even more opportunities for a slip up. He walked slowly to the two women, since he wasn't certain what he should say. Clearly, the valet had been misinformed.

Henry glanced over his shoulder, confirming the man had left the foyer. With the all-clear, Henry shifted his path to miss the two conversing women, although a twinge of regret flared. A small part of him wondered what would happen if he struck up a conversation with the woman who drew his gaze with such ease. But now wasn't the time for personal interests. Just as he passed within three feet of the women, a voice rang out, "Gilbert! Darling!"

Henry stopped and faced the woman who had in a brief span sparked such an intense interest in him. She'd used his alias. It all became clear in an instant.

She was his wife.

Hell.

He plastered the biggest smile he could on his face. "Sallie, there you are." He went to her and planted a kiss on her cheek, the softness branding his lips while the scent of honeysuckle surrounded him, warm and fruity.

His Sallie blushed, her cheeks a bright crimson, heightening her beauty and adding to his frustration.

He kept his expression amiable and besotted, playing the part of a happy and surprised husband, and said, "I had no idea you were coming." But beneath it all, anger threatened to uncoil in his chest.

He took some measure of pleasure when his new wife flinched ever so slightly, no doubt catching the flash of censure he allowed to escape his gaze. He could accept her as his wife, but it didn't mean he had to like it, whether she was compelling or not.

But still, where the blazes was Louise? Why had Jonesy sent this much too young of a woman with whom he had no acquaintance and could therefore not assess her skills as an agent? To make it all worse, his pulse had quickened as soon as he'd looked into her clear green eyes. She might be young, but a spark of intelligence snapped across the distance between them.

"It was last minute, darling," she replied, her voice tinged with excitement.

It was too late to turn back now. They had an audience with Lottie Wingate, who watched them intently. He couldn't afford to cast any suspicion upon himself. He'd managed to ingratiate himself with Arthur Wingate, posing as a writer hired to pen the man's life story, but Lottie had been cold from the start.

"I'm thrilled you're here," he said, taking Sallie's hand. He turned his attention to the older woman. "If you'll excuse us, I'd like to have a word in private with my beautiful bride."

"Certainly," Lottie said, her gaze speculative. She was a striking woman with fair skin and red hair that had yet to succumb to graying. "It was lovely to meet you, Sallie. I hope we'll have a chance to speak more. And you'll have to accompany Gilbert the next time he comes here." Henry didn't miss the hard flash in her gaze. Lottie hadn't liked him from the moment he'd arrived and the feeling was mutual. "We could have tea while the men discuss business."

"I'd like that," Sallie said.

Having abandoned his drink on a side table, Henry tucked Sallie's gloved hand into the crook of his elbow and led her into the next room. He wanted to speak privately but, in a flash, knew this would be impossible. It was too risky to engage in any kind of conversation beyond the benign while they were at this party.

"Would you like a drink?" he asked quietly. He could use another one.

Sallie smiled and nodded, sliding a quick glance at him, and then letting her eyes roam the room.

They found a waiter and his wife's gloved hand soon held a sherry and Henry's a whiskey, straight up. He drank it in one swallow. His wife narrowed her eyes, the first sign of some backbone in the woman.

"I know my arrival is unexpected, Gilbert," she murmured over the rim of her sherry glass, taking a sip. "But rest assured, I'm here to stay. You're not alone any longer."

CHAPTER 2

Kate used the glass of sherry as a shield. It was obvious undercover agent Henry Maguire was stunned to see her and less than happy with her presence. Luckily, she had known who to look for from a photograph Mr. Jones had given her, although it hardly did justice to the man before her.

Henry Maguire had presence. There was simply no other word for it.

His intense blue eyes accented the hard line of his jaw like the frozen slopes of Colorado where her cousin Molly Rose had lived. Kate couldn't help but notice his clean-shaven face and the citrusy smell coming from him. It was pleasant in a way that unsettled her, and she was entirely uncertain why.

But she had been warned ... Henry was expecting Louise Foster, and he would have no idea who Kate was. It was unfortunate that Mrs. Wingate had caught Kate right at the door and had started speaking with her, because it had made contacting her "husband" fraught with danger.

But it was over. Henry had accepted the charade, and they were now working together. He had said he wanted to speak privately, but as yet he hadn't, so Kate could only conclude it wasn't safe to do so while at the party. She vowed she wouldn't break protocol. She wouldn't say anything to Henry that his loving wife, who had been separated from him for nearly two months, wouldn't say.

"When did you arrive?" Henry asked.

"Earlier this evening."

"How did you get here?"

"A man named Francis O'Malley brought me. I hired him." The Pinkertons had hired him, but she couldn't say that aloud. "I believe he's a blacksmith in town, and he runs a livery too. He offered to stay, but I assured him that you would be here and see me home." Her lips stretched into a smile, but she couldn't hold Henry's gaze as he watched her rather intently, so she took in the room.

It was quite festive. The Wingate wealth was on grand display with sparkling crystal chandeliers hanging from tin ceilings, a tiled floor covered in ornate rugs, and stuffed chairs likely imported from Europe.

As she brought her attention back to her "husband" she caught him still staring at her, those ice-blue eyes holding her briefly spellbound. He must have been watching her the entire time she had scanned the room. She shifted, feeling a bit uncomfortable, wanting to clear the air more than anything.

Had she done something wrong? Was she dressed inappropriately?

But a second glance around the room revealed that while her gown might not be quite as fancy as the many ladies in attendance, it was good enough. It had been Louise's dress, after all, and Kate had to believe her mentor had been very prepared to enter this operation as Henry's wife.

That was it. Henry was upset about Louise.

She turned to him. "I'm sure you're worried about my dear sister, Louise."

He regarded her with interest. "I am," he replied in a measured tone. "Is she well?"

"Unfortunately, no. She's indisposed at the moment, but she should be better soon."

Henry accepted the news with a nod, his gaze conveying a glimmer of concern. Suddenly, Kate felt terrible. It had been clear from Louise that she valued Henry's expertise, as well as his friendship, but Kate hadn't thought any further than that.

The additional assignment that Louise had given Kate—privately and outside the dictates of the job—now seemed to take a different tone. Louise had asked Kate to keep an eye on Henry because eight years ago his father had died in an accident in Trinidad, apparently falling to his death down a mine shaft. Kate had inferred that Louise considered Henry compromised, and that it could place him at odds with the job the Pinkertons had been sent to do.

But now the worry in Henry's eyes, however brief, said something else. Did he and Louise have a relationship that extended beyond business associates? Is that what his irritation was about? Did Henry love her? And why did that thought cause another ripple of unease in Kate?

Ignoring it, she added, "She'll be all right. You've no need to worry. The bullet missed all vital organs."

His eyes flicked back to her, reflecting shock.

Oh, no. He did love her.

His flat, controlled expression was slowly being transformed into raised brows and ever so slightly widened eyes. "She was shot?" he asked, so quietly that his mouth hardly moved.

She brought the sherry glass to her lips and uttered in a low voice from the side of her mouth, "Barely."

She met his gaze again, and he held it for a long moment. Finally, he gave another nod, and it seemed to Kate that the gesture indicated a kind of acceptance on his part of the circumstances they were now in.

"Gilbert," an older gentleman boomed as he approached them.

"Lottie told me your wife was here." The man turned to Kate and took her hand, dropping a kiss on her knuckle, still gloved thankfully. "You never told us she was such a beauty."

"Sallie," Henry said, emphasizing her name. "I'd like you to meet Arthur Wingate. This is his gala."

"It's a pleasure to meet you, sir," Kate replied. "Your home is beautiful."

"Thank you," Wingate said, smiling. He was an imposing man with a confident air, but the flash of admiration in his eyes when he looked at her left Kate uncomfortable. Maybe even nauseated, but it was hard to say since her nerves were stretched to the limit this evening.

As she gently pulled her hand from his grasp, contact he had drawn out a bit longer than necessary, Henry reached out and completed the task for her, tucking her fingers into his elbow once again. The gesture reassured her, and she leaned into her "husband" ever so slightly, still holding the sherry in her left hand.

Kate had been briefed during her preparation for the job, but it had been speedy indeed. Louise had been incapacitated only two days earlier, and Kate had been brought in to replace her at the last minute.

What she knew: Arthur Wingate was a businessman with a controlling interest in several coal mines in the area. He had moved here in 1876 supposedly to be near his father, Ellis Wingate, who had a modest homestead nearby. But Arthur was flashy and bold with his wealth, causing an estrangement with his father, although nothing more was known. Ellis Wingate had died over nine years ago. It was reported that Arthur had his hand in many investments: exporting iron and steel machinery, with it mostly being engines, electrical machines, but also printing presses.

And now the First National Bank of Trinidad had reason to suspect that Wingate might have committed insurance fraud. It was also believed that a counterfeiting ring was active in the area. Could it involve Wingate? Was producing printing presses a cover for machines that could print U.S. currency? It seemed preposterous on the surface. The man had more than enough wealth if the preliminary investigation were true, so why would he commit a crime to gain more? But the bank had hired the agency to find evidence, and now it was Kate's job to assist Henry in the investigation.

"How does our fair town compare to Italy?" Mr. Wingate asked her.

She snapped her attention back to him. "Pardon me?"

"Henry told us that earlier this year you both traveled to Milan for a writing assignment he had. I have to admit, it's one city Lottie and I have yet to see. Should I take her?"

"Of course," Kate replied, trying not falter. She had never been to Milan and sincerely hoped that Wingate wouldn't pursue this much further.

Nervous, she withdrew her right hand from Henry and shifted the sherry to it. In response, Henry stepped closer and rested a hand at the small of her back, sending a sharp tingle along her spine. It was supportive, which she appreciated, but also disconcerting because Henry's presence was fast becoming a distraction for all the wrong reasons.

God help her. She was finding herself drawn to her husband.

Of all the ...

Unbidden, an image of Henry and Louise flashed through Kate's mind, annoying her. But truthfully, now that Kate thought of it, there had never been a moment when Louise had appeared starry-eyed over Henry. Was his attachment to Miss Foster one-sided? From what little Kate knew of Henry Maguire, the thought of him pining for a woman who didn't return his affection seemed a stretch.

"I think Sallie's favorite thing to do was visiting the Milan Cathedral," Henry said. "Right, darling?"

"Yes. The architecture is breathtaking. I'm certain Mrs. Wingate would have a lovely time if you were to take her."

Wingate nodded. "Then it's settled. Now I must entice my wife. She quite likes all her projects and art charities, so it can be difficult to convince her to travel with me."

"I'm sure you can be quite persuasive," Kate added. Henry's hand had remained at her back. She swallowed the last of her sherry and allowed a waiter to take her empty glass. Feeling a bit overheated, she removed first one glove and then the other. They had come only to her wrists, so weren't bulky, but her reticule was small, and it would be a challenge to stuff them inside. She resigned herself to holding them when Henry's hand brushed hers.

"Let me hold those for you." He placed them in the interior pocket of his jacket.

A woman in a peach-colored gown and coiffed blond hair suddenly appeared beside Wingate. "And who is this?" she asked, her attention fixated on Kate.

An urge to escape overtook Kate, but she remained beside Henry, who said, "This is my wife, Sallie. Dearest, this is Delia Wingate, Arthur's niece."

"Pleased to meet you," Kate said, but she didn't miss the slight pinch of Miss Wingate's delicate brows as she returned a half-hearted smile.

"Delighted to finally meet Gilbert's long-absent wife."

Kate's mind blanked and she couldn't think of a response. Instead, she was reeling from the possessive aura emanating from this woman, and it was surely directed at Henry. She had to swing her thoughts from his possible involvement with Louise to now considering that he was in a romantic entanglement with this Delia. Kate didn't have extensive knowledge of romance with the opposite sex, but Delia wasn't bothering to hide her displeasure.

Kate straightened her shoulders. If she were truly Henry's wife, then she wouldn't tolerate this behavior. "Well, I'm here now," she said. Henry had removed his hand from her when he'd taken her gloves, so Kate reached over and clasped his bicep, leaning against him. "I'll be sure to keep him well-occupied, so you all don't have to entertain him."

Wingate laughed, but Delia's cordial smile slipped a notch.

Kate's gaze was drawn to an older woman standing across the room, just visible over Delia's shoulder. The tight curls of her black hair were frosted with white, and she was so short that her neck was craned back to speak with her companion.

It couldn't be.

As alarm filled her, Wingate started talking again. Kate pretended to listen while she stole more furtive glances.

Her heart sank.

The woman across the room was acquainted with Kate's grandparents. She even had been to their home—the SR Ranch—once. What was her name? Ethel? Edna? Estelle. That was it. Mrs. Estelle Marsh.

Kate's mind scrambled to find a solution. *The food table in the other room.* Reluctantly, she released Henry and turned to the woman who was clearly her nemesis. "Miss Wingate, I haven't had anything to eat all day. Would you mind showing me where I might get some refreshment?"

Delia's demeanor was less than warm, so Kate reached over and pulled the woman to her, locking arms. "I so look forward to us becoming friends." She looked back at Henry, who watched her with intense speculation. "I'll find you later, Gilbert," she added.

With Delia between her and Mrs. Marsh, Kate was able to leave the room without being detected. Delia nodded at guests, but Kate kept them moving.

"You must be very famished," Delia said.

"Completely."

They entered a large dining room with a long table filled with a variety of finger foods. In truth, Kate *was* hungry. She released Delia, picked up a plate, and began helping herself.

"How is it that you came tonight? Gilbert never mentioned you were coming." Delia's composure had shifted to one of confidence, or had Kate misinterpreted the woman's irritation earlier? Perhaps she was wrong about Delia. And Henry.

Kate popped something sweet and flaky into her mouth. The food was amazing, and she *had* skipped supper so that she could make it to the party. "I wanted to surprise him," she said around her mouthful. It was basically the truth.

The preparations that Mr. Jones—and the Pinkerton Agency—had made for her had entailed transporting her to the small cabin where Henry lived on Wingate land. It had been Louise's idea for Kate to make an entrance at the party.

Kate plucked a meat cake from a large silver platter, took a bite, and once the flavor melted across her tongue, she placed two more on her plate.

She was beginning to think that Louise either didn't like Henry —which she was certain wasn't true—or else the woman had a wicked sense of humor. It was clear Kate's presence here had thrown Henry off-kilter.

"It'll do him good if you show up unannounced," Louise had said. "He won't be able to hide you. The community will know you've arrived. Henry thinks himself invincible, but agents shouldn't work alone."

Would Henry have really locked her up in his little cabin if she hadn't arrived in full view of the guests this evening? Kate found that unlikely. Besides, Henry couldn't command her in that fashion. Not only was he *not* her husband, he also wasn't her boss. Louise had made that clear as well. Henry was a senior agent and therefore carried more experience, but Kate was given free license to pursue leads as she saw fit.

Kate finished her circle of the long table having piled her plate with every form of hors d'oeuvre available and stopped before Delia who sipped a glass of champagne. Kate considered switching to the same drink, if only to indulge the novelty of it, but there was no need to overdo it. She was better off with a ginger ale or a sarsaparilla, or even a Hiawatha mineral water.

"Do you live here with your aunt and uncle?" Kate asked.

"Yes. I never knew my mother and my father is away much of the time, so they've raised me."

Kate gave a nod since her mouth was full. As soon as she swallowed, she said, "My mother has been ill, which is why I was unable to join Gilbert sooner." She warmed to the lie she had told Francis earlier. Henry's cover story regarding his absent wife entailed her spending time with her family. Kate had simply decided to take it a step further, because one look at Henry's handsome face, and she knew she needed a compelling reason why she would be separated from her dashing husband for such a length of time.

"I'm sorry to hear that," Delia said. "Gilbert never mentioned it, I'm afraid."

The use of Henry's *alias* first name on Delia's lips set Kate's teeth on edge, ruining her appetite, but only for a moment, thankfully. She consumed what remained on her plate, trying to get her annoyance under control. An agent needed to be cool under pressure, not emotional. If for some reason Henry were romancing this woman—which would be dangerous and foolhardy on his part—then he obviously had a reason. Kate assessed Delia again. Perhaps she should try to befriend the woman.

"I hope your mother is doing better," Delia added.

"She is. Thank you for your good wishes." Making a quick decision, she leaned close to Miss Wingate and added, "Might I confide in you?"

"Of course," Delia replied coolly.

"My marriage to Gilbert is a bit rocky."

"Oh." The woman's blue eyes flashed with calculation. "I see."

"We've been spending time apart. It just seemed to be for the best. But I've come to try and make amends, at my mother's urging. You can't give up on love when you hit the first bump in the road, can you?"

"I would imagine not." Delia's brow marred in what Kate could only construe as guilty confusion.

Mrs. Marsh entered the room, jolting Kate out of her play-acting. She brought her napkin to her mouth and plastered the delicate cloth over the bottom half of her face, trying to conceal herself. When Mrs. Marsh walked toward them, Kate tossed the napkin to the floor and bent over to retrieve it, remaining in the position until she saw the whoosh of Mrs. Marsh's maroon skirts move past her.

Standing again, she said, "I'm parched now. Shall we go back to the ballroom and get a drink?"

Delia agreed and Kate hustled to leave the dining room, not looking back lest Mrs. Marsh catch sight of her face. The sooner she left this party, the better.

CHAPTER 3

Henry rode his horse in the darkness, his wife astride a borrowed mare from the Wingates. He hadn't brought a carriage because he'd come to the party alone. And Wingate didn't have any buggies to spare as he had loaned out what he had to several other guests. But the woman portraying his wife sat tall in the saddle, clearly at home on the animal, and hadn't uttered one complaint about her dress being ruined or the discomfort. She had embraced the situation and happily befriended the animal before climbing atop her.

The stable hand had offered a side saddle, but she had chosen a regular one, so now her skirt and petticoats were bunched up around her knees. That didn't seem to bother her either. Henry would have taken this opportunity to learn the details about her arrival and why the agency had sent her without his knowledge except that they had company. Three gentlemen rode behind them, their path back to town coinciding with Henry and his "wife," so he'd been forced into silence. Even when they came to a crossroads and the men took their leave in an opposite direction, Henry held his tongue.

Although he had no reason to suspect a spy following or an

errant person hiding in the underbrush who might overhear them, it seemed prudent to have the discussion he and this woman needed to have in the privacy of his home. *Their* home.

Whether he approved of her working with him or not, their fate was already sealed. Her arrival at the party had guaranteed that, and Henry couldn't turn the tables now.

Why had she suddenly appeared at the party? Had Jonesy had a particular reason for that?

Louise. It had to be her, which in a small way made him feel better about her situation. A knot of worry had taken residence in his gut when "Sallie" had told him that Louise had been shot. Louise had always been a bit reckless. He had to hope she would recover from whatever she'd gotten herself into.

The appearance of this agent as his wife, catching him off-guard in such a public setting, had Louise's fingerprints all over it. He could just imagine her happy chuckle over his discomfort. It was that fact that made him a feel a little more tolerant of the girl beside him. If Louise had given her stamp of approval, then "Sallie Holmes" must be capable.

"It's a lovely night," she said. "Thankfully not too cold for May."

He gave a silent acknowledgment, glancing at her profile, and his chest tightened. She was a stunning woman, and this was bound to be a problem. Not for himself, but Wingate. During the past week it had become more than clear that the man had a penchant for liquor and an eye for women. How far he took that admiration, Henry didn't know, but perhaps that was why Mrs. Wingate was perpetually in a sour mood. And Henry hadn't missed the assessing look Wingate had given "Sallie" earlier.

When they reached the house, he dismounted and moved to help her down, but she was already off the horse.

"I'll see to the animals," he said. "You can go on inside. Or ... have you been inside already?"

"No. The door was locked, so my trunk is on the porch."

"I didn't know you were coming. My apologies. And your name?"

"Kate Ryan."

She reached out and he shook her hand. Her grip was firm and business-like.

"Henry Maguire," he replied.

"I know."

"How did you get into your gown?" he asked, realization hitting him.

She smiled, unruffled. "Behind that bush over there." She nodded toward the side of the house. "I had a buttonhook. It was a difficult, I'll admit, but I got it done."

She didn't whine, and she was resourceful. He didn't know whether to be pleased or worried.

"I'll see to your trunk after I finish with the horses, and then we can talk."

"Of course."

He handed her the key to the house, and she went inside. He got the horses unsaddled and brushed and left fresh hay in the stalls as well as checking their water. When he came to the porch, however, there was no trunk. He stepped inside.

"His wife" had lit the lamp on the wooden table in the kitchen. She had somehow dragged the trunk inside and was bent over sorting through the contents. She didn't glance up.

"You can have the bedroom," he said. "I'll get my belongings."

He went into the small room and retrieved a few items of clothing, but as he was about to grab everything, he paused, then returned to the outer room.

"I don't think I should have all my things strewn about the house. It'll look suspicious if anyone stops by. And now that you're here, I'm guessing I—we—may have more visitors. Ladies do like to have tea and gossip."

"I understand."

"You're a bit of a surprise," he said.

They watched each other for a moment, then he broke the spell by lifting the trunk and carrying it into the bedroom.

As he returned to the kitchen, he said, "I imagine you're tired," Then he remembered the gloves in his jacket, so he retrieved the items and handed them to her.

"Thank you."

"Why don't you have a seat." He indicated the table. "I won't keep you long."

Miss Ryan sat, as did he.

"Louise?" Despite everything, his concern for her rushed to the forefront.

"She's fine, as I said. She was shot during a job in Albuquerque. I'd been in training at the agency and was immediately brought in to replace her. She's on the mend, I can assure you. And she filled me in on the particulars of this case. Well, as much as she could. There haven't been any reports from you since you arrived. Louise, and Mr. Jones, thought that I should come as soon as possible. There was concern about your welfare."

"I see," Henry said. "I didn't send word because I didn't want to bring any undue attention. I won't lie, you *were* a surprise this evening."

"I apologize. Louise insisted that I ...."

He laughed. "I can well imagine what Louise said. She must think highly of you."

Miss Ryan hesitated. "She's been training me. I think very highly of *her*."

"So do I. What do you know?"

"I've been briefed on your mission, as well as information about the Wingates."

"Can you shoot? Ride?"

"Yes."

"How long have you been with the agency?"

Miss Ryan hesitated, then said, "Four months."

Ah, hell. She was as green as they came.

"I lead, you follow," he said. "Understand?"

He wasn't certain, but he glimpsed a flash of rebellion in her eyes.

"I do." But her flat voice and closed expression told him more than she knew. Good. She had fire in her. But he had to hope that he could keep her out of his hair regarding his father's death.

"How old are you?"

"Nineteen."

He swore under his breath.

That knocked him. She looked young, but he'd been certain she couldn't be *that* young. A streak of protectiveness hit him. While he didn't anticipate anything violent happening on this case, it still might. He did believe that Arthur Wingate had murdered his father, after all. And Louise getting shot was the perfect example of why women shouldn't do this job. And especially not young women with their entire lives ahead of them.

"Why are you here?" He tried to temper his voice so it wouldn't sound like an accusation. "You're young. You're beautiful. You could have a far better life than this."

"Why are you here?" she countered.

He didn't answer.

After a moment, she spoke. "I'm here because I want to help people, to see that justice prevails. It's why I became a Pinkerton. I promise that I'll work hard and that you can count on me."

The determination in her gaze and her earnest expression got to him.

Dammit all to hell.

She was an idealist.

He used to be one. Not anymore.

KATE TOSSED and turned all night.

Come morning, she rose early, dressed, and set out to quietly explore the kitchen. The pantry was well-stocked with everything a good wife would expect—flour, sugar, sorghum, dried beans, rice, and many canned items. A quick inspection revealed peaches, tomatoes, and green beans. In the larder were eggs, a hunk of ham covered in cheese cloth, and butter. She also discovered a half-used loaf of bread.

Henry kept a tidy home. Kate was impressed. The men in her life—her father, her older brother, Eli, along with her uncles Logan, Nathan, and Cale—weren't nearly as organized when it came to domestic matters.

She glanced over at her "husband" and undercover partner. He was asleep on the stuffed burgundy couch, his tall frame spilling out over the bottom edge. It didn't look enjoyable. She wondered how they could remedy the situation, but nothing came to her. The bed he'd given her was very comfortable and she'd slept better than she had expected, notwithstanding the faint smell of his aftershave that lingered on the pillows. She had flipped them over, not because it bothered her, but because it didn't.

She wasn't sure what the day would hold. She had been trained to stay alert, to search for clues, to befriend certain individuals if it seemed advantageous, but it had all been instruction only. Theories. Now she was here, on a live case, and her stomach fluttered with nerves.

She would ingratiate herself with the women surrounding Arthur Wingate. So far, the most prominent were Lottie Wingate and her niece, Delia.

She glanced over at Henry. In sleep, he appeared less stern. Maybe it was because his hooded eyes were closed and couldn't watch her with ... what? She had sensed annoyance and even disdain, but there had also been surprise in that first moment when she had called his name as he had been about to walk right past her, as if he hadn't known who she was. He hadn't known, of course, so the surprise was understandable, but still ... for the briefest of moments, there had been something else, a worry, maybe even a slight fear.

What in the world did Henry have to fear from her?

She perused the kitchen once more, supposing a good wife would prepare a hearty breakfast for her husband, especially one she had been parted from for such a lengthy time. Especially one in which she was trying to patch up her shaky marriage.

Kate sighed. Why on earth had she told Delia that? But she knew. It would throw the woman off, making her think she had an advantage. It might give Kate a way into that inner circle, whomever was in that circle. Kate had been briefed on some of the men acquainted with Wingate, along with their wives, but she had no way of knowing the true state of the friendships and relationships until she was able to spend time with these women. And Delia, in her early twenties, was closer to Kate's age than Mrs. Wingate. It would be easier to befriend Miss Wingate.

Should she share her strategy with Henry? He had given her a very brief overview the night before. She had been hoping for more, but perhaps he had been tired. However, her gut told her she would have to prove herself to her "husband." He hadn't wanted a partner to begin with, despite that he'd been parading around with the open knowledge that he had a wife ... somewhere.

Her conversation with Louise came back to her. Henry's father, Hugh Maguire, had been killed in a mine shaft fall in Trinidad in 1891. It had been ruled an accident by authorities at the time, but coincidentally, Hugh had been friends with Arthur Wingate. Their boss, Edgar Jones, had overridden Louise's suggestion that a different agent take this assignment since Henry clearly had a conflict of interest, but apparently Henry had convinced Jones that he was the best man for the job, that Wingate couldn't possibly know of Henry's connection to Hugh, and that he could remain impartial.

So, unbeknownst to Jones, Louise had given Kate a secondary assignment. Kate was not only to assist Henry in the investigation into Wingate's possible counterfeiting and insurance fraud, but she was also to watch Henry himself, to step in if necessary if he became emotional.

After having met Henry, Kate didn't believe he would ever be swept away by his feelings.

But it didn't escape her that the reason he might not want her here was because of the history between Wingate and Henry's father. Did Henry have another agenda? Louise had spoken so highly of him and with such obvious warm affection, indicating a strong friendship, that Kate didn't believe he could do anything outside the jurisdiction of the Pinkertons. And Hugh's death had been an accident, right? Or did Henry perhaps think otherwise?

Kate filed her observations away. She would need to keep her eyes and ears open for the next few weeks.

She thought of Jebediah, the stray dog her mother had found five years ago. He'd been in poor shape, too skinny with ribs showing, matted black hair, and crusted ears. But her mama had been determined to clean him up, to feed him, and to give him a warm place to sleep in the barn. Kate loved animals but she was a bit ashamed to admit that she hadn't welcomed Jeb with open arms. Their pup, Marley—acquired at the Denton Fair two years prior—was more than enough for her. She had been quite bonded to the tan dog who'd frequently slept in her bedroom at night. She hadn't wanted anything to interfere with that relationship.

But at the end of the first week, her ma had announced that Kate would care for Jeb.

"Why?" Kate had complained, fourteen years old and resentful of being bossed around.

"Because Jeb needs to learn to trust, and you need to learn patience."

"I take care of Marley," she had rebutted.

"And now you'll take care of Jeb, too." Her mother's voice had been quiet and firm.

"Have Josie do it, or Eli." Her younger sister had an affinity for animals, especially broken ones, and her older brother was such a rule follower that he'd do the job whether it suited him or not.

"He's broken, Katie. I know you're the best person for this job. Sometimes things happen for a reason."

Kate had gone resentfully silent. All her free time not spent on schoolwork or chores or playing with Marley would now be consumed with an animal that didn't even want to be around her.

"Spend time with him," her mother had said. "Give him space. Forgive him for not being what you want him to be—whole and happy. You don't have to love him. But kindness and respect are traits that can be freely given. Sometimes, angels come in disguise."

"You're saying this dog is an angel?"

"No. But maybe *you* are."

Kate had done what her ma had commanded, although it hadn't really been an order. Molly Hart Ryan wasn't a strict mother in the sense that rules always needed to be followed, but she was a woman who expected her children to exhibit a compassion for the creatures around them. Her mother had been captured by Comanche when she was a child, during which Kate's grandparents—Molly's folks—had been killed. Kate knew her mama carried deep scars from that time, but mostly she spoke of love and forgiveness. Of moving forward. Of not only finding one's place in the world, but of making one's mark upon it.

And Kate knew her mother was trying to teach her a lesson.

Jeb eventually became Kate's constant companion, along with Marley, and the three of them had many adventures. The hardest part of growing up and pursuing her dreams had been leaving those two adorable mutts, but they were in good hands with her ma and pa. Her pa even let *both* dogs sleep in his bedroom, her ma often teasing him about the soft spot he had for those two.

But her ma had been right about befriending Jeb. It had taken time. An adherence of space had to be observed. Kate decided this could be applied to her relationship with Henry.

She needed to prove herself, not just to the agency, but to Henry before he would trust her as a true and full partner.

She could live with that. It was time to get to work.

She would make Henry breakfast.

CHAPTER 4

Henry awoke to the smell of bacon and coffee. Swinging his legs to the floor, he sat for a moment and rubbed a hand down his face. It hadn't been his best night's sleep, and the cause was currently making herself at home in the kitchen, but he thought maybe it wasn't so bad having a partner.

Without warning, a wave of homesickness hit.

Aunt Lydia and Uncle Jim had raised him and his older brother after their mother had passed during Henry's birth. Their father had been too consumed with his work to maintain a normal life for his sons. On a morning like this, Aunt Lydia would have been humming in the kitchen while she prepared the morning meal for three always-hungry males.

He pushed aside the longing for simpler times, because even the simple times had been tainted with resentment. Working for the Secret Service, his pa's absences had been frequent, and as a boy, Henry had concluded that his father hadn't loved him and Ian enough to stay close. It had all reached a boiling point when Henry was sixteen with an argument that had kept Hugh from returning for a visit again. A year later he'd died.

Ian still blamed Henry for driving their pa away.

Maturity, however, had a way of replacing anger and bitterness with grief and regret. That's why Henry had come to Trinidad, finally. He would make amends. He would lay his pa to rest and discover what really had happened with his death. Henry hadn't told Ian, now a U.S. Deputy Marshal, that he was here, or about the map he'd discovered in an old cigar box Aunt Lydia had given him recently. He and his brother hadn't agreed about much in the last eight years, and Henry didn't need more of his censure.

That brought him back to his new partner.

As a new agent, she would likely rebuke his focus on his father's death, implying that it jeopardized their assignment. Because if she was anything like he'd been when he'd first joined the Pinkertons—hungry for justice and the desire to prove himself—she would insist on everything being handled by-the-book.

And if Henry had learned anything in the last seven years as an agent, it was that sometimes rules needed to be bent.

He'd had every intention of keeping Louise away as long as he could, and it would seem he'd gotten his wish with her unfortunate injury. Although she had trained other female agents, she'd never confided in him about Kate Ryan. She'd never given a hint that she had an up-and-coming agent that could possibly replace *her*.

Dammit, but Ryan would be in his way.

He stood. He'd slept in long underwear as a concession to his houseguest, but he still managed to startle her as he entered the dining area.

"Good morning," she said, a hand to her chest as she abruptly stopped at the sight of him. Her pink cheeks and bright gaze stirred that damnable interest that he'd briefly indulged in the night before when he'd seen her in the Wingates' foyer, before he'd known she was to be his partner.

Pushing aside his inopportune attraction to her, he said, "Mornin'. Sorry about the state of undress. You and I are going to have to agree to a certain amount of familiarity." *Until I can figure out how to send you back.*

Squaring her shoulders, she flashed him a brilliant smile. "Not a problem. I have an older brother. You can't shock me."

He suppressed a grin. Normally he slept with little clothing. He would bet that'd shock her. Should he behave inappropriately with the hope that she'd flee? It was a thought, but one he quickly dismissed. He valued his job, and his aunt and uncle had raised him to be a gentleman. And it wasn't Kate Ryan's fault that Louise had sent her headfirst into Henry's case, much to his annoyance. It also wasn't her fault that despite her youth she was a handsome woman, her figure trim, her curves hinting at what might lie beneath her practical ivory blouse and brown skirt. Curves that had been on display the night before.

"Is it all right if I go into the bedroom to dress?" he asked, inwardly chiding himself for letting his thoughts wander into such territory.

"Of course," she replied. "I've taken the liberty of making breakfast. It should be ready by the time you're done."

"Thank you." He paused at the doorway and turned back. "You don't have to cook for me, by the way."

"Since we both need to eat, and as I'm technically your wife, it would be prudent for us to have the appearance of a normal married couple." She cleared her throat. "Your kitchen is orderly and well-stocked. You've made it easy for me."

He nodded. "My Aunt Lydia's influence."

"You must be close with her."

"I am." He went into the bedroom and shut the door. A short time later he was seated at the kitchen table eating a plate of sunnyside-up eggs, fried potatoes, and crisp bacon. It was accompanied with a cup of richly brewed coffee.

"I don't know what to say," he said, enjoying the meal. "It's not often a woman cooks for me."

"What about your mama?" Kate asked from across the table. "Or your aunt?"

"Well, my mother died when I was an infant."

"I'm sorry."

"Thank you. I have no recollection of her, however. My aunt and uncle raised me, but I haven't seen them in some time."

As they ate their meal, he was aware that he was the senior agent, and this young woman was now under his supervision. Maybe he didn't need to get rid of her altogether. Maybe it would be enough to simply *misdirect* her. Even that niggled his conscience. He well remembered his early days with the agency and how much he wanted to prove his mettle. He could only assume Kate Ryan was the same, or else why would she be here when she could be tucked away somewhere with a husband and babies underfoot.

Annoyed by the vision, he said, "I guess I should tell you about the schedule for the week."

She waited, attentive.

"I usually go to the Wingates' each morning to discuss the memoir with Arthur, and then return here in the afternoons to write, although sometimes I've remained at the main house to work. It helps to keep an eye on the comings and goings of Arthur's business associates, but I can't be too obvious."

"I understand. So you're really writing the book?"

He nodded. "Arthur has insisted on seeing some of the drafts, so I've been forced to."

"Would you like help with that?"

"Are you a writer?"

"My cousin Sophie wants to be, so she and I would write stories together when we were young. I'd be happy to free up some of your time."

Henry considered it. To be honest, scribbling out those drafts from notes he took during conversations with Arthur was a bit tedious.

"I have to warn you that my penmanship isn't stellar."

"Have you been able to search the house?" she asked.

"No. I've yet to be alone, so there's been no opportunity."

"Perhaps I could accompany you during your meetings with Wingate?" she asked, raising a brow.

It wasn't a bad idea, but Henry really didn't want to be tied to Kate Ryan all day. He also didn't relish her being with Arthur. He was concerned that such a young woman wouldn't be able to hold her own with a man such as Wingate, who had no doubt spent his life lying and manipulating others to make his way in the world. And then there was the fact that his Civil War stories were rife with blood and violence.

He was also less inclined for her to search the house than him. She would no doubt botch it.

"We'll see," Henry replied. "Today is Sunday, so there won't be any work today, but Arthur has invited us to supper this evening."

"What time?"

"Be ready around three."

She nodded. "Do you have any leads on the counterfeiting ring? Or any proof that connects Wingate to insurance fraud?"

"Not yet. The Wells Fargo stage carrying the funds for Wingate's account was attacked and the money stolen. Wingate collected the insurance on the funds."

"But weren't there also other monies in that shipment that were stolen?" she asked.

"There were. But Jonesy investigated and none of them were insured."

"Jonesy?"

"Sorry. Edgar."

"You two must be friends."

Henry nodded. "For the most part." He didn't want to belabor the point. He didn't want Ryan to think that he got special treatment from Edgar, although Jonesy had made some allowances for Henry this past year.

"So, somehow, we need to connect Wingate to the men who stole the money?"

"Yes," Henry said. "I've been looking for some kind of communication system but so far nothing."

"Do you think they'll attempt another stage robbery?"

"Anything is possible."

"But so soon? Wouldn't that seem suspicious?"

"Yes," Henry replied. "But a man like Wingate likely believes he's above the law. We need to stay alert."

"I can pursue a friendship with Mrs. Wingate as well as Delia Wingate. And what about the neighbor, Mrs. Beckett?"

Henry paused. Kate Ryan was well-briefed. He supposed he had Louise to thank for that.

"Unknown whether she can offer any information, or whether she might be involved somehow."

"Aren't she and the Wingates engaged in a boundary dispute?"

"They are."

"Perhaps I should try to befriend her as well," she said.

"That might prove challenging since I gather she doesn't like the Wingates, but yes, let's pursue that."

It turned out Henry didn't need to misdirect Ryan—her focus on the women in this case should take care of that for him.

He had finished his meal so stood and took his empty plate to the wash basin. He retrieved Ryan's dishes as well and proceeded to wash and dry them.

"You don't need to do that," she said, standing near him. "I can clean up."

"It's all right." He focused on the task, avoiding her green eyes. "We can share the chores. It's only fair."

She put the rest of the kitchen in order while he finished the dishes, a scene of domestic wedded bliss. It was both awkward and comforting at the same time. Time to put some distance between them.

He dried his hands with a dish towel then headed to the door and grabbed his hat.

"I'll be back later," he said.

"Where are you going?" she asked, a slight frown marring her brow. With hands on her hips, she was like any new young wife chastising her husband for rushing out to spend time without her.

He'd already had his day lined up, and Kate Ryan wasn't going to change that.

"I need to run into town and handle a few things," he said. "I'll be back to accompany you to the Wingates' for supper."

"Shall I go with you?"

He settled the hat on his head and shrugged into his jacket, turning away from her. "No." Looking at her would test his resolve about withholding information. But it had to be this way. He wasn't about to change his agenda simply because she'd shown up.

"I'd like to be useful." The edge in her voice conveyed her irritation. "Can I transcribe any of your notes?"

He hesitated but then couldn't think of a reasonable explanation as to why she shouldn't, except that maybe Henry hoped that somewhere in Arthur Wingate's ramblings, the man would slip up about his connection to Hugh Maguire. Kate Ryan wouldn't be attuned to such things, so letting her look at his notes should be fine.

"Sure."

He walked over to his leather briefcase and removed several sheets of paper. "Here's the newest stuff," he said, handing it to her. "There's blank paper and pen and ink at the desk." He nodded toward the corner of the room where a modest wooden desk sat.

She took them and immediately became immersed in the top paper, moving over to the desk without looking up.

Henry walked out the door, saddled his horse, and headed south down the main road leading into Trinidad.

He tried to shake the feeling that he was betraying the confidence of his "wife."

This isn't real, he reminded himself.

So why then did it seem as if the part of his life that had always been ill-fitting had suddenly clicked into place, like a missing puzzle piece?

Kate Ryan's intelligent gaze and attractive countenance came to mind.

My wife.

He pushed aside the flicker of emotion it ignited in him, an unnamed sentiment he immediately recognized as out-of-place and entirely unprofessional.

He had a job to do.

A beautiful partner wasn't about to change that.

CHAPTER 5

Henry spent the first part of his time in town doing something that would seem obvious—shopping for a gift for his newly arrived bride. He browsed the mercantile and ultimately purchased a collection of lavender soap. Then he headed to the blacksmith to have his horse reshod.

As soon as he entered the building, an older man froze when he saw Henry.

"I need new shoes for my horse," Henry said. "Can I leave him and come back in an hour?"

The man nodded, appearing to regain his bearings. "Yep. I can do that."

He remembered what Kate had said about getting a ride to the Wingate party. "I believe you escorted my wife last evening to the Wingate ranch."

"Sallie Holmes."

"Yes."

"She's a nice girl. You're lucky to have her." The man's gaze beneath bushy gray brows shined with intensity.

Concern for Kate washed over Henry. Why was the blacksmith so focused on Henry's "wife?"

"Thank you." Henry extended his hand. "I'm Gilbert Holmes."

The man shook it. "Francis O'Malley, but most people call me Dutch. What are you doin' out there with the Wingates?"

"I'm working with Mr. Wingate to ghostwrite a memoir for him."

"Is that so?" Dutch gave a dismissive shake of his head. "Watch out. There's likely to be a lot of ghosts out there to trip you up."

"Do you know him?" Henry asked.

Dutch shook his head, a little too quickly in Henry's book. "Nah. Just heard things around town. The Wingates don't like people in their business, so why the hell would he need to write a book?"

Henry considered the rough-edged blacksmith. While Henry agreed with the salty attitude of Dutch, he couldn't, for obvious reasons, come out and agree with the man. "Perhaps he wants to leave a legacy for his family."

"What family? He and Lottie ain't got no children."

The use of Mrs. Wingate's first name struck Henry as odd. "How long have you been in Trinidad?" he asked.

"Not long. Just a few months. I best get to your horse."

It was clear that Dutch didn't want to continue the conversation, and Henry had to consider that perhaps Kate could get more information out of the man. He would instruct her to pursue the lead.

Henry left the blacksmith shop and made his way to a house about three blocks away. Innocuous. Just the way Henry liked it. It was his point of contact that Jonesy had set up prior to Henry arriving in town, although this was the first time Henry had come here. In truth, he hadn't had a reason to until now. Until his "wife" had arrived. Jonesy had thought it better to exchange missives here rather than the post office, and since Jonesy was currently in Albuquerque, a courier would be dispatched immediately once Henry left his correspondence.

Henry knocked on the door and was greeted by a housekeeper.

"I'm here to see Mr. Emmons," he said.

"May I say who's calling?" the older woman asked.

"Gilbert Holmes."

"Please come inside." She ushered him into the modestly decorated foyer and then into a sitting area.

A short balding man wearing spectacles and a suit appeared. "Mr. Holmes." He smiled and shook Henry's hand. "It's a pleasure to meet you. Please sit. I'll have Gertrude bring us coffee."

The housekeeper arrived and deposited a tray with cups, saucers, and a pot of coffee, pouring them each a cup before departing and shutting the door behind her.

Henry took a sip and then considered the man sitting across from him. "I'm sorry I've not come before this."

"Well, I was beginning to wonder. But Mr. Jones instructed me to wait until you made contact."

Henry nodded. "Would you have any correspondence for me?"

"I would." Mr. Emmons reached inside his jacket and pulled two letters. "I don't like to leave them lying around. Gertrude doesn't know about this, and I don't want her finding it by accident."

"Can I read these in private and then write a response?"

"Not a problem. I'll tell Gertrude that you're reviewing a contract and not to disturb you. I'll check back in thirty minutes."

"That would be fine." The man left the room.

Henry opened the first letter. As expected, it was from Jonesy.

Gilbert,
Starling will arrive on May 12 to add to your collection. How is the book going?
Smith House Publishing

Henry frowned. The date was the day before the party, so it

must be referencing Louise, although Starling was code for any female agent. He opened the second one.

Gilbert,
We've found a new Starling for your collection and will be sending it along shortly. Look forward to hearing about your progress on the book.
Smith House Publishing

Henry sighed. Damn. He could well imagine Jonesy's irritation over Henry not responding. Henry went to the desk in the corner where paper, pen, and ink rested atop it. He sat and composed a response.

In Care of Smith House Publishing:
Dear Sir,
Bird arrived safe and sound. Not my usual but I'll make it fit in my collection. Book is still in draft phase. More later.
Gilbert Holmes

When Mr. Emmons returned, Henry gave him the letter and departed. By the time he returned to the blacksmith, his horse had been reshod, but Dutch was nowhere to be seen. Henry left payment with a boy tending the animals, and then headed to his final destination for the day.

HENRY GUIDED his horse south of town, as if he were returning to the cabin he shared with his new partner, but when he came to the first fork in the road, which led northwest, he took it.

He had another goal—the abandoned mine shaft where Hugh Maguire had died. It had been weighing on him whether to visit the location. It were as if he'd been channeling his brother since he'd arrived in Trinidad. *It was an accident. Let it go.* Avoiding the hard places wasn't going to get Henry the answers he'd come for.

In the distance, Fishers Peak filled his view with its flattop mesa, and fluffy white clouds emphasized the blue sky. As his horse left the main road, the open terrain shifted to forest, and while Henry liked the cover, he didn't like the fact that someone could be watching.

Still, he behaved as if he were simply out for a Sunday afternoon ride, exploring a piece of Wingate's property. He was soon headed uphill and finally came to the remnants of the Ellis Mine, named after Arthur's father. Henry's research had revealed that while it had been intermittently in use in the late 1880's, after the death of Hugh Maguire in 1891 it had been completely shut down.

He came to a boarded-up entrance and dismounted, tying off his horse at a hitching rail that still stood. Henry came as close as he could to the dilapidated opening and paused, thinking of his father.

Why had Hugh come here that night? The police report had stated that he was investigating something and had likely slipped and fell. What had he been investigating? Local law enforcement hadn't pursued it further, and surprisingly, the Secret Service for whom Hugh had worked had also done nothing, filing it as a tragic accident.

At the time, Henry had been seventeen and Ian nineteen, and neither of them had had the wherewithal to dig any deeper. Aunt Lydia had accepted the death certificate of her only brother with misty eyes and a grief that she'd largely kept to herself. And Henry had let his anger toward his father keep him warm at night, fueling his desire to act out. It wasn't until he'd found the Pinkertons that he was able to channel his energy into something worthwhile.

But now, the grief of what he'd lost squeezed his chest. Ian had blamed Henry for pushing their pa away, and maybe his brother had been right.

"I'm sorry about that fight," he whispered under his breath.

He would never be able to make amends directly with his pa, but at least he could figure out what had happened eight years ago.

His downward gaze caught sight of footprints in the dirt. He sank to his haunches and inspected them more closely. They were fresh, maybe a day or two old. Rising, he followed the trail to the right, coming to another entrance, but this one had a sturdy wooden door with a padlock on it. Certainly not old.

"Can I help you?"

Henry spun around at the sound of the man's voice. He appeared to be about Henry's age, dressed well as if he'd recently been to church, his brown hair combed back.

"I was just out for a ride," Henry said. "I'm always fascinated by old mines."

"I'm Walter Beckett." The man settled a bowler hat on his head and reached out to shake Henry's hand.

"Gilbert Holmes," he replied, clasping Walter's hand.

He must be Clayton and Jean Beckett's son. From Henry's research, he knew that Clayton, Arthur, and Hugh had been friends back in Ohio before the Civil War.

Recognition shined in the man's gaze. "You're the writer that Arthur hired."

"I am. Are you close with Mr. Wingate?"

"I work for him."

That was news to Henry.

"Weren't Arthur and your father friends?" Henry asked.

Walter nodded.

"But I've heard that your family and the Wingates are in a boundary dispute," Henry added.

"That would be my mother. I worry that maybe she's become senile in her old age. She's never been the same since my father died four years ago."

"How does she feel about you working for Arthur?"

Walter shrugged. "She doesn't like it, but I'm not a child. I can do what I want."

"I thought this mine was abandoned. I read that a terrible accident happened here eight years ago."

Walter's friendly expression dissolved. "Well, despite that, this is still Wingate property. Arthur stores equipment here."

"What kind of equipment?"

"For the mines. Stuff like that. It's easier to keep it out here than at his warehouse in town."

Henry hadn't known about a warehouse. He'd need to look into it.

"Mind if I have a look?" Henry asked, trying to keep his countenance innocent and curious.

"Sorry. You'd need permission from Mr. Wingate."

Right. Walter Beckett was hiding something.

"So you have a wife?" Walter asked.

"Yes," Henry replied.

"And she showed up last night?" Walter wore a slight smile. "Delia must've hated that."

"Why would you say that?"

"There's been talk that she was pursuing you."

"I'm not encouraging it," he replied. It was only a slight lie. Delia's interest in Henry had been obvious from the start, but he'd done little to smother it in the hopes she might let slip useful information for the case.

"That doesn't usually matter with her. Just watch out."

"Why would you say that?"

"I used to be engaged to her."

CHAPTER 6

By late morning, Kate had made her way through Henry's notes, writing a new version that cleared up confusing passages. Of course, Henry would need to proofread it, since she may have made a few errors, but overall, Kate was proud of her efforts, feeling rather accomplished.

She thought to make a list of suspects, but then decided against it. Such a document could be found by someone, so it was best if she kept such information in her head. Also, truthfully, she didn't have many, just the few people she'd met at the party the previous evening.

She considered again that she should've followed Henry when he'd left this morning, to document his whereabouts, but her conscience had stopped her. Truth be told, she wasn't entirely comfortable with the extra assignment Louise had given her. What if Henry caught Kate questioning his actions while on the job? How would she explain herself? Any headway she had made as his partner would be lost.

So much had been in the realm of theory when Louise had trained her to be an agent, and that had continued even when Kate had been brought in suddenly to replace Louise at Henry's side. But now that she was here, it felt ... different. Henry was a flesh and blood man, clearly capable and in control of the assignment he'd been given. What right did Kate have to question his actions? His possible motives? In truth, she had much to learn from him.

And there was no doubt that she wanted to be in Henry Maguire's good graces.

To pass the time until he returned, she made herself a cup of tea and sat down on the sofa with a copy of *The Time Machine* by H.G. Wells. She and her cousin, Sophie, had a great love of reading and often exchanged books, and it was Sophie who had recommended this one to her. Kate wondered what it would be like to be a time traveler. It might make her career as a Pinkerton easier because she could jump to the future, figure out the culprit, then return and impress everyone with her deductive skills.

Or maybe she could just do something nice, like go back in time and meet Henry's now-deceased father.

When a horse and buggy drew close to the house, Kate went to the window. But when her gaze fell on the passenger, curly hair beneath a sun bonnet, she ducked, her heart racing.

Mrs. Marsh!

She didn't want to ruin her cover now, not when she'd just begun. And by default, it would ruin Henry's alias as well. Kate couldn't let that happen.

She shuffled on her hands and knees to the bedroom, the skirt and the single layer of petticoat beneath it giving her grief the entire distance. She was finally forced to bunch it around her waist. Once in the bedroom, she carefully and quietly closed the door. Footsteps on the porch echoed back to her.

Her gaze landed on the window. Did it open? She stood and tiptoed to it. The latch was stiff, but with some effort she pushed it open. It was a narrow opening and the drop to the ground was a little far.

A knock on the front door was followed by Mrs. Marsh's voice calling for ... someone. Was it for Henry? Or had the woman come to greet "Sallie?" Kate couldn't be certain, but it didn't matter. She couldn't let Mrs. Marsh see her face. She hauled herself up on the windowsill, and wedged her leg through the opening, but her dress snagged, stopping her progress. She became stuck, half in and half out. Struggling to free herself, she began emitting grunting noises when suddenly the fabric ripped, and she careened through the opening. She would have landed face down in the dirt if her left hand hadn't caught the window ledge. She let go and landed with a thud on the ground.

Pain shot through her wrist, her palm now bleeding from a cut, and she suppressed a groan. Closer inspection revealed a giant splinter from the wooden sill had become embedded on the edge of her hand.

Kate grimaced.

"Are you all right?"

Kate stood and spun around, finding herself face to face with a young girl wearing a lemon-colored dress that was a bit dirty. Her brown hair was in disarray, as if the trees had reached out to touch this wild child during her sojourn through the forest.

"Where did you come from?" Kate asked, making sure to keep her voice low, guessing the girl to be about ten years old.

The child pointed to a spot in the hills behind the house. "I live back there with my granny. You're bleeding. Should we go in this house and fix you up?"

"No. I'm fine. Really."

"Do you live here?"

Kate decided to come clean. "I do, but there's a woman at the front door that I'd rather not speak with."

"Oh. I can help. C'mon." The girl turned and waved for Kate to follow.

They were soon swallowed up by the tall pines, and Kate's heartbeat calmed to a steady rhythm. A glance over her shoulder showed that even if Mrs. Marsh decided to inspect the back of the house—which Kate decided was doubtful—she would be unable to see them.

She inspected her hand again. The pain had increased, and the blood continued to flow.

Kate walked quickly to keep up with the young girl's fast feet. "What's your name?"

"You can call me Nell." Droopy curls the color of coffee bounced as she walked.

"Is your name not Nell?"

"Nah, that's my nickname, and the one I prefer."

"What's your full name?"

The girl wrinkled her nose. "Penelope. But I don't like being called Penny. That's what my brother calls me. I like Nell. It sounds more grown up."

"I'm Ka—Sallie."

"Hiya, Kasallie."

Kate laughed. "No, just Sallie. I'm a little like you. I have one name, but I prefer another." Kate scanned the pathway they were following. "Where are we going?"

"I'll take you to Granny. She'll fix your hand."

This surprised Kate. They were within walking distance of another property? This wasn't in any of her briefings.

It ended up being a good walk to Nell's grandmother. They climbed not one but two hills. As they descended the second, a valley revealed itself, along with a small homestead.

"This is beautiful," Kate said. "Whose land is this?"

"Wingate."

"How long has your grandmother lived here?"

Nell shrugged. "Her whole life, I guess. At least, the life she had with Grandfather. But I didn't know him. He died the year I was born. I visit here sometimes. Right now, it's just me and not my brother. He's back with Mama and Daddy in the city. I like roaming in the countryside better than brick streets and too many people. I can breathe here."

"I know what you mean." Kate thought of the Rocking Wren, the ranch where she'd grown up with her older brother and younger sister, and a large collection of cousins within spitting distance. "What's your brother's name?"

"Howard."

"Is he older?"

Nell nodded. "He's thirteen. I'm nine."

"I have an older brother," Kate said. "His name is Eli. He can be obnoxious, but we get along better now that we're older." Worry crept over Kate. Maybe she shouldn't be talking about her real brother. Perhaps she should fabricate her entire family. This undercover work was proving to be a challenge.

Nell released a heavy sigh. "Then I'll look forward to the future when I'll like him better."

They came to a low fence and entered through a latched gate. An older woman sat on the porch, knitting.

"Granny!" Nell waved to her. "This is Sallie, and she's hurt her hand."

Granny stood, revealing a stout body. She stepped forward, taking Kate's hand. "It's a pleasure to meet you, Sallie."

Her smile was infectious, and Kate resisted the urge to pinch the woman's full cheeks like one might a child. Granny's black hair was streaked with white and pulled back in a single braid, and she reminded Kate of her mama's Comanche sister, Running Water. Seven years prior, Kate's mother, Molly, had found Running Water when the family had been at a fair in Denton, Texas, and since then had rekindled a relationship with her.

Was Granny of Comanche heritage? And what was she doing living on Wingate land?

"There's a deep splinter," Kate said.

Granny nodded. "Come inside. I can help you."

Kate followed Nell and the older woman through a screen door and then into a rustic kitchen with pots of herbs lining a deep shelf below a window. Sitting atop a counter was a bounty of freshly picked carrots, turnips, and potatoes. The kitchen smelled of earth and lemons and life, and it made Kate's chest swell with homesickness.

Time spent cooking with her mama and younger sister, Josie, in the kitchen at the Rocking Wren filled her with memories of mirth and laughter. And she always loved being at her grandparents' ranch, the SR, named for Susanna Ryan, her grandmother. The much larger house was always filled with family since Kate's uncle Logan and her aunt Claire lived nearby, as well as Uncle Nathan and Aunt Em, and Uncle Cale and Aunt Tess. And Kate's many cousins were always around. She had never been lonely.

Granny motioned for Kate to sit and then retrieved a bowl, towels, tweezers, and a bottle of antiseptic. Setting to work, Granny took Kate's hand and carefully wiped away the blood with a wet towel, then poured the carbolic over it, letting the bowl catch the runoff.

Kate hissed as her hand stung. Then Granny spent several minutes focused on the splinter. Kate fought to keep her composure through the pain and discomfort as the tweezers did their work.

Finally, Granny sat back. She poured more carbolic acid and then wrapped Kate's hand in a bandage, tying it off.

"You'll be fine," she said with kind eyes and a smile that seemed to hint at mischief.

"I can't thank you enough," Kate said.

"You're welcome. Now, let's get to know one another. Go sit on the porch with Nell, and I'll bring refreshments."

Kate followed Nell to the front of the house, noticing the artwork that hung in the hallway. It depicted outdoor scenes of Indians in various settings. Kate was certain they were Comanche and the style seemed familiar to her, but she continued to the porch and took a seat on a wooden chair. Granny brought a tray with a pitcher of lemonade, three glasses, and thick molasses cookies. Kate gulped down the sweet liquid and ate two cookies before she came up for breath.

"Hits the spot, doesn't it?" Granny chuckled.

"It does. Everything is delicious."

"Sallie is living in the Purcell cabin," Nell said.

Granny raised an eyebrow. "Are you?"

Kate nodded, reaching for another cookie. She'd always had a sweet tooth. "Why is it called the Purcell cabin?" she asked.

"About eight years ago a man named Charlie Purcell lived there," Granny said. "The Wingates own it, as you must know, and he worked for them. But one day he disappeared."

"They say he stole a fortune from Arthur Wingate," Nell cut in.

"That's terrible," Kate replied, wondering why none of this had been in her briefing, but she supposed the news was too old. It didn't really have a bearing on the current case.

"And Lottie Wingate probably cursed him," Nell added.

Granny shushed her.

"I've heard of her séances," Nell continued, her eyes wide and her chin set in defiance. "She summons demons and sets them loose on people."

Granny gave her granddaughter an amused look. "I hardly think so. And maybe Charlie Purcell did steal something, but he was never heard from again, so I guess we'll never know."

Nell turned to Kate. "Have you seen any demons in your cabin?"

"No." Kate added a smile for reassurance.

"But your hand." Nell's face tensed as it dawned on her that Kate's injury might have been prompted by a supernatural entity.

"That was just me being silly. There was a woman at the door I didn't wish to speak with, so instead I made a mad escape out a back window."

"Was she a demon?" Nell whispered.

Kate laughed. "No. Nothing like that."

"Then why were you trying to get away?"

Kate's mind blanked. Why indeed. "She ... well, she wanted my husband to write a book for her, the same way he's writing one for Mr. Wingate. She's very long-winded. I just wasn't up for a conversation with her."

"I had heard there was a handsome bachelor staying at the cabin," Granny said.

"Oh?" Kate cleared her throat, unsure if she were referring to Henry or not.

"Delia Wingate told me," Granny added.

Not an error at all. Delia had lied about Henry's marital status. The thought was a burr under Kate's skin. "Not a bachelor," she clarified. "That's my husband, Gilbert."

Enlightenment spread across Granny's face. Kate couldn't say why exactly, but she was certain that Granny didn't like Delia. Or maybe it was just the Wingates in general.

"Then I'm glad you're here," Granny said. "We could use another face in the neighborhood. How long will you be staying?"

Kate shrugged. "I'm not sure. At least until Gilbert's business is concluded."

"The book?"

"Yes. He's ghostwriting a memoir for Arthur Wingate."

Granny looked genuinely shocked, then she snorted a derisive laugh. "Arthur trying to rewrite history? That sounds like him. How smart is that husband of yours?"

Kate had only just met Henry, so in truth she had no idea, but something told her his intellect was keen and his eye sharp.

"I believe he's quite smart." She sounded like a besotted wife. Good. Except she wasn't acting.

"Tell him to watch himself. He's sure to get a load of hogwash from those people." Granny poured more lemonade into Kate's glass and indicated for her to drink.

Kate gladly did, and then asked, "I take it you don't like the Wingates."

"Just some of them."

"Is there a reason why?"

"Let's just say that the snakes in this area aren't always in the woods."

"I'm afraid I didn't catch your name."

"You can call me Minnie."

Kate waited, sensing that she wasn't finished.

"Minnie Wingate."

CHAPTER 7

Henry sat in the grand dining hall with Kate at his side while the Wingates' wait staff served supper—succulent roast beef, Brussels sprouts swimming in butter, and warm biscuits. Henry didn't want to enjoy it, but Wingate wealth did have a few perks.

Henry glanced at his wife, wondering if she could cook this well. If her breakfast this morning was any indication, then he suspected the answer was yes. For some reason, the thought cheered him, which was good since his meetings with Wingate often left him in a dark mood after. There was no denying the man possessed charisma. Henry wasn't immune to it, and it left a knot of ambivalence in his gut. He once again reminded himself that Arthur Wingate's wealth was no doubt ill-gotten, and it was very likely he had caused Henry's father to meet an untimely end.

Arthur and Lottie bookended the ornately carved dining table, with Henry to Arthur's right, Kate beside him, and Delia beside her. Across the table were two gentlemen: William Phelps, the First National Bank manager who had been at the party the night before, making his presence even more suspicious this evening. Was he in on the insurance fraud? The other younger man was Ralph Moller, an art dealer. Apparently, Lottie liked to buy and sell paintings.

Both men had wives present. Mrs. Phelps was considerably younger than her husband, and while it certainly wasn't a crime the pairing did seem unusual to Henry. And Mrs. Moller, while congenial enough, tried much too hard to be the center of the conversation. She had just finished questioning Henry about what it was like to be a writer, how Wingate's memoir was coming along, and what kind of wild stories would be included.

Henry didn't miss the gleam in Arthur's gaze as he looked at the young Mrs. Phelps. How did Arthur get away with his womanizing, especially chasing the wife of a business associate? Surely it had to spoil his relationship with the husband.

Charisma or not, Arthur Wingate was getting sloppy in his old age. And Henry would exploit it.

Henry chanced a glance at Kate beside him. Her gaze was fixed on Wingate and his leer toward Mrs. Phelps. "I met Minnie Wingate today," she suddenly blurted out.

The table went silent.

Henry turned more fully to his "wife," and instead of a gleam in his gaze he offered a bit of reproach.

She returned a small smile, and Henry knew she'd instigated the interruption on purpose. Was she protecting Mrs. Phelps?

Kate shifted her attention to Arthur. "Is she related to you?"

Henry reached beneath the table and sought to grab Kate's hand, but belatedly he realized her injured one rested beside her plate. His fingers instead found her leg, which he gave a slight squeeze, and a blush blossomed on her cheeks. It was too forward of him, he knew, and the intimacy sparked an unexpected heat in his solar plexus, but he hoped she would get the hint to stop talking about the Wingate woman.

Arthur cleared his throat. "Yes. She's my stepmother."

"She was so lovely to me. She helped me with a scratch on my hand." Kate indicated the bandage on her left hand.

When she had returned home in the early afternoon with her

hand bundled up, she'd told Henry about meeting the woman, and he'd told her to keep her distance. When he'd questioned her further about the injury Kate had said she'd tripped while walking outside and then had run into Nell. They had been closer to the Wingate woman's house than to their own cabin, and so Nell had taken her there. Henry sensed there was more to the story but had let it go. He had neglected to tell Kate not to bring it up, hence the leg squeeze, which was sending his thoughts in a different direction, an irritating distraction that was more pleasant than he cared to admit.

"I'm glad she was helpful," Arthur said. "We're not very close. In fact, I'd advise you to stay clear of her. She hasn't been right in the head for some time."

"Oh, I'm sorry to hear that. She seemed perfectly lucid to me."

"She has her moments."

"Perhaps Nell shouldn't be staying with her then," Kate said. "Is there some reason the girl doesn't stay here?"

Henry squeezed Kate's leg again, earning him a quick frown from his wife, but she quickly recovered.

"My apologies," she amended. "This isn't any of my business." She took a sip of water from her crystal goblet.

"Sallie," Lottie said from her end of the table, "we would love you to join our Ladies' Group. We have meetings at six o'clock on Tuesdays right here."

Kate smiled, acquiescing. "That would be lovely. Thank you."

"It's settled then."

The rest of supper went forward without scandal, much to Henry's approval, but although he didn't know Kate Ryan well at all, he couldn't help but feel she was far from the timid and meek wife she had forced herself to be throughout the remainder of the meal.

Once concluded, the men retired to the library while the women headed to the salon. Henry smiled and gave a peck on the cheek to Kate. It was unnecessary, and he wasn't entirely sure why he'd done it, but he felt the need to share a private moment with her. To perhaps let her know that despite her earlier questioning, he wasn't angry with her.

When he pulled back from her, her slightly raised brow spoke volumes. She wasn't thrilled with his behavior.

"Sorry, darling," he murmured, aware that others might still overhear them. "I just wanted to let you know how happy I am that you're here."

"Are you?"

He held her gaze. "Of course."

Ambivalence flickered in her eyes. "Try not to drink too much brandy, dear."

He narrowed his eyes, taking the teasing and handing it back. "I suspect you could drive the buggy home if I'm too deep in my cups."

She leaned close and he caught her flowery scent. "You suspect right." She turned and walked away, her hips sashaying beneath her lavender dress.

He schooled his features, although he wasn't sure why. He was allowed to watch his wife. He was allowed to let a dash of hunger escape.

He entered the library with Arthur, Mr. Phelps, and Mr. Moller, taking the brandy the valet offered, as well as a cigar, and settled into a comfortable chair. And did his best to put the image of Kate Ryan's fine figure out of his mind.

"Do TELL us how you met your dear Gilbert," Lottie Wingate said, her focus on Kate. Her tone was pleasant, but Kate couldn't help but sense an undertone of dislike in the woman's voice.

Delia sat beside Kate on the sofa, looking annoyed, which Kate could only chalk up to her obvious attachment to Henry, or rather to "Gilbert." Kate couldn't decide if Henry was returning the woman's affections or not, as he had been fairly remote to Delia during supper. He'd been attentive to Kate, however, and she was ridiculously pleased by it.

It was funny that she could feel so territorial over a fake marriage, but she assured herself that it was important for appearances. It meant that Kate could do her job. And it wasn't lost on her that she needed a good showing on this case if she were going to continue with the Pinkertons and not get demoted back to office staff. Being a field agent had been her dream from the beginning.

"We met at Ohio State University two years ago."

"You went to college?" Delia asked, gasping.

"Yes," Kate replied, settling into the story given her by Louise.

"But you're so young," Laura Phelps said, her gown almost as yellow as her hair. "And you're a woman."

Kate smiled. "Believe it or not, there were a handful of women in attendance, so I wasn't alone. The College of Arts and Sciences allows applicants to be as young as sixteen years old."

"Was it difficult to gain entry?" Helen Moller asked, her elegant brows marred in a frown.

While the story was a lie, it annoyed Kate how stunned these women were that a female would try to make something of herself. She wanted to tell them they could be so much more than merely a wife.

"An entrance exam is required as well as a solid background in arithmetic, geography, English grammar, and American History." She spoke succinctly, trying to educate them. "You must also write an essay. My topic was 'The Most Remarkable Person I Ever Met.'"

"And who was that?" Mrs. Wingate asked, accepting a sherry offered on a tray by her wait staff.

"My mother, of course."

The answer appeared to delight Lottie, although Kate wasn't sure why. As far as she knew, she and Arthur didn't have any children.

"Gilbert and I met in an English Literature class," Kate added, the detail helping to lend credence to Henry's cover as a writer.

Laura sighed. "That sounds romantic. Did you fall in love over Shakespeare?"

Kate laughed. "Why yes, we did. He quoted 'A Midsummer Night's Dream' to me, and I was smitten."

"And it was your mother who was ill, right?" Delia asked. "That's why you didn't come with Gilbert when he arrived?"

"Yes."

"How is she now?" Helen asked.

"Much better, thank you," Kate answered.

Mrs. Wingate smoothed out invisible wrinkles in her gown. "What was she afflicted with?" she asked.

Luckily Kate had thought about this the previous night. "She was thrown from her horse and suffered a head injury."

"That's terrible." Delia's eyes reflected genuine concern, or perhaps she was simply a good actress.

Kate swallowed a twinge of guilt for seeking false sympathy from these women, but it also stemmed from the fact that she was doing her mother a disservice. Molly Ryan had been raised with the Comanche, arguably the most powerful tribe in the area encompassing parts of Texas, Oklahoma, Kansas, and Colorado, including the wilderness around Trinidad. The various tribes had possessed knowledge of horse husbandry that was legendary. Kate's mother had never been thrown from a horse.

"It took her some time to recover," Kate added.

Laura leaned forward. "But she's well now?"

Kate nodded. "Yes."

"I'm happy that she's on the mend," Mrs. Wingate said. "I'm sure you're glad to finally be here with your husband. And now that you *are* here, I should like to invite you to a little get-together I'll be having on Tuesday evening."

"You mean the Ladies' Group?" Kate asked.

"This meeting will come after that," Mrs. Wingate said.

"Oh?" Kate hid her confusion. "It sounds lovely."

"Maybe," Delia murmured behind the crystal goblet she held to her lips.

"I'm afraid I don't understand," Kate said.

Delia arched an eyebrow. "How do you feel about talking to the dead?"

Kate paused, not bothering to hide her surprise, not because she found the topic shocking—her aunt Em had a knack for such things, so she'd grown up with an abundance of stories concerning the unknown—but rather to buy her time to respond. Something told her she needed to tread carefully. She recalled Nell's admonition about Lottie summoning demons, and it would appear there was some truth to the girl's fears.

"Oh, Lottie," Laura said, being awfully chummy with the older woman considering their age difference, "I'd heard you do séances. Is that what you're doing Tuesday evening?" Eager curiosity shone in the young woman's eyes.

"Yes," Mrs. Wingate replied. "It will follow our women's meeting. You're welcome to join us as well, of course."

Laura beamed and said, "I should like that."

"Would you like to join us, Sallie?" Mrs. Wingate asked, her voice ringing with an understated challenge. "For *both* meetings?"

Kate plastered an appeasing smile on her lips. "Let me check with Gilbert first, and I'll get back to you." She sought to change the subject and shifted her attention back to Laura. "Do tell me how you met your husband."

CHAPTER 8

Henry was loath to admit it, but he'd drunk too much brandy. He was forced to hand the reins of the buggy over to his "wife."

Had he taken her earlier admonishment as a challenge? Or was it that she'd portrayed him as sometimes drinking too much in front of the others, and he'd simply taken it to heart? It surely wasn't because he'd been to the mine shaft earlier and was feeling melancholy about his father.

Henry never wallowed.

Somehow, however, he had managed to lose track of how much brandy he had ingested. Drink after drink had soothed the irritation of having to listen to Arthur pontificate about Wingate wealth to the other two men.

Finally, he'd stopped, but as Kate took silent charge of getting them home, handling the mare and the buggy with a deft hand, a wave of dizziness told him it had been too late. All Henry could do now was focus on staying upright.

She slid a sidelong glance at him. "Did you learn anything this evening?"

Only that you're an enigma, and I can't fathom my reaction to you.

"I did." He hoped he wasn't slurring his words.

When he didn't elaborate, Kate said, "Well?" Her tone was tinged with annoyance.

"You sound upset."

"When I told you to watch the brandy, I didn't tell you to go and *drink the brandy*."

"I'm not happy about this either," he muttered under his breath. He never let his guard down while working. Until now. *Until Kate Ryan.*

It was easier to blame her than the fact that he had been unsettled about spending time with Wingate more than he had anticipated.

Her eyes lingered on him, and he held her gaze, drinking in the fierce intelligence reflected there. He'd never had much use for meek women. Kate Ryan's ambition, dedication, and obvious independence matched his own.

But she was so young. What could she possibly bring to the table? Except that she was beautiful and confident and capable. In that moment, he knew she would go far in the Pinkertons.

The hunger for her ignited in a flash, far more intense than earlier. He turned away before she sensed it, before he did something stupid like try to kiss her. Not that she'd given any indication of sharing the attraction.

He clamped down on his very male reaction, knowing it would ruin whatever working relationship the two of them might have. He needed to concentrate on that, because if she were as intelligent as he suspected, he would have a hard time keeping her away from his true mission of ferreting out what had happened to his father.

That was why he was here. It was also why he wouldn't compromise her by getting her involved in it. She was just beginning her career, and he might very well be ending his.

She nodded. "Fine. Tell me what you learned."

His mind blanked as the buggy rocked and a wave of nausea sloshed and pitched in his stomach. *Hell.* How much brandy had he downed? He honestly couldn't remember, which was never a good sign.

"Wingate has a warehouse on the edge of town. I'm gonna search it." While knowledge of the existence of the building had come from Walter Beckett, Henry had managed to get Arthur to speak of it this evening.

"For evidence of counterfeiting," Kate stated.

"Well, apparently Lottie stores art there, but yes, I'm thinking more along the lines of counterfeiting equipment."

She flicked the reins. "Then I'll go with you."

"No."

"Why?"

"Because ...." His words floated away like smoke. What the hell was happening? He couldn't seem to hold much of a thought with this woman. *No, it's the brandy, not Kate Ryan.* After all these years of avoiding the web of love and lust for a woman, he was not about to fall for this young, pretty girl, no matter how soulful her eyes were.

She laughed. "You can't even come up with a good excuse. Louise warned me that you were stubbornly independent."

"Yeah? Well ...." She was right.

"Why is everyone so hell bent on avoiding Minnie Wingate?" she asked, thankfully changing the subject.

"I don't think Arthur likes her very much."

"Why?"

"The story, as near as I can tell," he said, his thoughts swimming, "is that Arthur's father, Ellis, married her after traveling through this area and eventually settled here. Arthur never accepted her."

"Because she was a stepmother?"

"Because she's Comanche."

Kate's profile took on a frown, revealing a lovely ridge between her brows that distracted Henry. "I thought she might be."

"When Ellis died, Arthur had every intention of throwing her off the land where she lived, and he set out to discredit the marriage because she was Indian, but then, for some reason he dropped it and she stayed in her home. But Arthur wants nothing to do with her. I should've told you to avoid talking about her. That was my mistake."

"Well, I suppose the leg squeezing was your way of putting me in line." There was an edge to her voice.

"I'm sorry about that. I didn't know what else to do. And I'm sorry about the kiss, but we may have to appear affectionate in public at times."

Her dark gaze searched the shadows of his face before she gave a nod. "I understand. I accept your apology, and I would like to make a request of you."

The rocking wasn't helping his stomach any.

"I would like to ask that you not encourage Delia Wingate in her infatuation with you."

He groaned. "Can you stop the buggy?"

"No, Henry. I have a right to have a say in how we proceed with this job."

"I'm not feeling well."

She pulled hard on the reins, and he jerked back in his seat. He barely made it to the ground before retching.

Hell.

He wiped his mouth with the back of his hand, stood up straight and adjusted his jacket, then returned to the buggy.

"Are you feeling all right?" she asked.

"Yep. Sorry about that." He climbed onto his seat. "And about Delia Wingate—I haven't encouraged her, but I haven't exactly spurned her either."

Kate flicked the reins, and they were in motion again. Henry took a steadying breath to ward off the dizziness.

"I just thought it was better not to raise any suspicions," he added.

"And you don't think it was suspicious to let her think she had a chance with you when you're a married man?"

Henry laughed. "No. There's no crime there, except that I look like a cad."

"With that I can't disagree." Kate kept her gaze on the road ahead.

Her tone and countenance were that of a jealous woman. Damn. Ryan was a good actress, a skill that came in handy in their line of work. He pushed aside the twinge of regret that her response wasn't real.

He might find Kate Ryan attractive, but he had been around attractive women before, both in the job and outside of it. He'd never had this problem before. He could handle it. Hell, he'd been fending off Delia Wingate for the last week, and by all accounts she was a very attractive woman. But it was obvious even in his inebriated state she was no Kate Ryan.

Ryan was as green as they came and far too young, but as she sat there with her back ramrod straight, her eyes narrowed with cool disdain, and her mouth pursed in consternation, he couldn't miss the steely edged resolve in her demeanor. There was more to Ryan than met the eye, and he would do well not to underestimate her.

Kate brought the buggy to a halt in front of their house.

"I'll see to this," he said, referring to the buggy and horse.

Kate released an exasperated huff. "Of course, you won't. Good for you that I know my way around such things."

As she disembarked and came around to his side, he was determined not to be coddled. But as he stepped down, his foot twisted, and he crashed into her. She held onto him, keeping him from hitting the ground, and his body ignited with awareness as her breasts briefly made contact with his chest. His face came perilously close to hers, and he recalled the kiss he'd placed on her cheek earlier.

"Do you have a real husband I should know about?" he asked, trying to ignore the faint floral scent of her hair.

"I don't." She shifted to his side and began guiding him up the steps and onto the porch. "Are *you* married, Henry?"

"Nope. You're my first wife, Kate Ryan."

In the moonlight he could see a faint smile tug at her lips. "Then I guess we're even. You're my first husband."

She opened the door and helped him into the house. His vision was spinning. She gently laid him on the sofa, pulled off his shoes, and tucked a blanket around him.

She must have lit a nearby lamp because she was bathed in a soft golden glow, and he gazed into her lovely face. "You always remember your first," he murmured.

He didn't miss the flash of uncertainty in her eyes, and it tugged at his primal male side. She wasn't immune to him. It both flattered him and left him with a sinking dread. Not only was his concentration slipping on this job, but he couldn't very well romance his brand-new partner, who was also brand new at the agency. Jonesy wouldn't be happy, and Louise would flog him ... or worse.

"Thank you, Kate, for your help."

She arched a brow, giving him a frosty glare. "Well, I couldn't very well leave you face-down in the dirt, now could I?"

Good. She wasn't going to succumb to this attraction any more than he would.

Content they'd reached an understanding, he closed his eyes.

CHAPTER 9

Henry awoke with a pounding headache.

Kate strode into the living room with a glass of something. "Good morning. You're not going to sleep the day away on this Monday, are you?"

He very carefully sat up, pressing a hand against his forehead. "I suppose I deserve this."

"I never said that. Here." She handed him the glass. "Drink this. It will help. My aunt Claire is a doctor, and she gave me the recipe."

He eyed the concoction. "Well, it looks like wine, but it smells like medicine."

She stood before him with hands on her hips. "Quit complaining. I could've given you rabbit dung."

He jerked his gaze up to her. "What?"

She laughed. "I've finally frightened Henry Maguire. Don't worry, there's no excrement in there, although cowboys swear by it. This is a fruit-infused spirit with chamomile, cardamom, peppermint oil, and myrrh, and a few other things. This blend isn't quite the full recipe since I had to work with what was in the pantry along with my own supplies."

Henry frowned. "You carry myrrh with you?"

"It's a good pain reliever. Go on." She waved a hand at him. "Drink the whole thing."

He grimaced but did as she said. She took the glass back to the kitchen, then returned.

"We need to look in that warehouse," she said.

"I agree. But I'll do it."

"I'll help you. You shouldn't go alone."

"But it could be dangerous."

"I appreciate your concern for my welfare," she said. "But what about yours? Who will watch your back? Is there anyone here you can trust?"

"No."

"Then you're stuck with me. We can go tonight once it's dark."

Since he wasn't feeling himself, and the thought of further conversation was exhausting him already, he agreed.

"I'm going out. Will you be all right?"

He nodded, then looked at her. "Where?"

"Delia has invited me into town to go shopping."

"Sounds like fun." But it really didn't.

"Well," she said, "I'm guessing she would rather invite you, but that would hardly be appropriate."

"There's nothing going on between me and Delia." Nothing beyond the woman's friendliness. Henry knew what the signals meant but had so far managed to avoid an entanglement. "I'm sorry if she implied that we were anything more than friends. I can assure you, we aren't, and never will be."

"Because of Louise?"

"What?"

"Never mind. It's just ... if there's a valid reason for your interest in Delia, then I understand. All I ask is that you tell me, so that I won't be blindsided by her. You and I communicating will help both of us do our job."

He sighed. "Agreed." He leaned back into the sofa. "The only reason I didn't spurn her outright is because she brings something unique to the table."

"What's that?"

"She's part owner of a company with her father."

"Her father being Arthur's brother?"

"Yes. Arthur has two brothers—Delia's father, Wallace, and Nell's father, Roy. He's not particularly close with either one, but he and Lottie have basically raised Delia."

"Why do you think the company is important?"

"I'm not sure," Henry replied. "Wallace buys and sells art with it."

"That could be a way to launder counterfeit money."

Henry nodded. "It's crossed my mind. I also learned something else interesting about Delia. She was engaged to Walter Beckett."

"Jean Beckett's son?"

"Yes. The engagement ended, although I'm not sure when."

"Part of the Wingate/Beckett feud?" Kate asked.

"There's a little twist there," he said. "Walter works for Arthur."

"That seems like a conflict of interest."

Henry couldn't disagree.

"Oh, I meant to tell you," she added. "Yesterday when I was at Minnie's, she and Nell said that Charlie Purcell, who used to live in this cabin many years ago, supposedly stole from Arthur and ran off, disappearing."

"How long ago?"

"I'm not sure exactly. Do you recognize the name?"

"No." But Henry wondered if it could be related to his father. "I'll have Jonesy check into it."

Kate gave a nod of agreement. "You should eat something. I've made porridge."

She stood and pinned a hat atop her hair, which she'd left flowing down her back, and Henry's gaze was drawn to the curves visible beneath the simple calico dress. When she sat to put on her black boots, Henry was able to fully gawk since her attention was on her footwear. When she finally looked up at him, he allowed a smile to cross his face.

"What's so funny?" she asked, fluffing her skirt and petticoats back into a modest position.

"Nothing. I just wanted to say thank you for taking care of me."

She pulled on riding gloves. "Isn't that what partners do?"

"I suppose."

"You know, Henry, you're awfully young to be so cynical."

She turned and left before he could respond, and the house was immediately less of everything—less warmth, less excitement, less energy. Less Kate Ryan.

KATE STROLLED DOWN the wooden walkway with Delia, looking at the window displays as they passed. The clip-clop of horse's hooves on the red-brick road resonated in the background, and the Victorian architecture visible across the street lent Trinidad a worldly atmosphere. Kate could almost imagine they were in New York City instead of Colorado, and one day she hoped to see the eastern United States for herself.

Delia wore a fitted navy jacket that matched her skirt, her blond hair tucked beneath a fancy bonnet. Kate's long-sleeved day dress suited her fine since it was thankfully a bit warm in the sunshine, but she still felt a tad underdressed beside the woman.

"Do you think you and Gilbert will be able to reconcile your marriage?" Delia asked casually, as if chatting about the inner workings of the Holmes's marriage was the most normal thing to speak of. Kate found herself regretting taking this tactic.

"I think we'll be fine," Kate said happily. "Since I've arrived, Gilbert and I have spent some very special time together, having long conversations. I'm feeling much better, and I think he is too. We're both committed to making this work."

"That's wonderful. You patched things up so quickly. Perhaps you should open an office and help other married couples find the same happiness." Her comment was curt and flippant, and Kate chose to ignore it.

Despite everything, she didn't exactly dislike Delia. There was something compelling about her, almost driven, and it spoke to Kate's own ambition in pursuing her career as a Pinkerton.

"Have you ever been engaged?" Kate asked, wondering if Delia would tell her the truth.

Delia nodded. "Yes, twice. Does that surprise you?"

"No, of course not," Kate lied. "What happened?"

"The first was Walter Beckett." Delia was being honest.

"Don't the Becketts have land bordering your uncles?"

Delia nodded.

"What happened?" Kate asked.

"I realized we weren't suited, and I broke it off. That was four years ago. Soon after I became engaged to Joseph Crump, but he was simply too old. I admire Laura Phelps for being married to a mature gentleman, but I just couldn't do it. Of course, I didn't love him, but Aunt Lottie tells me I'm too picky in that regard. But it didn't matter, as he passed away before we could marry."

"I'm so sorry."

Delia squared her shoulders. "I've decided I don't really want to marry at this point. Uncle Arthur and Aunt Lottie think differently, of course. On behalf of my father, I suppose. I've always been closer to Aunt and Uncle than to Papa—I never knew my mother—but at this point I'm feeling that marriage isn't for me. That maybe it's too restrictive."

"Then don't marry," Kate replied. "You seem to be in a unique position. Your family has wealth. You don't need a husband."

"But I'm completely dependent financially on my uncle at the moment, and he wants me to wed." She didn't mention the company she supposedly co-owned with her father. "Uncle has been looking for a match for me. I have to admit, I rather fancied your Gilbert for a bit." She cast a mischievous smile at Kate. "I didn't know he was married at first."

Kate suppressed her surprise that Delia was all but admitting to her infatuation.

"But don't worry," Delia added. "Now that I've met you, I can see that he's quite taken with you. I thought it would be fun to be married to a writer, to travel to places like Italy. I would love to get out of here."

"I appreciate your candor," Kate said slowly. "I rather like my Gilbert as well. And yes, it's lovely to travel. But marriage is much more than that." And since Kate had no experience whatsoever in this area, she relied on her parents' union. "Marriage encompasses not only a great love, but also friendship, and tolerance, and forgiveness. You must compromise and have good cheer about it so there's no bitterness that might fester and rot if left to grow."

Delia glanced over, a look of awareness in her gaze. "You've quite convinced me, Sallie."

"Of what?"

"That I want a marriage like yours and Gilbert's."

Kate went silent. No reason to go overboard.

They entered a dress shop and spent the next hour ordering two gowns for each of them, which required measurements and fittings. The garments would be ready for pick-up in three days. Afterwards, they went for tea at a small establishment, and Kate rather enjoyed the outing. Delia was quite intelligent, and despite that she'd never been to Italy, she had traveled to London and described her visit in such detail that Kate decided she must go one day.

With her job at the Pinkertons, she was now earning her own income. One day, she planned to travel. And despite that her folks, Matt and Molly, had such a strong marriage and an obviously loving bond, Kate wasn't certain she would ever have that. She dreaded marrying for anything less and being stuck running a ranch in the middle of nowhere.

She longed to see the world.

As they left the café, an older woman stopped before them.

"Delia, what a surprise to see you out today."

"Hello, Mrs. Beckett." Delia's expression didn't appear congenial. "May I introduce you to Sallie Holmes. Sallie, this is Mrs. Jean Beckett."

Mrs. Beckett gave a nod toward Kate, her brown eyes wide and forthright. She was a handsome woman with only a hint of gray in her dark hair. "It's a pleasure to meet you," she said.

"Likewise, ma'am."

"Are you new in town, Sallie?"

"Yes."

"Her husband is ghostwriting Uncle Arthur's memoir," Delia said.

Mrs. Beckett's face registered genuine surprise. "Memoir? Just when I think Arthur can't do anything more shocking, he manages to prove me wrong." She released a short laugh, amusement dancing in her eyes.

"Have you known the Wingates long?" Kate asked, trying to make the most of the encounter. Perhaps she could draw out something useful that she could report back to Henry.

"Yes," Mrs. Beckett replied. "My dear Clayton, may he rest in peace, knew Arthur from when they were boys in Ohio. They even enlisted in the War together."

"And they both ended up in Colorado?" Kate said. "They must have been good friends."

"I suppose. Once, maybe, a long time ago."

"You know that Uncle Arthur didn't ruin their friendship," Delia cut in.

Mrs. Beckett narrowed her eyes. "Is that what your uncle told you?"

Delia looped her arm with Kate's. "We really must be going."

Delia pulled her along and Kate was forced to give a wave and a *good day* and be on her way.

"Is Walter her son? Is that why you don't like her?" Kate asked as they walked briskly down the wooden boardwalk.

Delia sighed, looking straight ahead. "It's most definitely awkward to be friendly with your ex-fiancé's mother."

CHAPTER 10

Henry peered around the building, looking for signs of anyone on the street. It was deep in the night, so it should be clear.

"Are you certain you can get inside?" Kate asked in a whisper from beside him.

He nodded. They were both dressed in dark clothing so they would blend with the shadows, and Kate had even donned trousers. He had to applaud her practicality while at the same time trying to ignore the striking figure she presented.

There were some field agents who didn't care to partner with a woman. While Henry generally preferred working alone, he had never minded collaborating with Louise, who was capable, intelligent, and possessed the same work ethic he did. Luckily, he wasn't married in his civilian life, as some of the other male agents were. He'd heard from more than one that their wives didn't like them in close contact with female operatives.

Louise had never been a distraction for him.

Kate Ryan on the other hand ....

A sense of prophecy settled over him and he shook it off. This young slip of a girl wasn't going to be his undoing.

He moved quietly along the side alley to the front boardwalk. The warehouse wasn't in the main part of town, but at the west end, so there was unlikely to be any passersby at this time of night. Or early morning. He guessed it was around two a.m.

As they came to the front door, Kate whispered, "Would you like me to pick the lock?"

"No," he said, and pulled out a key. "We'll use this." He unlocked the door and they slipped inside. He quietly shut the door behind them.

"How did you get that?"

"I borrowed it from Wingate."

They moved through the front room. It was so dark they had to stop so Kate could strike a match and light the kerosene lamp she had carried for that purpose. Without speaking, they inspected the shelves in the warehouse, staying near one another so they could share the light.

"What is all of this?" she asked.

"Equipment, I'm guessing. Wingate does own several coal mines in the area."

When nothing that looked like a printing press appeared, they headed to the back of the building. In one corner were at least half a dozen wooden barrels.

Kate brought the light closer and inspected one. "What do you suppose is in these?"

Henry withdrew a small knife he carried inside his boot and pried the lid off. It was empty.

"Wine?" she asked.

He sniffed. "Doesn't smell like it." He replaced the lid and motioned her toward two offices. There were signs affixed to each door.

Kate held up the lantern.

Wallace Wingate.

Walter Beckett.

"We'll search both," he said.

Before he could get his tools from his coat pocket, Kate had dropped to a knee and with a long metal file she picked the lock on Wallace's door in less than ten seconds.

"Louise's tutoring?" he murmured.

She flashed a smile, and he lingered on her profile a moment longer than was proper.

"It's her favorite subject to teach," Kate replied, turning the handle. "That and cryptography."

They entered the office. A quick inspection revealed a clean and orderly desk with a plush chair.

Henry searched the desk drawers but came up with nothing. As Kate turned back toward the door, she gasped.

"What's wrong?" he asked.

"Look at that painting," she said, staring at the wall beside the doorway.

It seemed fairly standard in Henry's mind: An outdoor scene with trees, blue sky, white clouds, and water bubbling from a spring.

She leaned in to look at the name in the corner. "It's a J. Montgomery," she said.

"What's so special about that?"

"They're just very hard to come by. My grandmother collects them. Well, she only has one so far, but she's been trying for months to get another. Normally his work focuses on the Comanche and is filled with a gritty realism alongside a sense of the divine. You can see some of that here, of course."

Henry frowned. "Of course," he replied, but he didn't know art.

"Usually, his work has a high level of detail of various tribal activities."

"Then how do you know this is the same artist?"

"The style is very similar," she replied. "If it truly is one of his, how did Wallace get it? And since it's not the normal focus of

Montgomery's work, how did this painting come about? But even more important, my grandmother isn't aware of this one."

"How do you know?"

"She's become a bit of a collector in the past several years and has taught me a lot about art. It's something she and I share. J. Montgomery has been one of her favorites because of his depictions of the Comanche. She's always been protective of my mother and her time with them."

"Your mother lived with the Comanche?"

She nodded. "She was abducted when she was a child."

"But she was rescued?"

"Partially. It's a long story. Maybe I'll tell you sometime." She went back to staring at the painting. "If Wingate is trying to launder his counterfeit money, then art is a great way to do it. Don't you think? And wasn't Mr. Moller from supper the other night an art dealer?"

"Yes." Damn. She was right.

"Doesn't Wallace Wingate buy and sell paintings?"

"I believe so. I'll have Jonesy do more digging into Wallace's company."

They left Wallace's office and locked it, then went next door to Walter's. His work area was messier, with papers strewn across the desktop and a file cabinet in the corner. Henry inspected the paperwork as well as all parts of the desk but nothing consequential showed up.

"Would you set the lamp on the desk?" he asked. "I want to look through the file cabinet."

There'd been a case he'd worked on a few years back where the guilty person hadn't bothered to hide any evidence, and in fact had left it out in the open the entire time. The technique had almost worked, because no one expected it to be right under their nose, so they naturally discounted several clues. Finally, however, it had dawned on Henry.

He glanced across the room and Kate was crouched beside a collection of men's shoes.

"Looking for evidence of mud?" he teased.

"Not exactly. Just a theory. One that Louise shared with me."

Kate began inspecting the shoes in earnest, lifting them up and turning them this way and that, then looking inside.

Henry closed the file cabinet, silently admitting defeat and crouched near Kate.

"How did you get Jonesy to hire you?" he asked.

"You make it sound as if I was completely unqualified," she murmured.

"I didn't mean it that way. It's just that the agency doesn't hire many women."

"I know," she replied. "My grandfather knows Mr. Jones's father."

Henry chuckled. "You pulled strings."

She flicked her eyes to his. "I'm aware that I'm very young *and* a woman. I needed a foot in the door, but it was Louise who helped me keep that door open."

"I'm not surprised. She must have felt you were qualified, or she would never have fought for you."

"I'd like to think that I *am* qualified. I'm not here to rest on my laurels."

"I can see that."

"Was that a compliment, Maguire?"

"Maybe."

She raised a delicate brow. "Thank you. How often have you and Louise worked together?"

"Several times. It makes it a little easier when you know your partner."

"You mean when you *trust* your partner."

"Yes." No reason to sugarcoat it.

"You know, I'm in the same boat as you," Kate said.

When he gave her a questioning look, she added, "I must learn to trust you as well. This is my first assignment, and yes, I'm inexperienced, but wouldn't that have been the case for you on your first assignment?"

"My first case was nothing like this one," he said.

The silence between them stretched until Kate finally spoke. "Would you tell me what happened?"

"It was the Homestead Strike."

Recognition lit her face.

"I take it you know of it," he added.

"Yes. You must've been very young."

"Eighteen and wet behind the ears, but full of determination about doing right. But sometimes what's right and wrong gets muddled."

"Hadn't workers of the Homestead Mill armed themselves and sealed off the town? And the Pinkertons were brought in to establish order?"

"That was true. And those who were striking had valid reasons—Andrew Carnegie was cutting wages and jobs." He sighed. "But I did as I was told, and I fired on them when our barge arrived on shore."

"But didn't the Pinkertons ultimately surrender only to then be attacked?"

He gave one curt nod. "Agents I had trained with were killed."

"I guess you're right," Kate said, her voice soft. "This job is nothing like that one. I wonder that you remained an agent after that."

"When it was all over, I was one of the fortunate who hadn't been badly beaten by the mob. It made me more determined that justice should prevail. Rather than shake my confidence in being a Pinkerton, it strengthened it."

"Has it been worth it all these years?" she asked, her earnest expression indicating how much she wanted to know his answer.

He thought to lie to her, to tell her justice always did prevail, that right always outweighed wrong, but he found he couldn't. She deserved the truth.

"Sometimes," he said.

She took his answer with a forthright acceptance. "I suppose all we can hope is that we've done our best and know that it was enough."

He found himself believing in her optimism, if only for a moment. To be standing in her shoes, where the world seemed bright and cheery and good prevailed over evil—it was a place he had never really occupied. His mother had died when he was young, and his father had been largely absent. The world had always been unsteady in Henry's mind. When his father had died, it had gone full tilt.

"I hope you can hang onto that perspective, Kate."

She watched him, her eyes clouded with compassion and something more. Henry feared the *something more* was also in his gaze. He wanted very much to be an agent that Kate Ryan could look up to, and along with it was desire—for her.

She averted her gaze, breaking the spell, and shifted her attention to a pair of boots sitting against the wall.

She picked up one of the shoes and popped off the heel, revealing a cavity along with a piece of paper.

"I think we've discovered something," she whispered.

She went to the desk where the lamp would offer better light and smoothed out the paper on the surface. Henry moved beside her and scanned the contents.

"Is that what I think it is?" he asked.

"I believe so. It's a cipher."

A way to send encoded messages. And now they possessed a key.

"I can't believe you found that," he murmured.

She smiled at him, and the gesture sprouted a seed in his chest, something akin to besotted admiration. He was beginning to think he should give up trying to suppress it, since it didn't seem to be working anyway.

"But we can't take it," he said, "or else they'll change the cipher, and it won't help us."

"Agreed. Look for a piece of paper. If you can wait, I'll copy it."

He did as she asked. It took her forty-five minutes to transfer the code. During that time Henry went back into the main warehouse, but since Kate possessed the only light, his explorations in the partial darkness didn't turn up anything further. Once she was finished, they replaced the folded paper in the boot heel, tidied the office so that it wouldn't look as if they'd been there, and quietly slipped out of the warehouse and back into the shadows. They had left their horses a mile away in a wooded area, so they returned to them and rode home.

Before Kate retired to the bedroom, she handed the copied paper to Henry. "You should keep it."

Henry hesitated. "I think you should. You're less likely to look suspicious. You're less likely to be searched if someone thinks something is going on."

"All right. I've got a hidden pocket sewn into my undergarments. I'll keep it there."

Henry tried not to imagine where that piece of paper might reside on her person.

"Good work tonight," he said.

"The same to you." She headed to the bedroom. "Good night, Henry." She shut the door.

He kept himself busy getting ready to bed on the sofa. It was late and he was tired, except that once he lay down, sleep eluded him. And it had nothing to do with the current case, but everything to do with the woman in the next room. He cast an arm across his eyes. He couldn't help but wonder if Louise had sent Kate Ryan to him as a test. Louise had always said that he should try to get a life outside of work. But that was a stretch. Louise valued the agency as much as he did. She would never have sent Ryan if she hadn't felt her competent. If she hadn't felt that she could protect Henry.

At last, sleep found him, but his dreams were filled with a dark-haired woman with green eyes.

CHAPTER 11

Kate settled onto the settee holding a cup and saucer and sipping her tea. She was at the Wingate house in an open and airy sunroom, where a group of eight women had gathered. Lottie Wingate presided over the meeting of the Women's Christian Association, to which she had invited Kate in her capacity as Sallie Holmes.

Delia Wingate was also present, but thankfully Mrs. Marsh was absent. Kate had almost said no to the invitation, worried that she would run into the woman, but a discreet inquiry had revealed that Mrs. Marsh had departed.

Kate still didn't know why the woman had come to the Holmes' cabin that day, but Mrs. Wingate had alluded that Mrs. Marsh was an art collector. Was that how she and Kate's grandmother were acquainted? Did they both share a mutual love of J. Montgomery paintings? Kate would've asked Lottie about it, but a quick inspection of the Wingate home showed no Montgomery art hanging on the wall. She decided not to press any inquires that might look suspicious.

Kate also hadn't told Henry about knowing Mrs. Marsh, but

now that the woman was gone, she wouldn't concern Henry with what was possibly an unnecessary detail.

A glance around the room showed the additional six women to be of varying ages. A few of them Kate remembered being introduced to at the party three days ago during her sudden appearance at Henry's side, along with Laura Phelps and Helen Moller from supper on Sunday.

"Let's bring this meeting to order," Mrs. Wingate said as she began flipping through a pile of papers on her lap and looking down her nose through narrow reading glasses, her red hair glistening from the oil lamp light. "First, we would like to welcome Sallie Holmes." She raised her gaze and planted a serene expression on Kate.

The other ladies murmured a welcome, and Kate cast a smile around the room.

"Some of you have already met her. Her husband, Gilbert, has been working with Arthur these past few weeks and we're so happy to have her here at last. A man shouldn't be without his wife, right, ladies?"

There was a hum of agreement. "We hope she'll stay permanently in our little community, which is why I've invited her to our meeting." Mrs. Wingate cleared her throat. "All right then, let's get started."

Delia sat beside Kate on the settee, and she offered a plate with small cucumber sandwiches. Kate snatched up two and prepared for what was certain to be a boring meeting. All she really hoped for were introductions to the women in the area. Henry had managed to compile a list of possible suspects, but they were mostly men. It was up to Kate to investigate the wives and female acquaintances.

"So our big event coming up is the art auction," Lottie said.

The maid entered the room. "Sorry to interrupt, ma'am. Mrs. Beckett has arrived."

Jean Beckett entered the room, a waft of strong perfume coming from the swoosh of her pale blue skirts. Kate didn't miss the steel in her gaze.

"Jean." Lottie's voice was flat. "I wasn't expecting you."

"I gather since you failed to notify me about the meeting. But Helen let me know." Jean nodded toward Helen Moller.

Lottie arched a brow. "An oversight on my part. Please join us."

Mrs. Beckett conveyed quiet greetings to several of the women, including Delia. Then she sat beside Kate. "It's nice to see you again, Sallie. You're jumping right into our community, aren't you?"

Kate nodded. "Yes, ma'am."

"Now," Lottie continued, "let's get back to the art auction. Arthur and I already have several pieces to offer, but if any of you know of artwork that we could include, please let us know. There's still time to purchase pieces, which we're willing to do ourselves."

A murmur of surprise and gratitude rippled through the room.

"That's so generous of you and your husband," Jean said. "Who will be receiving the proceeds from this auction?"

"All monies will be donated to Reverend Father Persone and the Holy Trinity Parish to benefit the work they do with the underserved of our fellow humans."

"How commendable," Jean murmured under her breath.

It was clear that Jean Beckett thought Lottie Wingate was full of hot air.

"Will you be donating anything, Jean?" Lottie asked, an edge to her voice.

"Let me think on it, as this is the first I've heard about this auction."

"The event came together rather last minute," Delia said.

"When is it?" Jean asked.

"Next Thursday evening," Lottie replied. "It will be here at our home."

Jean's expression brightened. "I look forward to my invitation."

Lottie cast a withering glare toward the woman but quickly

recovered. For the next thirty minutes, she spoke about details of the auction—placing an announcement in the local newspaper, organizing the art the day before, deciding on what food should be served.

When the meeting ended, most of the women departed.

Delia leaned close to Sallie. "Stick around for part two."

The séance.

Kate smiled.

This should be interesting.

"You're staying?" Lottie demanded, not bothering to be congenial.

"Yes," Jean said. "Helen also mentioned the séance. I've always wanted to attend one. You don't mind, do you? I thought maybe I could reach Clay." Her voice cracked as she said her husband's name.

Lottie sighed. "Are you a believer? That's crucial."

"What do you mean?"

"Do you believe in spiritualism?"

Jean appeared taken aback. Kate wondered why Lottie hadn't interrogated her in this way.

"I want to," Jean finally said, her voice quiet. "I do miss my Clayton."

Lottie appeared to give in. "I guess that will be enough."

The servants brought in a large round table and placed a tablecloth over it. Helen and Laura had remained, and along with Kate and Delia, and Lottie and Jean, they had six people. Chairs were added, and they all took their seats.

The butler announced the arrival of Mrs. Ramona Palmer. She was a short, robust woman with rosy cheeks and a jovial air to her, quite the opposite of what Kate imagined a medium might look like.

But then her aunt Emma, who possessed similar skills, appeared to be nothing more than a rancher's wife and mother of five sons to anyone looking in from the outside.

"Hello, ladies," Mrs. Palmer said, her energy optimistic and uplifting. "Are we ready to speak to the spirits?"

"I believe so, Ramona," Lottie said.

They all took their seats, with Delia and Lottie on either side of Ramona, who smiled and said, "I see some new faces here. Welcome."

Lottie introduced everyone to the medium, and then Ramona retrieved a large round crystal from her bag and placed it on a bright blue silk cloth at the center of the table. She added two white candles in holders, a glass bowl, and a swinging pendulum in a stand.

The entire setup had Kate feeling skeptical, since her aunt Emma didn't require any equipment for her second sight.

One of the maids placed a piece of paper, pen, and ink before each woman.

Frowning, Kate leaned close to Delia, and whispered, "What's this for?"

"It's Aunt Lottie's special twist on the séance."

"Now," Ramona said, taking a deep breath. "Each of us shall write down a sin for which we need atonement. Don't worry, no one will see this, but the spirits will know what's in your heart, and perhaps they'll come to us this evening with guidance and forgiveness."

Kate's mind raced with this new revelation. She was pretty sure this wasn't normal séance protocol.

"What will happen to these slips of paper?" Laura Phelps asked, her brow furrowed, voicing aloud what Kate was thinking.

"We'll place them all in this bowl," Ramona said, indicating the item on the table. "Then we'll burn them. It adds an extra punch to contacting the spirits."

As everyone took pen in hand and dipped it into the inkwell, Kate searched for something to put down. It needed to be from Sallie's point-of-view because Kate wasn't altogether convinced that no one would read it. Was Ramona Palmer a charlatan of such degree that she didn't even bother to hide it?

She quickly scratched out the only thing she could think of: *I thought of leaving my husband when we started having marital problems.* At least this would align with what she'd already confided to Delia.

She folded her paper a few times and dropped it into the bowl as it was passed around. When it reached Ramona, she set it before her, near the edge of the table.

"Please take a hold of one another's hands," Ramona said. "Then relax and shut your eyes."

Kate took Delia's right hand and Laura Phelps's left one into her grasp and shut her eyes, but she leaned her head back a little more than normal so she could see through the barest crack of her eyelids.

Ramona didn't waste any time. She switched the glass bowl with an exact duplicate hidden somewhere in the folds of her skirt. This one was also filled with slips of folded papers. Kate was sure they would be blank if she demanded to see them.

Bold. And clever, Kate supposed. Ramona Palmer was a top-notch fake.

Ramona continued, her demeanor becoming serious. "Let us pray for protection from beings that would do us harm. We ask God that only good spirits be allowed in our circle tonight, that no evil beings come near. Tonight, we are here to contact the spirit of Lottie's mother, and we seek guidance from the supernatural world. Lottie's mother, please join our circle when you're ready. We also welcome any good spirits who are near us as well. Please make your presence known."

"We have a dog," Ramona's voice boomed, causing Kate to jump. "I keep hearing Texas Ranger."

Kate froze. Her pa had been a Texas Ranger before he married her ma, and her family had had a dog named Ranger. How could Ramona have possibly known that?

"He's sitting beside Sallie."

Kate cracked an eye open, but Ramona's eyes were closed.

"You can speak to him," Ramona added.

Was her beloved Ranger here? Kate was surprised by feeling a sense of ... his presence.

"Please tell him I miss him very much," Kate said, unable to keep the emotion from her voice. She'd been twelve years old when he'd died, and it had been a terrible loss. "My pa still speaks of his amazing herding abilities."

"He's with you quite often, I believe. He keeps trying to show me something."

Trepidation filled Kate. Had she somehow inadvertently blown her cover? Could the spirit of her cherished Ranger really expose her? She held her breath, waiting.

"He's brought you a bone. It looks like it might be from an animal."

Kate released a silent breath of relief. "He did that a lot." Kate paused and then couldn't help but ask, "Is he well?"

"Yes. His love for you is still shining so bright. You lost him some time ago?"

"Yes."

"Is there anyone else here but a dog?" Lottie cut in, her voice quiet but tinged with the slightest amount of annoyance.

"You know how this works, Lottie," Ramona said. "The spirits come when they want."

Kate couldn't discount that maybe Ramona had some abilities.

"My mother?" Lottie prompted.

"No," Ramona replied. "But we'll keep the channels open. Anything can happen. Now, let me see who else is here."

Kate was grateful to have the spotlight off her, but a sense of

Ranger remained, truly lifting her spirits. She hadn't expected such a rush of emotion over this unexpected turn of events.

"We've got an older woman."

That resulted in an eager gasp from Lottie. "What does she look like?" she asked quietly, her voice quivering with anticipation.

Kate felt a pang of sympathy for Lottie, clearly desperate for a connection to her mother. But was Lottie part of Ramona's charade?

"She's tall and willowy, and she has a birthmark on her right cheek."

"I have an aunt on my mother's side who looked like that," Laura cut in.

"That would also describe my husband's mother," Helen said. "She died last year."

"It must be my mother," Lottie insisted. "Are you sure the birthmark is on the right side?"

While the women fought over the identity of the spirit, Kate noticed that Delia's breathing had changed. Sneaking a peek, her head was hanging down.

"Delia," Kate whispered. "Are you okay?"

Her head snapped up. "Lottie, dearest."

Everyone opened their eyes and stared at Delia.

"Mama," Lottie cried. "Is it you?"

"Yes, darling." Delia's voice had changed, both in tone and cadence.

Kate couldn't decide if it was real or not, but if it weren't then Delia was quite the actress.

"I've tried for so long to reach you," Lottie said, her voice filled with anguish.

"I'm always here. You've done well."

"Thank you!" Lottie all but gushed the gratitude, completely out-of-character.

But this couldn't be real, could it? On the other hand, why

would Delia agree to dupe her aunt? Unless Lottie was in on it too. It was quite a performance, but to what end?

Delia looked around the room, but Kate didn't see anything familiar reflected in her eyes.

"Is she possessed of a spirit?" Laura asked, her voice filled with panic, and Kate wondered the same thing.

"My mama must've chosen Delia because she's family," Lottie said. "Delia has always been an open book."

Kate wasn't so sure about that.

"Lottie, my dear," Delia continued, her voice sounding like that of a much older woman. "You've kept the family business going. I didn't think you had it in you."

"I will always honor everything you've taught me, Mama."

"Good girl." But Delia's voice was already fading, and she slumped back in her chair.

Lottie glared at the medium. "Ramona, do something."

"I can't force a spirit to return."

"Sallie, shake her," Lottie cried.

"What?" Kate looked at Delia, who had hunched over again. She really had no desire to touch her. In fact, she leaned further away. What if Lottie's mother jumped into *her?*

"Lottie," Ramona said, her voice soothing. "I don't sense any spirits now. They've all gone. But I would say this has been a most productive session."

Kate glanced around as Helen and Laura mutely nodded, their faces a bit paler than when this entire fiasco had begun.

CHAPTER 12

Henry sat across from Wingate. They were tucked into his office while the ladies had a charity meeting, which Kate had joined.

"I wanted to tell you about my time in the War of the Rebellion," Arthur said.

Henry readied his pencil over his notebook to jot down pertinent notes, rallying himself not to roll his eyes. Arthur really liked to embellish his accomplishments.

"My family lived in Ohio. When Union forces surrendered at Fort Sumter and the war began, I knew I wanted to join. So with my friends, Hugh and Clayton, I set out to join a regiment."

Henry's pencil froze above the page.

"Hugh?" Henry said, his voice quiet and thankfully steady.

Arthur paused. "Hugh Maguire. He was my good friend."

Henry raised his gaze, a bit shocked to see that Arthur looked ... upset. It was the only word for it, and it made Henry angry.

"Why do you say *was*?" Henry asked.

"That's a long story, one that I'll tell you at a later time." Arthur took a fortifying breath.

It was all Henry could do not to demand that Arthur tell him what had happened to Hugh, but he swallowed down the words threatening to erupt from his throat.

"You might recognize the other man's name, Clayton Beckett."

"He was Jean Beckett's husband?"

"He was. He passed about four years ago. The three of us were determined to join the fight, but we were too young, you see. We were only sixteen, so we ran away from home and lied about our ages."

Henry tried to calm his roiling mind and write down what Arthur was saying because this was all news to Henry. His father had never shared the details of the War with him or Ian, and Henry hadn't known just how deep the connection to the neighboring Becketts was.

"You became soldiers?" Henry asked.

Arthur nodded. "Even more unbelievable, the three of us became spies. And I was the best of them."

Again, Henry was shocked, and not just at Arthur's bragging. Hugh Maguire had been a spy in the Civil War?

"Why would they let you do that?" Henry said.

"I think it was our youth. We were able to infiltrate into the south easier than the older gents, and we were reckless enough to embrace the danger. I suppose that was the bigger reason."

A part of Henry didn't want to ask, but he had to. "Where is Hugh now?"

"We'd remained in touch over the years, and then, a while back, he came to visit and there was a terrible accident ...." Genuine pain crossed Arthur's face, and Henry couldn't believe how far the man would go to keep up the charade. He couldn't know that Henry was Hugh's son—Jonesy had been very careful with Henry's alias.

"He died about eight years ago. Here, in fact, in Trinidad. It happened at one of the Wingate coal mines."

"That's terrible," Henry heard himself say. "You're certain it was an accident?"

The question seemed to snap Arthur out of his melancholy. "Of course it was an accident. What are you implying?"

Henry realized too late that he had overplayed his hand. "Nothing," he said, trying to backtrack. "I guess my imagination was getting the better of me. You said you'd been spies. Did the three of you have unfinished business?"

That seemed to catch Arthur up short. "You mean like a job that may have been lingering? As if one of us had done something criminal and the other two had learned of it?"

Was Arthur all but confessing? Shit.

"Those are your words, not mine," Henry said.

Suddenly Arthur laughed. "You're definitely a writer, Gilbert. You have an overactive imagination." His countenance sobered. "My relationship with Clayton became strained over the years, but Hugh was my good friend."

Dammit, but a part of Henry wanted to believe that.

"You know he told me once that I should divorce Lottie."

"Why would he say that?"

"He never really liked her." Arthur sighed. "Hell, sometimes I don't like her."

"Do you want this in the book?" But it was more a question to get Arthur off the subject. Henry didn't really want to know the inner workings of Arthur's marriage, and he was certain that the biography he supposedly was writing would never have a stamp of approval from Lottie if she was portrayed badly in it.

Arthur chuckled. "What do you think?" He leaned back in his stuffed leather chair. "Lottie and I suit one another. It's not always been easy for us, but she's got a backbone made of iron. If you're ever down and out, you want her in your corner. But she can rub some people the wrong way. She and Hugh ... well, they never saw eye to eye."

Another reason for Henry not to like her.

"But listen to me going on about such sad things. Don't let my marriage dictate what yours could be. Sallie is a catch. I wouldn't mind looking at her for the rest of my days." Arthur shifted in his seat. "I've heard you two are having marital difficulties."

"Who said that?"

Arthur shrugged. "Women talk."

"My marriage is just fine." Henry wasn't sure if the steel in his voice was fake or real. He was only protective because Kate Ryan was his partner, nothing more.

"Should we include Hugh Maguire in the book?" Henry asked, trying to steer the conversation back. This was the in he needed—a plausible way to investigate the death of his father with none other than the man who purported to be his best friend, and possibly his murderer.

When had *possibly* entered Henry's mind?

He'd been convinced before coming here that Arthur was responsible. But there was doubt now. And Henry hated that.

Arthur's expression shifted again, the humor and the light leaving his gaze. "Let me think about that. And while I do, I've got a proposition for you. Why don't you take a few days in the wilderness and get away from it all. Take Sallie with you and patch up that marriage."

"I really shouldn't. I have work to do." But Henry was finally getting the chance to poke around Wingate land, and with Wingate's blessing no less. Henry believed the map in his father's belongings was of the Wingate property, and now Arthur was handing him the opportunity to investigate it.

Arthur smiled. "Oh, a few days off won't matter. I've got acres of some of the prettiest land around Trinidad. And you can have access to it all, including an ancient spring that has some old native stories associated with it. You and Sallie can leave tomorrow. I'll prepare a map and supplies."

"Thank you, Arthur. I look forward to it."

Somehow, however, Henry would need to ditch Kate.

"WINGATE WANTS me to go into the wilderness," Henry announced to Kate the following morning.

She frowned, instantly not liking this turn of events. "Why?"

"There's a spring he thinks I should see. He suggests I take you along, but I think you should stay. He may be up to something."

"Well, just pretend to go but stay behind," she offered.

"It's a thought, but I'd like to go."

"How long will this take?"

"A few days maybe."

"I don't think you should travel alone," she said.

"Someone should stay and keep an eye on Arthur."

"But I thought you didn't want me around him when you weren't here." Henry had alluded that Arthur liked to compromise women, and Kate could well believe it after meeting the man. But she felt confident that she could handle the man if necessary.

"Just keep your distance," Henry said. "You don't want to come with me anyway. It'll be uncomfortable for a lady."

Kate took a deep breath and held back refuting his last statement. Living out on the land wasn't foreign to her—she'd shadowed the ranch hands at the Rocking Wren as much as her brother, and her pa and her uncles had never treated her as if she were made of porcelain and easy to break. She had spent as much time in the saddle alongside the men as her male cousins.

She was conflicted with two motivations, neither of which she could voice aloud.

If she went with Henry, she would be forced into close contact with him, closer even than the house where they currently resided. At least here, she had a bedroom where she could gain a bit of privacy. Being alone with Henry in the wide-open spaces seemed far more ... intimate.

On the other hand, she had a job to do, and while part of that job was to aid Henry in his investigation, it was, unfortunately, also to keep an eye on Henry himself, per Louise's instructions.

"I'm going with you."

"That's not necessary, Ryan. The conditions won't be optimal. And what about that séance? You need to find out what that Ramona Palmer is doing with everyone's self-professed sins, and if Lottie and Delia are somehow involved in it."

When she'd initially told him about the séance, he hadn't been very encouraging about that angle to the case.

"Since when?" she asked, her tone a bit defensive.

"I was thinking about what you'd said, and I believe it's worth exploring."

She couldn't help but feel that he was placating her, throwing her a bone to give her something to do. Busy work.

Kate set her shoulders. "I understand. But you would be alone out there and exposed. My job is to back you up. I can't do that sitting here, drinking tea and listening to idle gossip." She held up a hand before he could interrupt. "Which, by the way, I can do plenty of when we return."

"What will Mrs. Wingate say?"

"Why would she say anything? We're husband and wife, remember? I have every right to travel with you."

Kate sought to keep her expression from showing her concern. Henry really didn't want her to accompany him. Was he up to something?

Despite Henry's obvious difficulty with her as his partner, despite his aloofness and at times brusque manner, she found herself liking him. Louise had said he was a good man, and the woman's disappointment that he may have been compromised had spoken volumes. Still, this was Kate's first assignment, and her performance would indicate whether she got more assignments. She couldn't botch this, not even to spare Henry's feelings.

With an impatient sigh, he said, "All right. But this is no

vacation. This isn't a *honeymoon*. You'll have to carry your weight. I mean that literally."

"I understand."

"Get packed. We leave at first light tomorrow."

He left the house and Kate didn't follow, instead getting her gear in order. She assumed he'd gone to the main house to visit with Wingate, and when she arrived in the late afternoon, she was told she had just missed him. She met with Lottie to request items for their trip, as well as to let her know she would be accompanying Gilbert.

"Why on earth do you want to go?" Lottie asked, her frown transforming her face into stern judgment.

"I've been away from Gilbert for several weeks," Kate replied, having rehearsed her reply in anticipation of such a question. "I just can't bear to be away from him, not even for a night. And I'd love to see the land that you and Arthur manage. I can only imagine how impressive it is."

"I suppose."

"And Gilbert becomes impatient with closed spaces. It's long been an issue in our marriage. Sometimes it's best to spend a few days in the bosom of Mother Nature. It's amazing how it can give a fresh perspective and improve the spirits." But Kate's rebuttal was about herself. Still, it didn't hurt to give Lottie an emotional reason, despite what Henry had said about avoiding such nonsense.

Unable to offer a counter argument, Lottie had sent the butler to retrieve the items Kate had requested—a tent, food provisions, pots and pans, a Winchester and ammunition, extra blankets and rope, heavy duster coats for both Kate and Henry, and a pack mule to carry it all.

"I'm not sure why you need all of this," Lottie said. "We have staff that will see to these things."

But Kate had learned from her pa always to be equipped,

especially when heading out into the wilderness. Never rely on anyone. Survival might depend upon it.

"I like to be prepared," Kate replied.

"You won't need the Winchester."

"What about wild animals? Bears? Mountain lions?"

"I'm sure your husband will keep you safe."

"Would you rely on a man for your safety?" Kate asked. "I'm a fair shot. And I prefer to rely on myself."

Lottie watched her for a moment, an air of cool assessment to it. Then she made a sound of acceptance.

Strangely, it made Kate feel better, as if she had passed some kind of test. As if Lottie Wingate knew there was more to endanger Kate out there than merely wild animals, and she was agreeing that Kate should have the ability to protect herself. Kate's esteem for Lottie went up a notch, however slight it might be.

Of course, Lottie was a suspect. Everyone in the household was. Kate thanked her for the supplies and returned home. She ate supper alone and finally went to bed. Much later she heard the front door open and the quiet footfalls of Henry as he took to his bed on the sofa.

Kate rolled over and tried to reclaim sleep. Working undercover was different than she had imagined. The isolation seeped beneath her skin, threatening to amplify her insecurities, but at the same time it steeled her resolve.

Seeking out a job with the Pinkertons had set her on a singular course less than a year ago. While her folks had never held her back from pursuing a goal, whether it was learning to rope a calf or mastering calculus in her studies, they hadn't exactly been jumping for joy when she had told them of her plans to travel to Chicago and apply for a job. Ultimately, her pa had taken her because Kate had been determined. Her ma had hugged her so tightly and told Kate how proud she was, and to be careful, and to remember always to trust her instincts, and to please come home for Christmas. Kate had assured her she would try to do all those things, and with tearful hugs she'd left home at eighteen.

But in her mind, she had left far sooner than that. When she was younger, she had dreamed of adventure, and she had known that staying in Texas and becoming a rancher's wife would never be enough for her.

But the more time she spent at the Wingates, the more she was coming to see that it wasn't true. Homesickness had begun a slow and steady growth in her heart, and spending time on the Wingate property had made her realize that her childhood had truly been blessed. When this was over, she hoped she would not only still have a job, but perhaps she could get home to Texas for a few days to tell her ma and pa how much she appreciated them. She would also like to see Eli and his wife, Cassie, and their newborn second child. And she and Josie could head out to their favorite spot on the Brazos and race their horses like the ruffians they once had been.

As she drifted off to sleep, she could feel the steady chuffing of the horse beneath her as they galloped into her memories.

CHAPTER 13

Henry needed to shed himself of Kate Ryan. He didn't want her tagging along, asking unnecessary questions. Besides, she'd slow him down.

He entered the barn and noticed the mule in a third stall as well as the extra pile of gear off to the side. She'd been busy, he'd give her that.

She strode in and said, "I'll be ready shortly. Lottie helped me gather the extra items."

"I think you should stay and keep an eye on things."

She stopped and gave him her full attention. "But you're still leaving."

"Yes." He handed her a package.

"What's this?"

"A gift."

She removed the paper, revealing the lavender soap he'd purchased three days ago. "It's lovely," she said. "Thank you. But I'm still accompanying you, although I'll give you extra points for trying to bribe me to stay."

"It's not a bribe."

"Whatever you say." She settled an unwavering look at him. "I'm going, Henry."

A frisson of ... something snaked down his spine. Kate Ryan was keeping something from him. What it was, he could only guess.

Hell, she was proving to be more cunning than he'd expected. He was both impressed and annoyed, since any further objections to her presence were sure to alert her suspicions.

He would need to figure something else out so that he could investigate the map without letting on to what he was doing.

He resigned himself to spending the next several days with a woman he was better off keeping his distance from, and not simply because of his agenda concerning his father. It was bad enough sharing this small cabin with her; now they would be alone under the stars, with the cool air and the headiness that always came from being in nature.

"Fine." He didn't want to dwell on his conflicting emotions any longer.

The confusion in her expression as he accepted her ultimatum almost made him crack a smile.

"All right, then," she answered. "Fine. And good morning, by the way," she added.

He probably shouldn't let her get her way too often. She'd come to expect it. In some ways, they were like a real married couple.

The thought amused him, and his smile must have escaped because she breezed past him, saying, "I saw that."

"Since I'm about done," he said, feeling suddenly magnanimous, "I'll head back inside and make us breakfast."

Kate's brows furrowed. "Thank you. That would be very helpful."

"That's me," he muttered, as he left the barn, his horse sauntering beside him. "Mr. Helpful."

He cooked up a pile of fried eggs and bacon and a fresh pot of coffee. He didn't have the patience to make biscuits. Kate returned as he divided the food between two plates.

She sat across from him and poured herself a cup of coffee. "Do you know where we're going?"

He pulled a paper from his shirt pocket, unfolded it, and laid it on the table. It was a map he'd sketched out with Wingate's help. He pointed out the boundary lines with the adjacent properties.

"That's at least ten miles one way and twenty the other," she said.

"Wingate has men stationed at these areas." He pointed to three line shacks. "He also has men that patrol. It sounds like five or six, so we should be safe enough if we run into trouble." He raised his gaze to hers. "There's still time to back out. You could stay here, safe and sound, warm and dry. There's no agency rule that says we have to stay together all the time."

"Are you trying to divorce me, Gilbert?"

He sighed and dug into his breakfast, as did she.

"Have you spent any time outdoors?" he asked between bites of food.

She cocked an eyebrow at him. "Yes." She didn't elaborate. She wasn't much of a talker, which he both appreciated and didn't, especially when he was curious about her.

"Care to elaborate?"

"My pa and my uncles run large spreads in Texas. I can assure you that sleeping outdoors won't send me into a fit of vapors."

The corners of Henry's lips inched upward again. He hid it by downing the last of his coffee. "We're burning daylight. We best get to it."

She stood and collected the plates. "Yes, sir. Let me wash these real quick, and then I'll be ready."

Henry went outside to check on the animals. Kate had her horse and the mule tied at the hitching post, ready to go. In a few short minutes, she exited the house and placed a hat atop her head. She wore a split skirt and yellow blouse that wasn't clingy but certainly hinted at her attributes. It was chilly but she had secured her duster atop her saddlebags. She retrieved the reins of the mule and tied them to the back of her saddle, then climbed aboard her horse as Henry settled on his.

"Ready," she said with a broad smile that quite frankly mesmerized him.

Snapping his attention away before she saw him gawking, he guided his horse down the road away from Wingate Ranch, eventually turning northeast. They moved through the forest and then along an idyllic stream, before coming to a homestead.

"Minnie Wingate," Kate said, halting her horse beside his. She had trailed behind him all day. "We should stop and say hello."

"Want to show her the progress on your hand wound?"

"It's well-healed. Maybe she has magical powers."

Henry considered the homestead beyond the tree line where they now sat. Arthur had told him that Minnie had been a bitter woman who had never liked her stepsons, that she had bewitched his father, convincing him to uproot from Ohio and settle here. Henry didn't point out that Arthur had also done the same.

Why had Minnie stayed after her husband had passed? Surely, she wouldn't have wanted to remain neighbors with the stepsons that she was reported to dislike.

"Let's pay a visit," he said. It was time he met Minnie Wingate for himself.

They descended at a casual pace to the homestead. Smoke swirled from the stone chimney, and as they neared, a young girl came out of the house and skipped toward them, a brown braid swinging behind her.

"Sallie!" The girl waved.

"Hi, Nell! This is my husband, Gilbert."

"Hi, Gilbert." Nell came to a stop as they dismounted and secured the horses. "Gran will be happy to have visitors."

"I hope so," Kate said. "We won't stay long if it's an inconvenience."

Henry removed his hat. "It's nice to meet you, Nell."

Nell smiled, then grabbed Kate's hand. "Come inside. Gran is canning so you'll have to talk to her in the kitchen."

The thick smell of sweet jam filled the air as Nell led them inside, and a hunger pang rumbled through Henry's belly.

Nell laughed. "Are you hungry?"

"We are," Kate replied with a grin, briefly locking eyes with his.

Her admission had him thinking of a different type of hunger, and despite every obstacle between them, not the least of which was trust, he looked forward to being alone with her with nothing but a canopy of stars above and the sounds of the forest surrounding them.

"Gran?" Nell yelled. "Look who's here. And they're starving."

Recovering from a vision of Kate breathless and wanting from his touch, he focused on Minnie Wingate. She was very short. From the way Lottie had spoken of her mother-in-law, he had assumed her to be bigger, harder, and just a bit more stalwart. And the Comanche in her was hard to miss.

"Welcome," she said, wiping her hands on an apron stained with bright red splotches. "Please excuse the mess."

She came to Kate and clasped her hands, then peeked at the injured one. "It's so good to see you, dear. Your hand is healing nicely. And this must be your Gilbert. The rumors I've heard are true. He *is* a handsome devil."

Henry didn't miss the blush that blossomed on Kate's cheeks.

He let his gaze linger on her, enjoying for a moment that they were simply a married couple. Happy. In love. Truthfully, if he had chosen a woman to *really* be his wife, Kate Ryan would easily be a contender.

"It's a pleasure to meet you, Mrs. Wingate." He extended a hand to her. "Thank you for letting us stop by." His fingers engulfed hers.

She laughed and applied more pressure to his palm. "Don't

worry. I won't break." She gave him a knowing look. The intelligence in her sparkling eyes was easy to see. There was no doubt she was a force to be reckoned with.

"Please sit." She ushered them to the table at the window. "Nell, get the butter. I've got fresh biscuits, and I'll put on a pot of coffee."

"And the jam ..." Henry caught himself saying.

All the females laughed. He'd given away his longing for whatever it was she was canning. Now he needed to bury the longing he had for his wife.

"Strawberry," Minnie said. "I'll get you some."

She and Nell quickly set the table, and Henry was soon enjoying the meal. Along with Kate's cooking, he was certainly getting spoiled.

The freshly churned butter melted off the hot biscuits and he slathered them with jam in turn. He polished off four in no time at all.

"What brings you both out this way?" Minnie asked, stirring a large pot on her stove. She stood on a stepstool so that she could see inside the pot.

"Arthur has spoken often about the vastness of his land and the sights within," Henry said, finally sitting back and taking a break from the food, although he was contemplating one more biscuit. "I wanted to take a few days and really see it. Sallie decided to accompany me."

Minnie arched an eyebrow. "Sounds like a good idea considering that you two have been apart for a while now. Make sure you tend to your marriage. Without daily care, it can wither away before you know it."

Why did so many people assume that he and "Sallie" were having marital problems?

"Would you know of any good places to camp?" Kate asked.

Minnie placed a lid on the pot and stepped down from the stool. She wiped her hands on a rag and went to a shelf along a far wall near the doorway, pulling a book down and bringing it to the table. She opened it and started flipping through the pages. From his vantage point, Henry could see that it was a handwritten journal.

She stopped at a page and flipped it around to show Kate. Henry leaned closer to his "wife" so he could see the hand-drawn map. He recognized several of the landmarks from Arthur's descriptions as well as the outline he'd given Henry. There was also the third map that Henry possessed, the one from his father. Somehow, he needed to use all three to find the starred location on Hugh's.

Minnie pointed to a spot. "There's a spring here that eventually feeds the stream farther down. It's very special."

"Arthur mentioned an ancient spring," Henry said. He quickly committed to memory the landmarks on Minnie's map, including a symbol of what could only be three trees ... wasn't there something similar on his father's sketch?

Kate looked at him and she was close enough that the green of her eyes left an indelible impression. "Can you find it?" she asked.

"I think so." He cleared his throat and looked back at the book. "Is this yours, Mrs. Wingate?" He took a chance and reached out to casually turn a page or two, just as someone merely curious would do.

"Yes," she said, her eyes watching him with a shine of ... something.

A ripple of worry passed through him. Did she know he was a Pinkerton? Was she somehow involved in the fraud? It seemed unlikely, but one thing he had learned in undercover work was to expect the unexpected. At this point, anything was possible.

But he also couldn't help but wonder if her knowing look was something different, something deeper. It was almost as if Minnie saw him as something other than what he was. And maybe she would be right.

"I've always kept a journal. It's a memento of my time with my husband."

With a few page turns, Henry noticed diary entries and drawings, and a recipe. He would've loved to look at it more in depth, but there was no good reason to keep it. He closed it and returned it to Minnie. Although maybe he could convince her later to loan it to him under the guise of helping to write Arthur's memoir. But given that Arthur treated her as if she were an infected limb on his family tree, it seemed unlikely.

"Thanks for the tip about the spring," he said. "We'll try to find it."

"Take care and honor the spirit that abounds everywhere." Minnie folded her hands together atop the journal. "But I sense that you both are connected to the land. I especially saw it in Sallie when we met." She smiled warmly at Kate. "Be careful out there."

"Do you think it's dangerous?" Kate asked.

"Arthur hasn't always had the kind of friendships you would hope for after a long and fruitful life."

"Sometimes Uncle Arthur and Aunt Lottie aren't nice," Nell added.

The conversation chilled Henry, and it really shouldn't. He'd seen criminals before, and he couldn't discount that Minnie might be one as well, along with a master manipulator of emotions. He didn't know why, but in his experience on the job, he'd come across more women who employed this technique than men. Or maybe he simply kept the wrong company. But one thing was certain—in no scenario did Henry enjoy hearing children speak of ill treatment. It was unconscionable in his mind.

Minnie reached over and patted Nell's hand. "Don't you worry, my girl. We're safe here."

Kate shifted uncomfortably in her seat. "Do you have any protection out here?" she asked Minnie.

Minnie waved her off. “Don’t worry. Families will always have their troubles. We’re no different.”

Henry released an inaudible sigh. He truly wished they weren’t having this conversation in front of Nell. Whatever Minnie thought she knew, she shouldn’t share it with her granddaughter. Not only did it endanger the girl, but it no doubt scared her.

“If we can ever help, please let us know,” he said. “We should only be gone a few days, and then we’ll be back at the cabin.”

“The Purcell cabin,” Minnie said with a nod.

Henry had already sent a note to Jonesy via his courier, Mr. Emmons, yesterday asking Jonesy to investigate Charlie Purcell.

Minnie placed her hands on the table and pushed herself to a standing position. “Let me get you some food for the trail. Nell, why don’t you show them the garden.”

Nell’s face brightened considerably, and they all stood to leave. As Nell and Kate headed to the front door, Minnie beckoned for Henry to pause, stepping close to him.

“I can see that you have a good heart,” she said, her gaze thoughtful. “I hope you find what you’re looking for.”

Willing himself not to be unnerved by the older woman, he said, “Thank you, Mrs. Wingate.”

“You go on outside now,” she said. “I’ll bring the food shortly.”

Henry left the house and found Kate and Nell behind the house in a lush, very green garden. He had no idea it was here since it hadn’t been visible when they’d approached the house.

“We have potatoes and corn and tomatoes,” Nell was saying, speaking in an authoritative tone.

Henry came to stand beside them. “This is extraordinary,” he said. “Did your grandmother do this all by herself?”

Nell nodded. “But I help when I’m here. Mostly I pick what she tells me. We have pumpkins growing over here. Come look!”

A bevy of good-sized orange pumpkins sat in the corner. Henry couldn’t deny that it felt vibrant and full of life here.

"This is amazing," Kate said. "You must have such delicious meals."

"We do. And we share too. There's an old blacksmith I've been seeing by your cabin lately. I gave him a small pumpkin last week."

"Are you talking about Francis O'Malley?" Henry asked. When Nell didn't respond, he added, "I believe he's called Dutch."

"Oh yes. That's him. Will you come back when you're done traveling?"

Kate glanced at Henry, a question in her eyes about Dutch, then she said, "Yes, we'll make a point to. Will you still be here?"

"Yes. I'm going to stay through the summer."

"What about school?"

"Gran is teaching me. And my pa thought it good if I came to spend time with her." Nell paused. "She's no spring chicken."

"No," Kate said gently, soberly. "I'm sure she appreciates having you here."

Gran appeared with a bag of food. They said their goodbyes and Henry and Kate were soon making their way out of the valley. The late afternoon sun put them in the shadows as they entered the forest once again. Henry supposed they could have stayed the night at Minnie's house, but somehow, he hadn't felt right doing that.

"She wasn't what I expected," he finally said.

"Nor I." Kate guided her horse around a tree in the trail. "But there's something rather compelling about her, wouldn't you say?"

He smiled. "Yes."

CHAPTER 14

As the shadows turned to gray, Henry halted and suggested they set up camp. Kate proved to be very efficient. He tended the animals while she set up the tent Lottie Wingate had given her. It appeared big enough for the two of them, but he would sleep outside. It would give Kate privacy and Henry peace of mind.

Once he had the horses watered, brushed, and hobbled nearby with feed bags at their disposal, Henry returned to a cozy campsite, the tent set back about ten feet from a fire with a pot of coffee brewing.

"I appreciate your domestic skills," he said, dropping the saddle bags nearby along with the Winchester Kate had procured. It was still nestled in its scabbard.

Kate looked up at him. She was crouched near a flat rock, slicing potatoes. "I'll have dinner up shortly. You'll like what Minnie sent with us." She nodded at the canvas bag that contained the goodies from Granny Wingate.

He peeked inside. "Are those molasses cookies?" He couldn't hide the longing in his voice.

"They are. I've already eaten two, and they're as amazing as you can imagine." She stood and used a bandanna to lift the coffee pot from the fire and then replaced it with a frying pan. It took her a few tries to get it balanced, but just as Henry was about to help her, she got it secure and added the potatoes and copious amounts of salt and pepper. The meal was soon sizzling in the pan.

"Well, if you're going to ruin your supper," he said, retrieving two cookies, "I may as well join you."

"You can do what you want, Henry. I'm not your mother, and I'm certainly not your wife." She glanced at him with a smirk on her lovely face. She began to stir the potatoes, then reached for the canvas bag that held the cookies. After a quick search, she pulled out a slab of salted pork. "I think we should eat this sooner than later."

"Minnie was generous with us."

Henry sat down and poured coffee into two waiting tin cups. He handed one to Kate, who stopped slicing the meat to accept it. "Thank you. Have you been noticing Dutch around the cabin?"

"Not really," he said. "Maybe Nell was exaggerating. Do you trust Minnie?"

She shrugged. "We can't trust anyone, can we?" She watched him over the rim of her cup and her meaning was clear.

"Trust has to be earned."

She held his gaze for a moment, and then said, "I agree." She set her coffee down and went back to slicing the meat.

"Where are you from, Ryan?"

"North Texas. You?"

"Ohio."

"How did you come to be an agent?" she asked.

He used the tin cup to warm his hands. "I got into trouble."

"You? A troublemaker? I find that hard to believe."

He couldn't tell if she were being serious or mocking him, but the slight upturn of her lips as she worked suggested teasing. A bemused smile tugged at his mouth before he could stop it.

"My father died when I was seventeen. I started to run with a rough crowd after that. One day my luck ran out and I was thrown in jail for vandalizing a local bakery."

"I'm sorry about your father," she said.

"Thanks, but he was never around much anyway. My brother and I had mostly lived with my aunt and uncle for years. My pa's death just seemed to add to the anger I'd been carrying for a while."

Kate added the sliced pork to the potatoes and stirred the aromatic mixture. "So you became a hooligan." But her tone was light. "How much bread did you steal?"

"If it had only been that. We broke windows and threw the products into the street. I deserved to be in jail." He took another swallow of coffee. "I'm not proud of that time."

"How did that lead you here?"

"There were five of us in jail, and a man came to talk to us. He spoke about walking a better path, about saying we were sorry and making amends to the bakery owner. He said he would help any of us who were willing to help ourselves. I was the only one who said yes. He posted my bail, and that was the beginning of a long journey of redemption. He helped with my court hearing, he got me doing volunteer hours with the bakery helping to fix the damage, and he gave me money each week so that I wouldn't feel compelled to steal. Turned out he was a Pinkerton, although I didn't learn that until much later. He recommended me to the agency, so I was trained at eighteen and have been working for them ever since. He was really a blessing in my life. I can't ever repay him."

Having spooned food onto two plates, she handed one to him. "Who was he? Is he still with the agency?"

Henry shook his head. "No. His name was Joseph Merrimen. He passed away shortly after I made full agent. I'll always be grateful that he got to see that." He speared pork and potatoes with his fork. "This is good."

"You can cook tomorrow."

"I've got crackers and dried apples."

She wrinkled her nose, her plate of food perched on her lap. "I suppose that will work. In a pinch. We may have to divide up those cookies."

"You're smaller than me, so I should probably get more."

She narrowed her eyes. "We'll see."

"So your grandfather got you an interview with Jonesy," he said.

She watched him with a cool slant of her head. "What you're really thinking is how did a woman as young as I am manage not only to pass training but get placed on an assignment with you?"

"You're a mind reader. Excellent." He smiled to soften his retort.

Her eyes widened. "Well, how could I have possibly been good enough to make it otherwise?"

With his plate scraped clean, he set it aside and fully focused on the woman who it appeared had a bit of a sharp tongue to her. "You sound like Louise."

"And does that make me good enough for you?"

Henry paused, the question catching him off guard. He knew she meant in a professional sense, but the words burrowed deeper, slipping past his defenses.

"I would venture to say that you're better than me in almost every way that counts, except maybe experience."

He didn't miss the slight flinch in her gaze, the flicker of confusion that shadowed her gaze and then was just as quickly gone. Somehow, he'd gotten to her. That hadn't been his intention, but the conversation had gone suddenly off course, revealing the latent, simmering undercurrent of attraction between them.

Time to stop it in its tracks. He was the senior agent. It was his job to keep their focus on the job and nothing more.

"Why did you want to be a Starling?" he asked, referring to the nickname they gave the female agents.

She set her empty plate aside. "Once when I was young, my pa took me to town and we visited the marshal, and I was so fascinated by his badge and the jail and how he talked about keeping order and bringing the bad guys in ... it tugged at something deep inside me. My pa and my uncle Nathan were Texas Rangers, my uncle Logan was a deputy, and my uncle Cale was a manhunter after leaving the Army. I guess you could say my childhood was steeped in stories of justice."

"Your pa and uncles encouraged you to do this?" He found that hard to believe.

"Well, not exactly. But once I decided, they didn't stand in my way. My pa went with me to Chicago to interview with Mr. Jones."

"Jonesy is hard to get past, your connection notwithstanding. You must have made an impression on him as well."

She pursed her lips and Henry allowed himself one long look at her mouth before pushing his fascination back where it belonged. If she wasn't a coworker ... but then he never would have met her ... *Damn it all to hell, Louise.* How did this get so muddled?

"I was very determined," she said. "And as much as you say that Louise must have taken a liking to me, that wasn't the case. She was nothing but hard on me."

"That's her way of saying she likes you."

"Are you ...." Ryan cleared her throat. "Are you and Louise ... well, you know .... I mean ...." She pressed those intriguing lips together again.

Henry considered the implication. It was far from the truth. He held no romantic inclinations toward Louise. If anything, she was more like a sister who kept him in line, who looked after him, who gave him a dose of his own medicine when he needed it. But why, if he had been so careful about propriety in his career, did Kate think he was involved with Louise? For a brief moment, he considered confirming it, if only to permanently douse the flame, however faint, that he was sure he'd seen in her eyes when she looked at him. She was so young, this was her first assignment, and it would stand to reason that she might idolize him.

But one thing he had decided when Merrimen had saved him

was to be as honest and straightforward as possible. Of course, his job required the opposite, but what he did as a Pinkerton justified the journey to get there. However, he wouldn't lie about Louise. Besides, if she ever found out, at the least she would box his ears like a mother punishing a child, and at the worst she would exact her revenge, like maybe making Kate Ryan his permanent partner, leaving him in a constant state of admiration for a woman who was off limits in every way.

"I'm not sweet on Louise, if that's what you're implying." He added a log to the fire, busying himself with the task so that he wouldn't have to continue the conversation.

"You were so upset when I told you she'd been shot that I assumed there was more to it," she replied in a rush. "Or that there *could* be more to it."

He raised his gaze. "Louise is my friend, and I'm worried about her. She was supposed to be sitting where you are right now, so I was also justifiably surprised to see you instead."

"I'm sure I would've been surprised if I'd been in the same position."

"Maybe we should get some sleep," he said. "I'd like to get an early start tomorrow."

She nodded and cast a dark glance at the tent.

"I'll be bedding down with the horses," he added.

She swung her attention back to him. "You don't have to. I'm perfectly comfortable sharing a tent with a male. I did it plenty with my pa, my brother, and even my male cousins."

Was she inviting him to more? He didn't know much about her, and it was true his curiosity was a smoldering ember threatening to turn into a blaze if he wasn't careful, but he was certain she was innocent in knowing what she was implying.

"I'm not your brother, Kate."

"No," she answered quietly. "But you are my husband."

"Only for show. I won't compromise you. At least, not if I can help it."

"While I appreciate your honor, what if someone comes across us? They may wonder why you're sleeping away from your wife."

He smiled. "I'll tell them we had a fight, and you threw me out."

Her perfect brows crashed together, causing a frown on her face, a face that reminded him of a nectar too sweet to resist. She smiled and said, "How about we say we fought, and you stomped out like the oaf you sometimes are?"

A hearty laugh escaped him, baring all his teeth.

God help him. He liked her too much.

CHAPTER 15

Kate awoke early, dressed, and exited the tent that Henry had allowed her to have alone. Her *husband* snored softly near the ashen campfire. She went quietly to the horses and once she was assured that all was well, she returned to the firepit, gathered several smaller pieces of wood that Henry had stacked last night, and got a fire going. She had coffee brewing when Henry stirred.

"Mornin'," he said.

"Good morning. Did you sleep well?"

He yawned and ran a hand through his hair. "I did. Something about being outside ... it's good for you."

"Good for the soul, you mean." She offered him a cup of Arbuckles.

"Thank you." His long fingers clasped around the rim, brushing against her hand. The touch, although light as a feather, sent a tingle along her skin that didn't stop until it settled deep in her abdomen.

Unsettled, she withdrew to her side of the camp. She was accustomed to being around men of strong character and equally strong opinions—her father and brother, her uncles, her cousins—and she had been encouraged to think for herself and never doubt that she was capable, so Henry Maguire should hardly rattle her.

But he did.

She chose to believe it was because of her secondary Pinkerton assignment. The one that Henry knew nothing about. The one that only Louise had set upon her, that only the two of them would share in case it turned out to be nothing.

And Kate wanted it to be nothing.

It was why Henry's touch was so confusing to her. If he was corrupt, then she shouldn't respond to him. She shouldn't feel anything for him. But she already did. In frustration and a flash of anger, she shoved the burgeoning feelings aside.

I have a job to do. So do it.

She retrieved bread and jam from Minnie's care package. Breakfast would be simple this morning so they could get started as soon as possible.

"We're not far from the first line shack," she said. "It wouldn't hurt to sniff around Wingate's hired hands. Perhaps one of them was behind the Wells Fargo stage theft."

"Good idea."

Once their meal was finished, she busied herself breaking down camp to avoid any further conversation. Doubts began to whisper in her ear. Could she really be an agent? All this subterfuge was taxing on one's emotions and conscience. Her ma had worried about this when Kate had stubbornly announced she was going to pursue a career as a female detective. They had had several discussions not only about safety and trusting one's instincts, but also about the inherent trait of lying that would be required in this line of work. Kate had insisted that she could do it, that it wasn't as bad as her ma might imagine. And already, in her very first case, Kate was feeling a bit defeated.

What if she really couldn't do it?

Frustration welled up, and it was directed at Louise. Why had the woman given Kate the task of watching her own partner, planting a seed of mistrust when she should've felt safe trusting Henry?

For the first time since being hired by the agency and settling into her assignment, Kate felt completely alone. She could only rely on herself. As she mounted her horse and followed Henry—he had tethered the mule to his saddle today—the isolation was especially acute.

They rode all morning, leaving the forest and skirting a ridgeline. Dropping into a valley, they finally came to a small cabin with a much larger lean-to beside it. The animals were more important out here, obviously.

As they halted their horses and dismounted, a man exited the cabin. "Hello," he said. "Can I help you?"

"My name is Gilbert Holmes," Henry said, extending his hand for a handshake. The man completed the gesture. "This is my wife, Sallie." He gave a nod in her direction. "I work for Wingate."

"Which one?"

The question took Kate aback. According to what she knew of Arthur, his older brother Wallace wasn't involved in the running of the ranch.

"Arthur," Henry replied.

The man nodded. "I'm Mort." His long graying hair was pulled back in a ponytail, lending an oddly youthful look to his appearance.

Kate shook his hand as well. "Pleased to meet you."

"What brings you all the way out here?"

"Trying to get the lay of the land," Henry said. "I'm working with Arthur on an autobiography. He urged me to get out here and see the wilderness that's a part of his legacy."

"That so? Huh."

Kate thought she saw a smirk on Mort's face, but it was fleeting.

"How long have you worked for the Wingates?" she asked, getting a sense that he didn't like Arthur.

"I used to work for his pa, Ellis, but when he died, I had to take work from Arthur."

Kate shaded her eyes, having left her hat hanging from her horse's pommel. "Why?"

"I've been here nearly thirty years, and I didn't want to leave. Some places get in your blood and no other will do."

As much as Kate wanted to escape Texas, she was beginning to understand that her home would always be an essential part of her.

Henry had moved closer to her, and his hand clasped her elbow, giving a slight squeeze. His nearness was both comforting and exciting, but she pushed both thoughts aside. He was giving her a clear signal, and while she was vexed by it, she would concede to his command.

He wanted her to leave him alone with Mort.

"I'm quite tired," she said. "Would it be possible to rest for a bit?"

"You can go on inside," Mort said, nodding toward the cabin. "I just made a pot of coffee. I'll get your horses watered."

"I'll help you," Henry said, giving a friendly smile to Kate as she left them.

Frustrated at being dismissed, she opened the front door and inspected the cabin. It was small and a bit messy. There were four beds and a small stove meant for both warmth and cooking. A table with only two chairs had seen better days. There were playing cards atop it—obviously that was how the men passed the time—and a shelf with foodstuffs—flour, sugar, beans, coffee.

She pulled off her riding gloves and retrieved a cup from beside a wash basin, checking to make sure it was clean. It wasn't so she wiped it out with the edge of her split skirt and then filled it with half a cup of coffee. She walked around the room inspecting things, unsure what she was looking for.

She needed to visit the outhouse, so she left her cup on the card table and exited the cabin, taking a path behind it and heading toward her goal about fifteen feet away. As she passed the lean-to, Henry's voice drifted to her.

"Did you know a man named Hugh Maguire?"

Kate slowed her progress. Why was Henry asking this of a perfect stranger? And what if this Mort reported the conversation back to Wingate? Wouldn't it cast Henry under a suspicious light?

"Why're you asking?" Mort said.

"Arthur mentioned him, and I was curious about his death."

"That was a long time ago."

"It was an accident, from what I heard," Henry said.

"Yep. He fell down a mine shaft."

"What did you know about him?" Henry pressed.

Henry, what the hell are you doing? Trying to blow this entire investigation out of the water?

"He liked to come out here sometimes," Mort replied.

"Why?"

"How should I know?" Mort's voice was tinged with irritation. "But I sometimes saw him with that Beckett fella."

"Walter?" Henry's voice held a hint of surprise.

"Nah. The older one. Can't remember his name now, but it was no secret that him and Arthur hadn't gotten on."

"Clayton Beckett."

"Yeah, that was him."

Kate carefully stepped away from the lean-to where she had been eavesdropping and continued to the outhouse, before Henry realized she'd been there.

There could be no doubt now in her mind that Henry was here for more than a counterfeiting and insurance fraud investigation. He was here to find out what had happened to his father. That meant he suspected Hugh Maguire had been murdered. And if that were true, then Arthur Wingate was more dangerous than a mere criminal who gained wealth by engaging in illegal acts and schemes. He could very well be a murderer.

THEY RODE on an open plain as the sun sank to the west, the sky burning a bright orange. Kate took it all in, feeling the same way she had as a girl riding with her pa. Free. Humbled. Whole.

She embraced it rather than thinking about Henry and Mort's conversation. A part of her had hoped that Henry might share what he had learned while speaking to the ranch hand, that he might tell her of his father and what had really happened, but he remained quiet. Feeling a bit defeated, she had let it be. It wasn't simply that Henry was withholding information from her, but the fact that it put her in additional danger. She had thought that Henry was a more honorable agent than that, that maybe he cared for her despite that they'd known one another less than a week. On more than one occasion she had seen him watching her with what could only be male appreciation. She wasn't so naïve not to recognize it. But apparently his feelings toward her didn't extend to trusting her as a full and equal partner.

She, of course, would need to tell Louise, but for now it wasn't possible to send a message, so she would need to set aside what had happened.

"You've been awfully quiet, Ryan," Henry finally said, letting his horse fall back in line with hers.

"Just enjoying the day."

"You're upset with me."

"About what?" She glanced at him from beneath the brim of her hat.

"About me talking to Mort alone."

She shrugged. "Did you learn the identity of the thieves?"

Henry laughed. "If only it were that easy. I thought he would talk more freely if you weren't there."

"And did he?"

"Not really. But we're heading in the right direction toward the spring."

"Where do you want to make camp?" she asked, her voice sounding hollow even to her ears.

He nodded to a spot up ahead of them. "Let's get to the tree line. It'll offer more protection in case the wind picks up."

They found a good spot and set up camp. Henry offered to cook, so Kate tended the horses. Soon the aroma of sizzling bacon reached her nose, and her hunger caused her to hurriedly finish her chore. If nothing else, she and Henry made good camp partners. She was doing her best to focus on the good.

When she returned, Henry was stirring a pot of beans beside the frying pan.

A rustling caught their attention and they both froze. Henry moved the frying pan off the fire and then stood slowly, pulling the pistol from the gun belt at his waist. He looked at Kate and waved toward a dense set of shrubs. She nodded. They both moved as quietly as possible toward it.

The bushes rustled again. It had to be an animal. With hope, it was nothing more than a raccoon or possum. When a whimper reached them, Kate rushed forward and pushed past the shrubs.

"Kate, wait!"

But she'd already found the culprit. A dog, haggard and clearly anxious, looked up at her. Behind her, Henry stood so close she could feel the heat from his body. She stepped forward to escape it, but Henry's hand gripped her arm, stopping her.

"It's just a dog," she said.

"We don't know if he's friendly."

"He's whimpering, so he's obviously hurt. Thank goodness we found him before dark and a predator got him."

She resisted the urge to yank her arm from his grasp and luckily Henry released her, but the imprint of his hand burned her skin despite the barrier of clothing. Ignoring it, she knelt.

"Hi, sweet boy," she crooned. "Are you hurt?" She extended a hand. "It'll be all right. We can help you."

Henry released an audible sigh. "I don't think this is a good idea, Ryan."

"You can't be serious?" She kept her tone even and low, never taking her eyes from the mutt, not wanting to startle him. Despite being covered in dirt and sticks, his black fur looked pretty good. He raised his ears, but the right one flopped over, and his dark brown eyes watched her with a soulful gaze.

She scooted closer. "We can't leave him here." She extended her hand so the animal could give her a sniff. This went on for a few minutes until he was accepting of her.

"Henry?" she asked, still watching the dog. "Would you get some bacon?"

"You're gonna feed it?"

"Quit being so obtuse about this. You're beginning to make me not like you."

Another loud exhalation, but then he released a soft chuckle. "You like me?"

Before she could answer that, he left. Kate used the time to sit fully on the ground. Henry returned and handed her a few pieces of cooked bacon. She held a piece out to the dog, who started wagging his tail.

"That's right," Kate said. "Go ahead and eat. I bet you're hungry."

The dog took the food, wagging his tail even more.

She held her hand up and Henry delivered another piece of meat over her shoulder, which the dog eagerly consumed. They did the sequence several more times until Henry said, "That's it. No more food."

"Don't listen to him," she crooned to the mutt. "We have more where that came from."

She extended her hand, and the dog licked her palm this time. She moved closer and was finally able to pet his head. The mutt allowed the contact and even bumped her hand when she stopped, wanting more.

"You're quite the affectionate boy, aren't you?" She used the opportunity to inspect his body and legs, looking for an injury. When she ran a hand over his right front paw, he yelped. "Oh no, it's all right. Let me have a look."

She found a gash on the foot pad, deep and sliced open, somewhat dried over and crusted with dirt. "He's injured," she said. "Do you think you could carry him back to camp?" she asked Henry over her shoulder.

"If this hound bites me, then—"

"Let's make sure that doesn't happen." She moved to her knees and waved Henry forward.

He came to the other side and squatted. "C'mon, Dog."

Luckily the hound let Henry lift him up and carry him to their campfire as Kate ran to keep up. At the last minute, she bolted ahead, grabbed one of her blankets, and threw it on the ground. "Put him there."

The dog didn't resist, and the tail wagging commenced again once he was back on the ground.

"Could you cook more bacon?" Kate asked, retrieving several items from her gear.

"Why do I suspect this mutt is going to eat better than us?" But Henry added more bacon to the hot pan.

As Kate laid out her items, Henry asked, "Shall I fetch some rabbit dung for you?"

She cast a withering glare his way. He deserved it, considering his behavior with Mort. Considering his behavior in general. "He's not drunk," she said, not bothering to hide her annoyance with him.

"I think you missed your calling, Ryan. You should've been a doctor."

"I thought about it. My aunt Claire taught me to keep a first-aid kit."

"That dog's very lucky to have found you then."

Kate smiled at the mutt, and using water from her canteen, she began cleaning the wound on his foot. The dog whined and repeatedly pulled his paw from her, but she was firm and worked quickly, dousing it in carbolic acid and then adding several drops of myrrh for pain before wrapping the foot with strips of cloth and then tying them off as tightly as she could.

"I may have to watch you all night to make sure you don't chew this off and tear open your foot again," she murmured to the dog.

"You have a big heart, Ryan," Henry said as he brought her a plate of beans and bacon.

"Thank you." She sat cross-legged and began to break off small bits of the meat and feed them to the grateful animal. "Didn't you ever have a dog when you were young?"

"Can't say I did." He sat across from her and watched the two of them.

"That's a shame. Dogs are one of the great gifts of the universe. My aunt Tess says that. She's got six."

"That sounds unnecessary."

"You're wrong," she said. "They're more than just animals. Just look at this fella's sweet gaze. There's a soul in there, to be certain."

"Don't get too theological on me, Ryan."

They ate dinner, and then Kate had Henry help her lift the dog and place him in the tent beside her where she got him secured. Henry gave them both one long look and then he left to sleep on the ground once again.

Kate settled herself, scratching the dog's ears. He licked her hand and as she drifted off to sleep, she wondered if he'd been sent to soothe her battered soul. If so, it was working.

"It's awfully nice to meet you," she whispered. "You probably have secrets too, but I guess we're all entitled to them, aren't we?"

When she stopped petting him, he nudged her hand to continue.

"You're a rascal." Not unlike the man outside her tent. "But I like you anyway."

CHAPTER 16

Henry had told Ryan that taking the dog with them would be difficult and awkward and would slow them down. She had refuted by saying they weren't really in a big hurry, and that there was no way she was leaving the animal behind. So he had rigged a harness of sorts and had tried to put it on Ryan's horse since he was determined she would deal with carrying the dog for the duration of the day. Quickly it had become apparent that it was too much for her, and probably unsafe for the mutt should he tumble and hit the ground. That was how Henry ended up with Rascal, so named by Ryan, the mutt's ears folded back in submission and his gaze glassy with what Henry could only surmise was worry.

Ryan never should've named the beast.

But what was done was done.

He'd never admit it, but the little guy had begun to grow on him, especially after he had licked Henry's face as Henry secured him on his saddle.

They rode for several hours, and Ryan didn't question him further about Mort, for which Henry was glad, although she didn't speak much at all. He had to admit he missed it. Conversing with her was usually a high point of his day.

He considered what Mort had told him. Were his father and Clayton Beckett working together eight years ago? Could Clayton have been involved with his father's "accident?" Unfortunately, the man was also deceased, so Henry couldn't ask him. Henry couldn't help but think this all must go back not only to the three men's childhoods in Ohio but also their time in the War. But his father had never spoken of either to Henry, or Ian as far as Henry knew. Maybe he should've asked his aunt Lydia, but he hadn't. In true Maguire form, he had decided to go it alone and figure it out for himself.

It wasn't lost on him that he was more like his father than he cared to admit.

In the late afternoon, they came to a rocky outcrop. "According to Minnie, the spring is up that hill," he said.

Kate dismounted and immediately came to help him with the dog.

"C'mon, Rascal." She coaxed him away from the horses to do his business.

"Why'd you name him that?"

"He looks mischievous, don't you think?" There was a bit of mischief in her own gaze. She'd been rather distant with him since they'd been with Mort. Was she upset that Henry had sent her into the cabin so that he could speak with the man?

"I hope it's not prophetic," Henry said, choosing to ignore her mood.

The dog was able to walk now, although he limped. The bandage still covered the front paw and was becoming filthier by the minute.

"We should leave the horses and walk from here," he said.

Kate nodded. "I think Rascal can make it. But can you bring the harness we rigged? Just in case."

"In case what?"

"You have to carry him."

He really should tell her she was pushing the limit of their professional relationship, but the words remained on the tip of his tongue. If it weren't for the dog, he suspected she might not be speaking to him at all. And to be honest, he preferred interacting with her.

Should he tell her about his father? About why he was really here?

Could he trust her?

But more importantly, would telling her put her at more risk on this assignment?

The last thought kept him from considering that line of thinking any further. He wouldn't involve her in something that could endanger her. Period.

A wave of protectiveness washed over him. Whatever secrets she was keeping surely paled in comparison to his and were likely related to some Pinkerton rulebook that more experienced agents didn't bother to follow. A few more assignments and she'd learn soon enough as well.

They set off on a well-worn trail, clearly in use on a regular basis. As they went, a breeze rustled the trees with a loud rushing noise, and the climb became steeper. Ryan was in good shape and kept up with Henry, but when Rascal began to struggle, she fell back.

Henry secured the harness diagonally across his chest and went back to his traveling companions.

Without speaking, Kate helped Rascal into the cloth contraption. Henry briefly locked eyes with her before standing straight, and a grudging gratitude reflected in her gaze, but the wariness remained. He fought the urge to reach out and smooth the edges of her irritation with him. It was for the best, he told himself, although he couldn't deny he'd liked it when, however brief, the two of them had been in accord together this week.

He balanced himself against the added weight of the dog and continued the upward trek, and Kate scrambled to keep up, which she did admirably well. He was certain they were near the spot his father had marked on his map, and Henry kept an eye out for a sign of ... something. Why had Hugh come here? What was so important that he'd made a map of it?

The trail leveled out and they entered an alcove of trees. The cool shade was welcome after the strenuous exertion, and Henry viewed what could only be called an oasis. Tall, strong maple trees and cottonwoods grew in a tight cluster, and the ground was abundant in plant growth, green and lush. The sound of flowing water drew them toward an opening in a pile of rocks.

They had only ascended during their trek, so where was the water flowing from? Behind the spring, the hillside continued upward, indicating there was pressure behind it.

"It's beautiful," Kate said, trying to catch her breath.

She stepped in front of Henry and helped him free Rascal from the harness. The dog immediately dropped his nose to the ground and began a path that took him every which way as he investigated their surroundings, his big fluffy tail wagging the entire time.

"Minnie was right," Henry said. "This place is worth seeing." He scanned the ground, finding signs of animals who no doubt visited for the water, but his eye also caught something else. A footprint. Very faint and soft, with round edges. Not something a ranch hand would leave, with boots and spurs, but it was also too large to be a female.

Just as Henry was reaching the conclusion that the culprit was likely Indian, a man who fit the bill emerged from the green shadows as if he were a ghost, his white hair gathered into two long braids adding credence to the claim.

"Ryan," Henry said under his breath, alerting her. She turned and froze.

Henry met the man's gaze but held off on drawing his gun. He had no desire to start something unnecessary.

Rascal emerged from his wanderings from the other side of the spring and upon seeing the stranger bounded at full speed toward him. The Indian's face split into a grin and he dropped to the ground as the dog ran into his arms. Much licking and happy yipping ensued.

Henry glanced over at Ryan, who met his silent assessment with raised eyebrows. They waited until the greeting between dog and man had calmed to a manageable level.

The Indian stood and said, "You have found my dog."

"Yes," Kate replied. "We didn't know he was lost. His front foot was injured, so we cleaned it and fed him."

"My thanks. I've been looking for him."

Henry didn't miss the crestfallen look on Ryan's face. She had already become attached to the mutt. Hell, Henry had to admit that he was too. But it was for the best. It wasn't as if he and Kate were an actual married couple, ready to welcome a dog into their family, no matter how nice the idea was for a few short hours.

Henry stepped forward and extended a hand. "I'm Gilbert Holmes. I work for Arthur Wingate."

The man nodded and clasped his palm. "You can call me George."

"I'm Sallie Holmes, Gilbert's wife." Kate stepped forward and shook hands as well. "Does your dog have a name?"

"Yes. I call him Bandito."

Henry laughed. "My wife has been calling him Rascal. I guess it's hard to hide his true personality."

George squinted, amusement in his eyes. "There are those who speak dog. It isn't that hard, really." He nodded toward Kate. "Bandito spoke and you listened."

The dog came back to Kate and bumped her leg until she leaned down to scratch behind his ears.

"And he likes you very much," George said. Then he looked at Henry. "But not you." There was no malice in the assessment, just a hint of sarcasm.

"Do you live around here?" Henry asked.

"Sometimes."

Kate stood. "So you live on Wingate land?"

George paused. "Arthur Wingate believes this spring is his, but he is wrong."

"It belongs to Jean Beckett?" Henry said.

"She also wishes to believe that, but she too would be mistaken. This is a border, a place of two worlds. It belongs to no one. But I came here to find my dog."

George was quite old. How had he climbed the trail?

"My ancestors lived on this land," he continued. "If Minnie sent you, then she must have had a reason."

Henry tried to hide his surprise. They hadn't mentioned Minnie to George.

"How do you know Minnie?" Kate asked.

"She is my sister," George said with a smile. "She looks after the land. There are some who believe they can control the wind. Arthur Wingate is one of those men. It doesn't mean that he can."

The sharp intelligence in George's eyes belied his circular answers. This man was no fool. He knew more than he was letting on.

Henry kept his face impassive. It was clear that George had been following them. The question was, why? Was he here because of Minnie? Did she know what was on his father's map as well? Was Bandito's injury all for show?

The last thought angered Henry. He could never condone harming an animal ... for any reason.

"We never mentioned Minnie," Kate added, confronting George a little sooner than Henry would have. "How did you know she sent us?"

"A little bird told me."

Kate's gaze became hooded, and Henry remained silent.

"A starling, I believe," George added.

Henry's neck tingled, his senses on alert. Was it a coincidence that female Pinkerton agents were called Starlings?

"Why would you say that?" Kate replied.

George's face took on a look of innocence. "Everything is connected if you look. Let us sit by the water and talk. I don't get to visit very often."

A silent exchange passed between Henry and Kate, and he gave a slight nod for her to follow George. They would play along. For now.

They settled near the spring, gurgling from the earth in a tinkling flow, almost like a song from a piano. Henry offered his canteen to Ryan, which she accepted. Rascal lapped up his fill directly from the spring, and George sat on the ground with crossed legs. His clothing was more modern with a white shirt and dark trousers, along with sturdy boots.

"Are you out here alone?" she asked.

He nodded and gestured toward the dog. "Except for him." Rascal lifted his head, looking lovingly at his master with his tongue hanging to the side of his mouth. "And the spirit of the land."

"What's so special about this spring?" Henry asked.

"A long time ago, this place was used by the Comanche—the Yapa Tribe. Or you might know it as the Yamparikas."

"Are they still here?" Kate asked.

"No, but the spring is sacred ground."

Concern crossed her face. "Should we even be here?"

"Are you questioning your existence?"

"More often than I should," she replied with a laugh.

Kate's sense of humor washed over Henry like a warm breeze, and for the first time he imagined his life after this assignment, after her. It was stark, and lonely.

"We should probably get back to the horses," he said to her, suddenly wanting her to himself.

They all stood.

"Do you have a ride?" Kate asked George.

"No."

"Do you have far to go?"

"It is a distance. But I will walk. I've done it before."

"Well, you should be careful with Bandito. His front foot is injured. I don't think he should be walking long distances, at least not for a few days."

"Perhaps you are right."

"You could camp with us, if you like," she added.

Henry suppressed a groan, and not only because he had developed an irrational desire to have Kate to himself. This would further complicate his efforts to explore the area later. Alone. He also couldn't help but feel that Kate was playing right into George's hands.

George nodded. "If it's not too much trouble. I can show you a good place to camp. Follow me." He whistled and Bandito took off after him, despite the limping.

"I hope you know what you're doing," Henry said quietly for Kate's ears only as she walked past him.

"Don't want to leave any stone unturned," she murmured in reply.

CHAPTER 17

Kate sat by the fire that evening as George whittled a piece of wood. Bandito was curled up beside him, and while she was happy the dog had found his owner, she was trying to rein in the affection that had grown on its own since the moment she had found him behind that bush. Soon, they would part ways.

The campsite was lovely, with a natural windbreak and an open area with enough room for the tent and the horses. There was also a small stream which George said came from the spring.

But where would Henry sleep? On the ground as he had been? Wouldn't George find that odd?

As she considered how this might unfold, she didn't discount that she might need to pick a fight with Henry to justify him exiting the tent for the night. She glanced at Bandito again, sound asleep, and she hoped the dog might wish to snuggle up to her during the night.

Henry returned with more firewood. They had already eaten, and now they sat in companionable silence as the stars spread across the blackened sky.

Kate couldn't contain her curiosity any longer. "Are *you* Comanche?" she asked George.

He gave a nod.

"What tribe?" Henry said.

"The Yapa, as I mentioned."

Henry stoked the flames with a stick. "Why aren't you living on a reservation?"

George shrugged. "I did for a time, but it was hard. When I lost my wife, I decided to leave, to find a more peaceful place. And I missed Minnie. That was ten years ago."

"Why don't you live with her?" Kate asked.

"I do. Sometimes."

George looked at Bandito and said something in his native tongue, and Kate responded in kind.

Henry turned to her. "You speak Comanche?"

"A little," she said.

"You speak like a child of the People," George said with a smile. "Why?"

"My mother. She lived with the Comanche for many years when she was young. She taught me some of the language."

"Which tribe?" George asked.

"The Kwahadi. It was more than twenty-five years ago. She'd been abducted."

"I am sorry for that," George said. "Stealing children was long looked upon as a sign of stature."

Kate didn't reply.

"Your mother's experience must not have been all bad," Henry said, "if she taught you the language."

"I suppose not. She doesn't speak of it in great detail, as I imagine some of it was painful, especially because when she was finally able to come home, she discovered that her folks had been murdered and her sisters sent away to live with an aunt in California."

"The Comanche murdered her folks?" Henry asked.

"Actually, no. The guilty was another man who had worked for my grandfather. I think for a time she was happy with the Kwahadi and was integrated into a family unit. She even had two Comanche sisters to replace the two she had lost."

"That tribe was more violent than most," George said.

"I guess I should add that my uncle was taken prisoner for a time with Kotsotekas, but he eventually escaped. However, he was an adult, so his experience was very different."

George looked a bit sheepish. "I am sorry to hear of your troubles with my people. I can assure you I mean you no harm now. And I'm very grateful that you helped my dog."

"I do think my ma would like you, George." Kate stood. "I think it's time for me to turn in, so I'll wish you both a good night."

George made a pallet opposite the fire from the tent and turned in himself. At first, Bandito lay next to him, but as Kate got settled in the tent, the dog poked his nose through the entrance, which Kate hadn't tied shut since she wasn't certain where she and Henry stood when it came to the sleeping arrangements.

"Hi, sweet boy."

The dog's body wiggled as his tail started whipping back and forth, and he came inside.

"Don't you want to sleep with George?" she whispered, kissing the top of his furry head.

Bandito licked her face then began sniffing around while Kate lay down. He finally ended his investigation as if he were undercover as well, then settled beside her, curling into a tight ball.

Henry pushed back the tent flap. "I'm coming in."

"Okay." She had already bedded down on the right side just in case.

"I apologize for the intrusion," he said, keeping his voice low. "I can't really come up with a good reason to sleep beside George, but I see that I've already been replaced."

Bandito lifted his head but didn't seem to welcome Henry's presence. As Henry crawled inside, he dragged his bedroll and blanket in behind him. Bandito's ears were pricked in annoyance as he watched Henry make his bed. The quarters were tight, and Kate had to grab the small lantern she had kept lit so he didn't knock it over.

When he was finally lying on his back, she looked over at him. Bandito was curled between them.

"Ready for lights out?" she asked.

"Yes."

She doused the lantern and rolled to the side so that she faced Bandito. She scratched his neck and tried to settle in for sleep.

"What do you think about him?" Henry asked, his voice still low.

"Bandito?" she teased. "He's a little needy."

A soft snicker escaped from Henry.

A smile spread across her lips. "You mean George. I'm not sure."

"Yeah, try not to fall for him the way you have for his dog."

"Feeling jealous, *Gilbert*?"

"Just cautious. I'm sorry about your family ...."

"What? Why?"

"The death of your grandparents. The abduction of your mother."

"I accept your sympathy," she replied, "but as I wasn't alive for either of those things, I wouldn't say I'm exactly in pain, but there are times when my heart aches for my mother. She's a strong woman, though."

"Then I see where you got it from. I don't know anyone who speaks Comanche who isn't one. It's a difficult language, and I'm duly impressed, Ryan."

The compliment warmed her, causing a pleasant flutter in her belly. "Thank you." Until that moment, she hadn't realized how much she had been craving a kind word from her partner. This being her first assignment and all, she had had little encouragement up to this point. She would have continued the conversation, but she didn't want Henry to know how much his words meant to her. She didn't want him to think she was incapable at her job, as needy as Bandito was proving to be. She ran a hand along the dog's back, the feel of his fur comforting.

"Good night, Henry," she whispered.

"Good night, Kate."

KATE AWOKE WITH A START, the stillness in the tent telling her it was deep in the night. She sat up and felt for Bandito, but he was gone. Henry's bed was empty as well. She pulled on her boots and duster and crept out of the tent.

Bandito had probably slipped out to sleep with George, but where had Henry gone? George's pallet was several feet away and she carefully checked on him, but the dog was nowhere in sight.

Was Bandito with Henry?

She returned to the tent, retrieved the lantern, and lit it. Keeping it low to the ground, she searched for tracks. Were Henry and the dog in trouble, or was Henry off doing something he didn't want her to know about?

She needed to search for them without it being obvious, so she pulled the edge of her coat around the light to shield it. It had been busy around camp earlier in the evening, so finding a direction to pursue was challenging, but her pa had taught both her and her sister, Josie, how to track, and she soon located fresh prints of both man and dog in the damp ground.

She set off after them, but the trail soon ended. Searching for signs in the surrounding foliage, she stopped abruptly when she stumbled into a man tucked behind a large bush, asleep.

In the lantern's glow there was something familiar about him.

He awoke, shielding his eyes from the light.

"Dutch?" Kate said. "What are you doing out here?"

KATE SAT near Francis O'Malley under the cover of the bushes where he'd been hidden, because there was no doubt in her mind the older man was hiding. Was he following them? First George, now Dutch. It couldn't be a coincidence.

"Why are you out here all alone?" she asked, keeping her voice low.

"Sometimes I like to come into the wilderness."

"But you're on Wingate land."

"No. I'm on Beckett land."

The spring and its questionable ownership.

"Did Mrs. Beckett give you permission to be here?" she asked.

"Something like that. Why are you wandering around in the dark?"

"I'm looking for a dog. He's black and fluffy, and his right ear flops over. Have you seen him?"

"I haven't. Is it yours?"

"No. He belongs to a man named George. Do you know him?"

Dutch nodded. "Yes. George Ortes. You shouldn't be out here alone, Sallie. Where's your husband?"

"He's on the other side of those trees." Just a small lie, but she didn't think confiding in Dutch was a good idea.

He leaned forward. "Can I give you some advice?"

"All right."

"Take care poking your nose where it doesn't belong. People can get hurt."

Her lantern was still burning, and in the glow of the light, Dutch's gaze was stark and serious, sending a shiver from the back of her neck down her spine and goosebumps to her arms.

"What do you mean exactly?" she asked, her words quiet. *Who are you, Dutch?*

The hard lines of his face dissolved into a softer expression. "I wouldn't want anything to happen to you. Or your husband."

This entire encounter was bizarre and didn't make any sense ... unless ...

"How long have you known the Wingates?" she asked.

"Long enough."

"And you don't like them. Why?"

He shifted. "That's not important."

"Did you know that Arthur was a spy in the War when he was a young man?" She had read Henry's most recent notes after his last book meeting with Arthur, a perusal that Henry didn't know about. Now she was sharing it with Dutch, and she wasn't entirely sure why.

The slight narrowing of Dutch's eyes told her she was on to something.

What she was thinking was unbelievable, and for a moment she hesitated, because if she were wrong, would she be giving Dutch more information than she should in an ongoing investigation? But her Aunt Em had given her only one bit of advice before Kate had left for Chicago and the pursuit of her dreams—*Trust your instincts, Katie. They're always right.*

Henry's father had died in Trinidad eight years ago. He'd fallen down a mine shaft. A body had never been recovered.

How had she not seen it sooner? Dutch had the same serious countenance, the same tilt of head, the same quiet repose as someone she had been spending a great deal of time with recently.

"You're not really Francis O'Malley, are you?" she said.

"And who would I be?"

"Hugh Maguire."

CHAPTER 18

Kate sipped her second cup of coffee, waiting for Henry to awaken.

After her encounter with Dutch during the night, who was none other than Henry's long-dead father, she had slipped back into the tent and pretended to sleep when Henry finally returned, Bandito thankfully with him.

Kate had no idea what was going on but clearly everyone was operating on their own agenda, so she had decided she would too.

While Dutch had confirmed that he was indeed Henry's father, he'd given few details as to why he obviously had faked his death and left Henry believing him to be dead for eight years. Kate had been both stunned and filled with anger toward the man. How could he have done this to Henry? And didn't Henry have an older brother? What about him? What kind of man did such a thing to his own children?

But Hugh wouldn't elaborate, simply saying that it was complicated. And that he was worried about Henry poking his nose into Wingate's business. Hugh had made her promise not to tell Henry that he was alive. At first, she had refused to make any such pledge, but Hugh had told her it would throw Henry off his game. He would be unable to finish his job—yes, Hugh knew that Henry was a Pinkerton and on assignment, alluding that's why he had returned—and it could ruin any headway the Pinkertons were making toward putting Wingate in jail where he belonged. And then Hugh had told her something she hadn't known—he was Secret Service, at least he had been before his "death."

He had finally extracted her vow to keep his identity to herself. For now.

She didn't like it. She didn't like lying to Henry. Not about this. But what could she do? If she told him, it was very likely their entire case could blow up in their faces.

Hugh had said he was here to keep an eye on things, to keep an eye on Henry.

If he was Secret Service, then he surely knew far more than her. Henry would understand when all of this was over why she had kept Hugh's existence from him. Wouldn't he? And why did it matter so much that Henry would ultimately forgive her?

She had finally slept but awoke before dawn with Henry slumbering fitfully beside her. His evening activities had obviously left him tired. Unable to return to sleep, she'd arisen and stoked the cookfire to make a strong pot of coffee.

She chewed on her lip. She should send a note to Louise with this latest turn of events and ask for guidance. But again, Kate hesitated. Missives, no matter how careful, could be intercepted. What if her actions made things worse? Could she live with that? Could her budding career survive it?

She rubbed her forehead as if the action might clear her mind and give her insight in how to proceed. Bandito wagged his tail from his position near her feet as if sensing her distress.

"And what secrets are you keeping?" she whispered as she scratched the fur around his neck.

"Mornin'."

Kate jumped.

"Sorry," Henry said, confusion crossing his face as he poked his head past the tent flap. "Didn't mean to scare you."

Kate quickly composed herself. "No, I'm fine," she said in a rush. "And good morning."

He came to sit by the fire. "Are we alone?" he asked, scrubbing a hand down his face.

He was sporting a day's growth of whiskers, but Kate already knew he had a routine each morning of shaving, so she expected the shadow would disappear shortly. Henry was nothing if not fastidious. Part of his regimented personality, she supposed. She watched him from the corner of her eye trying to catch echoes of Hugh in him, but "Dutch" had taken on a scruffy disguise and the only true connection she could find was in the eyes.

"Yes. George is off ... somewhere." *Would he stumble across Hugh as well?*

Henry grabbed the rag and reached for the heated coffeepot sitting over the fire, pouring himself a cup. Kate busied herself with making breakfast and George returned in time to eat with them. Kate then shifted her focus to Bandito's paw, checking the injury. Thankfully the swelling around the gash had lessened and wasn't too filthy after his night's excursion.

They repacked their gear and headed down the mountain and into the valley. For a while, they all walked, leading the horses and the mule, giving Bandito a chance to go at an easy pace. By late afternoon, they entered an enclosed area surrounded by cliffs on two sides and a rocky hillside on the other, George atop her horse holding Bandito so the dog could have a rest.

Three men and their horses greeted them from an obviously well-used camp.

"Hey, George, good to see you."

The Comanche nodded.

"Who's your company?"

"This is Gilbert and Sallie Holmes. Gilbert works for Mr. Wingate. They found my dog, who had run away."

"You always gave that mutt a long leash," the man said.

They halted and Henry took Bandito from George, who then dismounted.

George introduced the men, all looking to be in their late twenties to early thirties. "Clint, Fred, and Jim."

They appeared as if they'd been on the trail for some time, their clothing dusty and their fingernails edged with dirt.

"Pleased to meet you," Henry said. Kate simply gave a nod. "Do you all work for Wingate?"

Clint nodded, his sandy colored hair hung to his shoulders from beneath his hat, his beard and mustache ungroomed. His green eyes were wary. "We do."

George cast a glance at the setting sun. "It's getting late. Can we bunk down with you all?"

Jim shifted a wad of tobacco in his cheek and turned to the side to spit. He was thick around the waist with a dark shadow of stubble on his cheeks, not quite enough to hide his double chin. "I suppose," he said. "We ain't getting back to the line shack by dark."

"We can't share our grub though," Fred added, his eyes round and his nose flat. He was short and scrawny, and his hat was far too big for him, and it didn't surprise Kate that he didn't want to share their supplies.

Henry ran a hand through his hair then repositioned his hat. "No worries. We have our own."

The next hour was spent tending to the horses and setting up camp. George settled near the three men. Henry, however, put their tent about twenty yards away, and Kate helped him.

"Don't you think we should stick closer?" she asked, keeping her voice low so they wouldn't be overheard.

"Maybe. But I think it's better for you if we've got some privacy."

Their eyes met and she understood his meaning, but for the most part she hadn't picked up any untoward feelings from the three men. And George was nothing but courteous with her.

"I'll be fine, Henry."

He cocked an eyebrow at her.

"Sorry. Gilbert," she amended.

"Maybe you should turn in for the night. I'll stay up with them and see if I can learn anything."

"Again, I'll be fine. Besides, I'm hungry. And wouldn't your wife make you a nice supper in the great outdoors?" She smiled and stowed the curry brush, having finished with her horse.

There was a watering hole nearby, so she led the two horses and the mule over to drink. In the near darkness, she didn't see one of the other men until he cleared his throat, startling her. She spun around, a bit embarrassed. Henry's comment had gotten to her.

She couldn't remember which one he was. Wait, he was the first one they'd met. His name was Flint. No, it was Clint. She was usually good with names. Damn Henry for making her skittish. Along with the Winchester, she had a gun in her saddlebags, but unfortunately neither were nearby. She did, however, have a derringer tucked into a hidden pocket in her split skirt. The agency didn't require it, but she felt it was prudent, never knowing what kind of situation she might get into. And her pa had insisted. Her brother, Eli, had also taught her how to fight with her hands, giving her hints about how to leverage herself if a man—or woman—ever physically attacked her.

"You've got some fine lookin' horses," Clint said, running a hand along the horse's flank. He appeared to be grinning, although it was difficult to see his mouth among the ratty facial hair.

"Thank you. How long have you worked for Mr. Wingate?"

"About a year now, but we mostly report to the missus. You would like that, I think, that we report to a woman."

"Are you talking about Mrs. Wingate?"

He nodded. *Why did they report to Lottie?*

"We don't see many women out here. You must like roughin' it."

She moved to the other side of her horse, trying to put a barrier between her and this man. "I was raised on a ranch," she said. "I'm quite happy being outdoors." She grabbed the bag of oats that she'd brought and tossed a big pile on the ground. The mare immediately went to work. Henry's horse and the mule lifted their heads, their ears perking up, and they moved quickly to get their share of food, so Kate threw out more of the feed.

"They seem happy," Clint said, moving closer to her once again.

A frisson of unease passed through her. She glanced back to where Henry was setting up the tent, but in the late-day shadows, she realized he had finished and was gone. She looked over at the campfire where the others were gathered and spied Henry's silhouette. He was tall, although Jim was almost his height, but Henry carried himself differently. He was quiet, purposeful, and never appeared to make unnecessary movements. She imagined his physique was quite defined beneath his clothing, and as soon as the image crossed her mind, she shut it down. Henry was her partner, not a man she was pursuing in a romantic way. Still, she couldn't deny the undercurrent of attraction that simmered between them.

And on that thought, she brought her attention back to Clint, guessing he was a man of little honor. Perhaps it was best to expose it. She immediately set herself on a new course.

She left the protection of her horse and stepped closer to Clint. "I bet you know horses really well." She smiled, folding her arms in front of her, shielding herself, however small.

"Yep," he said. "I've been working cattle since I was a boy. It's backbreaking work, there's no doubt about it. Are you and your husband living at the main house?"

"No, we're at the Purcell cabin. Did you happen to know Charlie Purcell?"

Clint narrowed his eyes. "It was years ago that he was here. He was fairly worthless, from what I remember. He passed himself off as some kind of foreman, but he ran off and disappeared."

"What do you think happened?"

The look in his eyes—assessing and somewhat lustful—almost made her bolt for Henry. Was this really a good idea? Was she going to get anything useful out of this man? Or was she going to have to dodge his hands?

As the sun dipped below the horizon, leaving an orange glow in its wake, he leaned close. "I don't think he respected the way things are done around here."

Kate swallowed past the dryness in her throat and stayed put, fighting the urge to run.

"You're awfully pretty, Mrs. Holmes."

She a took step back. "Thank you," she replied, forcing another smile on her face. "I've heard about another man who was here then. His name was Hugh Maguire." Her heart pounded as the words spilled from her mouth. She was crossing into Henry's secret agenda, but with Hugh being alive, she couldn't help but think his sudden appearance was no coincidence.

At least it stopped Clint's forward progress toward her. "He died in an accident. I don't know why people are talking about him."

"Maybe his death wasn't an accident."

"Says who?"

She shrugged. "My husband is a writer. I share his curiosity in local stories, especially those that might be mysteries."

"You don't need to worry about such things, ma'am." The glitter of interest was back in his gaze, making her queasy. "Me and the boys keep watch out here in the boonies. We won't let nothin' happen to you."

Kate wasn't so sure about that. "Is there something special about this area?"

Clint chuckled. "Has George been filling your head with Comanche stories? The truth is, this is a dangerous area. There are cattle thieves and criminals who might hide out. You and your husband really shouldn't be riding around by yerselves."

"Thank you for the warning. Are there hideouts around here?"

"Most likely. I wouldn't go looking though. People get hurt in the back country and are never heard from again."

She was beginning to regret being friendly to Clint. It was now dark, but she could see the fire blazing beyond. It was small, emphasizing just how far away she was from Henry, and how isolated she was with Clint. "I need to be getting back to Gilbert."

"Hey." Clint's arm shot out and gripped her upper arm. She suppressed a flinch and maintained her false smile. "You don't need to leave so fast," he said.

She rotated her arm in the way her brother, Eli, had showed her many months ago, quickly disengaging from Clint. She was about to land a punch to his crotch when Henry grabbed her wrist.

"Sallie, there you are," he said, his voice carrying a hint of worry beneath his friendly demeanor. His gaze flashed sharply at her, stunning her with its intensity.

Henry was angry. On her behalf.

Kate willed herself to relax, and he loosened his clasp on her.

"Gilbert, I was just coming to find you." Her chest heaved as she sought to catch her breath, her cheeks hot. She moved into his arms and hugged him, burying her face in his shoulder.

For a split second, she could feel his body tense, could feel his uncertainty about her gesture, and then he folded his arms around her.

She closed her eyes and inhaled the scent that clung to his shirt, musk and sweat and something more, a scent that comforted her and ignited a fire in her belly. She hugged him tighter, feeling safe.

"Thanks for keeping an eye on her, Clint," Henry said over her shoulder, his deep voice vibrating in his chest against her ear. His tone wasn't thankful. It was borderline threatening.

"My pleasure," Clint responded, but it was anything but congenial.

There was a rustling sound and Kate assumed he was walking away, but she sensed that he went slowly, taking his time.

She leaned back slightly and caught a glimpse of Clint casting a glance over his shoulder.

"What are—"

Kate kissed Henry, cutting off whatever reprimand he was about to speak. He stilled. She was crossing the line, but she knew Clint was watching. She rose on her toes, raised both of her hands to Henry's face and deepened the kiss.

He didn't kiss her back. She slipped her hands to the back of his neck and gave it everything she had, wanting to convince Clint of her passion for her husband. She only broke contact to grab a breath of air, and Henry's stunned expression threw a bit of cold water on the entire action.

In case Clint was still within earshot—she wasn't sure anymore—she whispered, "I missed you, darling." Her mouth hovered near his, his breath hot as he said nothing.

She shifted, creating an additional inch of space between them, giving her a view of the trail. Clint was gone.

She turned to leave, but Henry didn't let her go. "Sorry," she said, releasing an anxious laugh, fighting the urge to bury her nose against his chest once again. "I was missing you is all." In case Clint had turned back.

She dared a glance at Henry. His face was ... perplexed was the only word that came to mind.

She smiled cheerily, much as she had for Clint, but this one wasn't false, it was filled with nervous panic. Had she just ruined it for them? Would they still be able to work together now? And why was her heart hammering in her chest, her lips hot from the intimate contact?

She was about to say something, when Henry grabbed her hand and led her back to the campfire. The touch was almost more intimate than the kiss, and the kiss had been unlike anything Kate had ever had before, despite Henry's lack of participation.

She trailed after her "husband," and he didn't release her until she was sitting beside him, so close that their legs touched from hip to knee. He began talking to the men, and the conversation centered on cattle and horses and line shacks. Henry put an arm around her and squeezed her against him, and Kate was content to remain silent and pretend for one brief moment that he was hers.

Henry kept Kate close to him during the campfire discussion, and she didn't resist or pull away. In fact, she seemed to be all in as far as pretending to be his loving wife. The kiss had quite frankly stunned him, not because he hadn't ever entertained the idea of kissing her, but because there was no reason to cross that line. Not really. And it had shocked him that she had. Unable to process whether it was real or not—because of course it wasn't real although his body's response had other ideas—he pushed it into a box in his head and refused to think about it.

But he hadn't liked Clint from the moment he'd met him, and he especially didn't like the way the man looked at Kate. So Henry tucked her beside him, making certain that all the men knew Henry wouldn't be cowed when it came to his "wife."

Once the night wound down, he stood and took Kate's hand, leading her back to the tent. He didn't entirely trust Clint, and he wasn't sure about the other two, so there was no way he wasn't sleeping inside with her. While the other night had been fine, now awkwardness was setting in.

He released her hand. "I'm gonna check on the horses," he said quietly, making sure they were alone. "That'll give you some privacy."

She nodded, avoiding his gaze.

Yeah, this was now awkward. He would need to fix that. But not out here in the open.

"I won't be gone long," he added, in case she was worried about Clint. "Is your gun handy?"

She nodded. "With my gear." She motioned inside the tent.

He waited until she knelt and crawled inside, then he went to the horses. They didn't really need to be checked, but it gave a plausible reason why he wouldn't be with her, in case one of the men decided to pay a late-night visit.

Something on the ground caught his eye. He leaned down and retrieved a folded piece of paper. In the darkness, it was difficult to see what it was, but this was the spot where Clint had cornered Kate. Had it fallen from the man's pockets when she'd extricated herself from his aggressive overture?

Henry had acted entirely on instinct when he'd realized what was happening, but thinking on it now, it was clear that Kate could handle herself, her actions against Clint bringing a smile to his mouth. He tucked the paper into the interior pocket of his jacket and went to the horses.

After what he considered a reasonable amount of time for Kate to get settled, Henry returned to the tent, but on his way back, George intercepted him. The Comanche was so quiet that Henry hadn't heard him coming.

"Did you need something, George?"

"Is your wife well?"

"Yes. Why do you ask?"

George considered the night sky for a moment, then said in a low voice, "I would not trust these men."

"Tell me something I don't already know. But let me ask you, why are we here with them?"

"Because you're curious, aren't you? About who Wingate is? Information doesn't always come from the honorable."

"You're saying these men aren't to be trusted?"

George's face remained serene as always. "Goodnight, Gilbert." He returned to his pallet beside the fire.

Henry made his way back to Kate, his mind was still swimming from that kiss. And that was the problem.

Last night he'd left in the middle of the night to scout the area where they had camped, searching for any clues that might indicate the spot that was marked on his father's map, but he'd come up empty-handed. He would need to search again tonight.

He needed to keep his head on straight, not clouded with visions of the soft curves of his partner, and the enticing mouth that moments before had been all over his.

Kate Ryan was a distraction. And that made her a liability.

He came to the tent entrance. "Sallie, is it okay if I come in?"

"Yes, of course, darling."

The endearment sent a shiver down Henry's spine, but rather than discomfort it left a trail of heat in its wake. He came inside and crawled to his side of the tent, his bedroll and blankets already in place. There was no light, but Henry could tell that Kate was tucked into bed.

He pulled off his boots, shed his coat, and removed his suspenders. He got under the covers and lay on his back, taking a deep breath, willing sleep to come instantly. But it was all too clear that he wasn't tired.

"I'm sorry about earlier," Kate said, the dulcet tone of her voice slipping past his defenses, inflaming a desire he had no business feeling. "I didn't mean to throw myself at you."

He imagined his lips on her neck, his hand sliding beneath her shirt, his palm on her breast ... he closed his eyes. "It did catch me by surprise," he choked out, frantically searching for a way to douse the blaze that was threatening to engulf him.

"Clint ...." She didn't finish.

"Yeah, I don't trust him. And George just said as much." He forced air through his nose, and then remembered the paper he'd found.

He sat up and retrieved it from his jacket. "I found this near where you and Clint were talking."

She pushed to a sitting position and took the item from him, her fingers brushing his hand, jolting nerves along his arm he hadn't known were there. She was too close to him as she unfolded the paper and huddled over it, trying to read in the dark. The scent of her hair wafted to him and unbidden he thought of burying a hand in the dark tresses, guiding her head back, and taking her mouth in a kiss that would be nothing like the one she'd given him earlier.

It would be deep and carnal and filled with a dark longing that he could only hope she would respond to.

She's so young.

And he was out of line.

"It's hard to see in the dark," she said, every word a soft caress, "but I think it might be in code."

"The cipher?"

"Possibly."

"Do you have it with you?" he asked.

She straightened, her shoulder bumping his. "I don't. I left it behind to keep it safe. Should we keep this?" She indicated the paper.

"Yes."

"I'll hide it in my unmentionables."

He forced himself to swallow past the dryness in his throat. "Fine."

She turned away from him, and he imagined she was stashing

that slip of paper somewhere dark and enticing. He settled back onto his bed. He needed to break this spell.

"I was annoyed when you arrived," he said. "I was doing fine without a partner. I think Louise was still miffed about a job we did last year in which I misdirected her so she wouldn't be in danger. I think she sent you as payback."

Kate also lay down, staring at the ceiling of the canvas tent. "I get it, Henry," she said. "You really don't want me here." The edge in her voice told him he'd hit a nerve.

"I tend to work just fine on my own," he said.

"I'm sorry you've been forced to work with a partner you clearly don't want, don't really respect, and I'm guessing don't really like."

The edge in her voice told Henry what a monumental mistake he'd just made. He'd been looking for a little anger from her. It was either that or move the few inches that separated them and explore her mouth, slowly and thoroughly. But it was clear he'd pushed her too far.

"Kate, wait. Stop."

She looked at him now. "Louise warned me about you, but you think it's because of some silly game you two play, or some kind of rivalry, but I think she did it because she was right about you. You're stubborn, you like to work alone, and you don't particularly do well with authority. Mr. Jones has given you a lot of leeway in the past, but now that Louise oversees the day-to-day details of the cases, she's doing away with some of your autonomy, and you don't like it. But I'd appreciate if you didn't take this out on me. I'm here to do a job, and we're expected to work together, and I expect you to abide by that. If you don't, then it will all be in my report when this is over."

She rolled over, effectively telling him she was done.

Henry stared at her backside, bewildered by what had just happened. He'd only meant to push her away from this borderland between them where he wasn't sure he could remain immune to her. Instead, she'd erected an icy wall.

He should be happy, except for the damnable fact that he still wanted her. The frustration of his very aroused body was evidence of that.

It was lust. That's all it could be.

Because there was no way he could feel anything else for her.

He didn't need her good will, or her friendship, or the camaraderie of a job well done.

He didn't need *her*.

No way in hell.

CHAPTER 19

Kate arose early the next morning and tended to the horses before anyone else was awake. By the time she had finished, Henry was up, along with the other men. In a stony silence, she accompanied him to the main campfire and poured her own coffee from the pot brewing on the fire.

Her feelings were still bruised from the previous night and her conversation with Henry, and it only illustrated the need to keep strong boundaries in their undercover work. It was obvious to her she was having trouble separating her personal feelings from her professional ones.

It was shocking how easily Kate had slipped into an emotional tone with him. She needed to take a step back so that she could do an impartial job. Kissing him had been a huge mistake, mostly because she had felt ... *something*. And if anything was clear in this type of work, it was that attachments were a detriment, and possibly even dangerous. If Henry proved to have a hidden agenda ....

But she was a hypocrite, because she was hiding information as well—not only her additional assignment from Louise but also knowing that Hugh Maguire was alive.

Dammit!

It weighed on her, lessening her anger at Henry and increasing her own at herself.

While she couldn't say anything about Louise's directive, she could tell him about his father. He deserved to know.

She glanced around. Was Hugh still watching them? If he were, he was doing a good job because she hadn't detected him.

Squaring her shoulders, she made a decision. When the opportunity presented itself, she would tell Henry that his father was alive.

As Jim prepared a simple breakfast of biscuits over the fire, she and Henry stood bundled in their coats. It was chilly this morning.

"What are your plans for today?" Henry asked.

"We'll be riding the south range," Clint said. "Checking fence lines and looking for anything amiss."

"Mind if we ride along?"

She didn't need to ask Henry why he wanted to remain with these men. The paper he'd found last night was incriminating in itself. She had studied it early this morning in the privacy of the tent—Henry had already left—and she was certain it was related to the cipher they had found in Walter Beckett's office at the Wingate warehouse.

Clint shrugged. "Suit yourself. Can the missus keep up?" He leaned past Henry to give her a look.

Before Henry could speak, Kate said, "Yes, the missus can keep up."

Jim tossed each person a hot biscuit and Kate was surprised at how good it was. "Jim, you're a very good cook," she said, munching on her breakfast.

"During roundups, I run the chuck wagon." He added bacon to the hot pan, and it immediately began to sizzle. "But it's too much trouble to do it with just the three of us."

Bandito bounded up to Kate as George joined them. She broke

off some of her biscuit and offered it to the dog, who gobbled it down with his tail wagging feverishly.

Jim handed her two more biscuits. "So you have more to share," he said with a warm smile around the tobacco bulge in his cheek. So much for not sharing their food as Fred had proclaimed yesterday. Unlike Fred and Clint, Jim's gaze reflected compassion.

And although she and Henry were still not speaking to one another, she had nevertheless made sure that her "husband" was between her and Clint this morning. She was still uncomfortable from her encounter with him the previous night.

Kate added bacon to her biscuit and shared at least half with Bandito who stuck close to her. Then everyone tore down camp and were soon astride their horses. She and Henry had silently packed their gear, the only conversation between them concerning the pack mule. Henry redistributed some of the weight to their horses so that the animal could keep up with them, and he attached the mule's lead to his saddle. Kate didn't feel like arguing with him—as if she couldn't handle her own horse along with the mule—so she let it go.

The ranch hands had an extra horse so saddled him up for George. Bandito ran alongside him, but when he got tired, Henry lifted the dog into George's arms and the two of them rode together.

By mid-morning they descended into a wide valley. Wingate's land was rich and lush, restoring much of Kate's sour mood over everything that was happening. A slight chill in the air kept the sky very blue, setting off white fluffy clouds that hung picturesquely above them. There were clusters of cattle beyond. Wingate's men were heading to check the fence, but before they left Clint told Henry, Kate, and George to stay in the open area, and that he would return in a few hours.

Henry dismounted, and Kate didn't miss the guarded look he cast toward Clint's retreating backside. Still, she was grateful for a rest. She hadn't slept much the previous night after her argument with Henry. There was a water tank, so they watered the horses, and Bandito also took a drink.

"I'm not staying in the clearing," Henry announced, and indicated that they should shelter in a nearby copse of pine trees swaying slightly a gentle breeze.

Kate silently agreed. Once they were settled, she pulled food from her gear and the three of them sat and ate with little conversation.

Without warning, Henry stood.

"I'll be back." And with that he mounted his horse and rode off, not even looking back.

Kate's irritation must have been written all over her face.

"Sometimes it's best to give him time to cool off." George's gaze reflected understanding.

He thought she and Henry were having a marital tiff. She had to concede that he wasn't exactly wrong. The disagreement, however, was very real.

She gave an accepting smile. "I suppose you're right."

But when George lay down on a bed of pine needles and fell asleep, Kate retrieved her gun from her saddlebags, along with a holster she had brought, and buckled it around her waist. Henry wouldn't be rid of her so easily.

She had yet to tell him of Hugh Maguire. She was determined to do the right thing despite Henry's stubborn secretiveness.

She climbed atop her horse and guided the mare in the direction Henry had taken.

THE DAY HAD GROWN WARM. Henry had shed his coat but sweat still trickled between his shoulder blades. He lifted his hat and wiped the perspiration from his forehead with the back of his arm. He was frustrated by two things: Clint and the others had disappeared and Henry couldn't seem to find their trail, and Kate Ryan. The first was understandable. The coded note that likely belonged to Clint placed the man under suspicion. Henry was hoping to learn if Clint, Jim, and Fred were somehow involved in the counterfeiting theft, because it would make sense that Arthur would hire his own to perpetrate such a crime. The second point was simply general discontent—Ryan was getting under his skin. And thinking of *her* skin made his body ache and his blood heat, and he didn't need to be sweating any more than he already was.

He guided his horse onto a trail that cut through a patch of forest.

He wanted to make things right with her. He also wanted to kiss her senseless, to keep her in the wilderness for a few days—alone—to give them time to get this tension between them under control.

But who was he fooling? The only solution for getting this under control involved bedding her.

"Sonofabitch!"

The man's voice spurred Henry to pull his gun and turn his horse as a familiar face emerged from the shadows.

"Ian?" His brother was the last person he expected to see out here, let alone in Colorado. "What the hell are you doing here?" he demanded.

Ian lowered the rifle he'd had aimed at Henry. "I could ask you the same," he said.

Henry holstered his firearm and dismounted. "I'm here on assignment."

Ian's silence conveyed the same.

"Why does a U.S. Deputy Marshal need to lurk in the woods?" Henry asked.

"I'm not here in a professional capacity. It's more a private matter."

Looking at Ian put Henry in mind of their father. All three of them were close in height, shared the same blue eyes, and had the same dark hair, although Hugh's had started to gray before his death.

Realization hit Henry. "You're here for Pa."

Again, Ian didn't speak, just gave a slight nod.

"You said I was crazy to pursue this." Henry released a derisive laugh. "What made you change your mind?"

"Henry, it's not that I didn't believe you. I just felt there was no reason to dig this up."

"But now there is?"

Ian rotated his right shoulder and briefly stretched his arm. It was an old injury from a gunshot wound. "Jean Beckett reached out to me."

"Why?"

"She knew Pa through her husband, Clayton. Pa, Clayton, and Arthur go way back."

"I know. They were spies during the War."

Surprise crossed Ian's face. "I didn't know that." He seemed to consider that new bit of information. "Jean told me she'd always thought Pa's death was suspicious."

"That's not news to me."

"She asked me to come here—undercover—to investigate."

"And?"

"Honestly? I've not found much. The big issue between her and Arthur Wingate is this boundary line."

"Yeah, the spring." Henry adjusted his hat. "You think Jean Beckett is being honest?"

Ian sighed. "Probably not."

"Her son, Walter, works for Arthur, and has for some time."

Ian nodded. "I'm aware. You think he's a spy for her?"

"Why the hell not?" Henry said with a huff.

"Why are *you* out here?"

Henry hesitated. He'd never told Ian about the map he'd found in their father's cigar box. He found he didn't want to mention it. Yet.

Henry shrugged. "Arthur encouraged me to take my wife and see the countryside."

That brought Ian up short. "Wife?" he said.

"Fake wife," Henry clarified. "She's my partner."

"That's a good thing. Aunt Lydia would be beside herself if you married without telling her."

Henry couldn't be certain, but he thought he heard distress in his brother's voice. Would Ian be upset if Henry took a wife without informing his only sibling?

Their estrangement hovered in the air between them.

"Is she a good agent?" Ian asked.

"She's green, but yes, she's proven her worth."

"Your alias?"

"Gilbert Holmes," Henry replied. "She's Sallie."

"You're the writer." Ian's mouth lifted in a slight smile.

"I see my reputation precedes me."

Ian smirked. "Folks think Wingate is a blowhard. Writing his memoir has only solidified the sentiment."

"I'll be sure to keep a low profile while in town. Your alias?"

"Tobias Baker. What's the official Pinkerton assignment?"

"We were hired by the local bank to investigate possible counterfeiting and money laundering that Wingate may have committed."

"Any progress?"

"Nothing concrete. I haven't located any equipment," Henry said, "but Kate and I found a cipher in a warehouse."

"Kate?"

"My wife. Actually, she found it."

"You always hated working with someone else," Ian said with a chuckle.

"There's no crime in that. I was supposed to partner with Louise Foster, but at the last minute she was replaced with Kate Ryan."

"I've heard of Miss Foster. She cracked that case last year in Dallas involving those rather prolific bank robbers. Wasn't she undercover as a fortune teller?"

Henry laughed. "More like a lady of the night. She got one of the men to confess to her." But then he sobered. What if Ryan were forced to go undercover in such a way? What if a suspect actually touched her?

"What's wrong?" Ian asked.

"Nothing."

"I need to get back to the Beckett men I'm working with."

When Ian extended his hand, Henry took it.

"It was good to see you," Henry said, "despite the circumstances."

"Maybe we should spend Christmas this year with Uncle Jim and Aunt Lydia."

Henry nodded. "I'd like that."

Gunshots popped in the distance. Henry and Ian exchanged a glance and took off toward it.

CHAPTER 20

Kate walked her horse through a dense area of forest, Bandito accompanying her a few feet ahead. As soon as she had left, he'd jumped up and followed her, so she had kept her pace much slower than she would have liked for his sake. But it wasn't all bad. Kate was enjoying this respite of peace, highlighting just how strained it had been having to live in such close proximity to Henry.

In the distance, voices drifted back to her. Low but definitely male. It was probably Clint with the other two men, and for a moment, she almost turned around to trace her path back to George.

No. She would do well to eavesdrop. Perhaps she would learn something. She looked down at Bandito. He was a bit of a problem since he would surely give away her presence.

The dog gazed up at her, his tongue out and happiness emanating in every wag of his tail. It was if he were smiling at her. How could she resist him?

Maybe having him with her would be a good idea. He could be her alibi.

"Can you behave though?" she asked him. "At least long enough for me to investigate?"

He responded with excited and rapt attention.

She sighed. "Yeah. That's what I thought. Let's go anyway." She could've backtracked to George and tied up the dog, but that would take too long. And she wasn't sure Bandito would let her. He appeared to be a dog accustomed to freedom, if George's behavior was any indication. He hadn't trained Bandito, rarely reprimanded him, and generally let the hound do what he wanted.

Kate secured her horse within the forest and set off on foot, moving quietly, Bandito at her side, his nose to the ground sniffing some unseen pathway.

Just beyond were two men she didn't recognize. Their horses were grazing nearby. They had the look of ranch hands with cowboy hats, chaps, and spurs.

Bandito started barking loudly, causing her to jump.

"You lost, miss?" a third man said from behind her. She spun around, plastering a smile on her face.

"I believe I am." She had to raise her voice to be heard above Bandito's barking. "My husband and I are out exploring, and I went for a walk with my dog, but then I got turned around. I heard voices," she glanced over her shoulder, "and I thought maybe it might be my Gilbert. I'm sorry, I didn't mean to sneak up, but I wasn't sure if you all were friendly."

The sound of boots crunching pine needles told Kate the other men had come to investigate the ruckus.

"What's going on? Who's this?"

"I dunno. I found her here with her dog."

One of the men eyed her with suspicion, his beard thick and his brows bushy. "That's your dog? It looks like George's dog."

"Oh, yes," she answered. "George. I know him. His dog and I have become great friends." She laughed, trying to win them over. "Don't tell him but I'm thinking of keeping Bandito. I'm Sallie Holmes. My husband, Gilbert, works for Arthur Wingate."

The men exchanged a glance, and worry rippled down Kate's spine.

"Where's your husband, Mrs. Holmes?" the bearded man asked, sliding his eyes to the gun at her hip.

"He and I got in a bit of an argument, and I've come looking for him. Have you seen him?"

"Nope. You do realize you're on private land."

"Yes, of course," she replied. "Mr. Wingate gave my husband and I permission to ride."

"But this ain't Wingate land."

"Oh?" She pretended to misunderstand. She was certain she, Henry, and George were still within the boundaries of Wingate's property, but she sensed she was in trouble with these three. Arguing with them would likely go nowhere. "Whose property am I on then?"

"Mrs. Beckett's," the younger one answered, the one who had found her.

The tone of these men left no doubt in her mind that she was in trouble.

Her gun was in full view. It was probably only a matter of time before they took it from her, so she readied to draw.

Suddenly gunshots rang out, and Kate dropped to the ground. As the men scrambled away from her and opened fire themselves, she crawled away, barely grabbing the rope collar on Bandito and yanking the dog to her. She forced him to the ground and kept him in place with her body partially covering his.

Wood splintered around her as bullets hit the trees, but she feared moving and giving Bandito the opportunity to run. With more strength than she would have believed, she held firm, her muscles aching. No matter what happened, this dog wasn't getting away on her watch.

Gunshots ricocheted and men yelled, but the fight seemed to move away from her.

And then silence.

Kate waited, her ears ringing and Bandito breathing heavily. She loosened her hold on the dog. Raising her head, she glanced around, but she was alone.

She took a steadying breath. "All right, Bandito," she whispered. "We need to move. And I need you to keep up. You hear?"

She stood, clutching the dog's collar with her left hand and pulling her gun with her right. She steeled herself and then moved, crouching while holding onto Bandito. She didn't stop until they reached her horse, the mare's stance wary.

"Easy, girl," Kate soothed. She holstered her gun while still holding tight to Bandito and then grabbed the horse's reins. She began walking with an animal on either side. She was afraid to mount and possibly have Bandito run off.

It was slow going, but when Kate felt she could trust Bandito not to run off, she released him. Thankfully, he stayed by her side.

She made her way back to where George had been sleeping, but he was gone, as was his horse. The mule remained, safe and grazing, although his ears were flicking as Kate approached. The animal had no doubt heard the gunshots, as had George most likely.

Still no Henry.

Kate debated what to do, but clearly she needed to find both men and make sure they were safe.

"Bandito, I'm so sorry to do this to you." She retrieved rope from her gear that she'd left with George and tied the dog to a tree. "It's for your own good. I'll come back for you."

She backtracked to where she had encountered the three men who likely worked for Mrs. Beckett, first on her horse and then on foot. It didn't take long to find them.

From the cover of a notch in a rocky outcrop, she assessed the situation. The Beckett men were holding guns on Clint, Fred, and Jim. How did they all get caught? Had they been shooting at Kate and the other men? Didn't they see her? Not only could she have been hurt or killed, but so could have Bandito. She shook off the wave of panic either thought conjured in her head and focused again on the group.

To her surprise, Henry appeared in the distance walking beside another man, a man who looked familiar to her.

She didn't know him, but in a flash he reminded her of Henry. They both walked with a confident gait while possessing a guarded expression above the same square jawline. And they both approached the group of captives and captors without an ounce of fear or caution.

Could they be related?

Hadn't Henry mentioned having a brother?

Kate didn't like this. Had Louise's fears come true? Was Henry not just compromised, but actively working on his own agenda at the expense of their case?

"Are you hurt?"

Kate jumped at the sound of George's voice and spun around, a hand on her chest. That was the second time someone had sneaked up on her. She really needed to work on that.

"You scared me." She kept her voice to a whisper.

"My apologies. Are you hurt?"

"No. You?"

"I am fine."

She glanced over her shoulder. "There's a group of men and they're armed. They have the Wingate men. And now I think Hen—" She stopped and redirected herself. "Gilbert may be trying to help them by befriending their captors."

George nodded. "We should go."

"To where?" she asked.

"To talk to them."

CHAPTER 21

Henry stood beside Ian and surveyed the scene. Three men stood over Clint, Fred, and Jim, who sat on the ground with their hands bound behind them.

"What's going on?" Ian said.

"They attacked us," the bearded one replied. "For no reason. So we cornered 'em and got the better of 'em."

"We heard shooting," Henry cut in. "Is anyone hurt?"

"We weren't trying to hurt anyone," Clint said. "Just scare them. They were trespassing. Again. We told you last week, Frank. Enough's enough. But you didn't listen."

"We weren't trespassing," Frank said. "And you know it." His attention shifted to Henry. "Who's that?"

Ian paused, so Henry jumped in. "I'm Gilbert Holmes. I work for Wingate. I take it this boundary dispute has you all rather trigger happy."

"They need to stay out of our territory." Frank's tone was flat and firm. "You coulda killed that woman we found."

Henry froze as panic sucked the air from his lungs.

Frank looked at him. "Holmes, you say? I think she was your wife. She was lookin' for you."

"Is she hurt?" He forced the words out in a rush.

"Not certain. She must've run off with George's dog."

"I need to look for her." As Henry turned, his gaze locked with Ian's.

He didn't miss the concern in his brother's eyes. Henry was all but broadcasting his attachment to Kate Ryan, and he honestly didn't care.

"Frank," Ian said. "Let them go." He nodded toward Clint, Fred, and Jim, then looked back at Henry. "Go find your wife, Gilbert. Perhaps we can talk again later."

Henry silently acknowledged him, then glared at Clint. "Where was this gunfight?" He didn't need to fake the anger in his voice. If Kate was hurt ....

"We found them in the trees about a quarter mile to the northeast," Clint said. "But we didn't see her. I swear."

As Henry prepared to leave, a figure approached wearing a dark brown split skirt and a tan hat.

Kate.

Relief flooded him.

George was with her, and Bandito trotted beside them.

"See?" Clint said. "We didn't shoot her."

Henry met them halfway.

"Are you all right?" he asked, his eyes scanning her for an injury. There was no blood, but her skirt was streaked with dirt and twigs were caught in her braid.

She nodded.

"You're not shot?" he added, urgency in his voice.

"No, Gilbert. I'm quite fine." She glanced at George, and then awkwardly embraced Henry.

He pulled her close, knocking his hat to the ground and hers past her shoulder blades, held by the stampede strings, and molded her against him, leaning his face into her shoulder. Her response was less warm, but he didn't care. She felt so right in his arms, her curves tucked against him, as if she were made only for him. He resisted the urge to kiss her neck although with an audience he knew she couldn't protest.

She leaned back and he reluctantly released her. "Care to fill us in on what's happening?" she asked, her eyes shifting to the men behind him.

"Seems to be nothing more than a boundary dispute," he said, lingering on her lips.

"I was *in* the gunfight, Gilbert." Her gaze was hard. "It seems to be more than a boundary dispute."

He acknowledged her comment with a nod. They would discuss it more in private.

"It is about more than that," George said, coming to stand beside them. "It's about the gold."

"What gold?" Kate asked, stepping completely away from Henry. He resisted the urge to grab her hand and pull her back to him.

"Two months ago, a gold bar was found in this area. Now everyone is looking for more."

"Why would there be more?" Henry asked.

"Because eight years ago a man named Charlie Purcell took a stash of gold bars from Arthur Wingate and disappeared. Everyone thought he went back East and was living the good life. But then that bar turned up recently and a new story was circulated quietly—that Charlie met ill fortune here in the woods. That the gold he'd stolen is still in these hills, waiting to be found."

Kate glanced behind Henry and kept her voice low. "And who is Charlie Purcell?"

Of course, they knew. The question was merely for George's benefit.

"He worked for Arthur back then."

"So these men are fighting over gold?" Kate asked.

George nodded. "Why do you think it's so busy back here?"

Henry had to admit it made sense. "And why Arthur and Jean fight over this boundary."

"It will make a difference if the gold is found near it. I wonder that you both didn't know the tale." George stared at each of them in turn.

Enlightenment hit Henry. "You think *we're* looking for it?"

George arched an eyebrow.

Having been released, Clint, Fred, and Jim joined them.

"Glad to see you're okay, Mrs. Holmes," Clint said, a hard glint in his eyes. "But you both best be getting back to civilization. It ain't safe back here."

Kate moved to stand before Clint. "That's been made abundantly clear to me. Just so you know, if you ever shoot at me again, I will return fire. And I won't miss."

Clint narrowed his eyes and Henry swiftly moved between them, putting Kate behind him. "Stay away from my wife," he said.

"Maybe you shouldn't have brought her. Never know what might happen."

"You could've killed George's dog," Kate said, her voice vibrating with anger as she leaned past Henry.

Henry moved to the side to keep her behind him, but she grabbed his arm and pushed against him. He turned around and crowded her back a few steps. "Let's go," he murmured to her.

Outrage flashed in her eyes. He couldn't blame her but now that she was safe, he didn't want her in danger again.

"Let's go." This time he was more forceful, and thankfully she conceded her position and walked with him to where they had left the mule grazing. George and Bandito followed. Clint did not.

KATE STARED into the flames of the fire. She and Henry had made camp, had supper, and now Henry was splitting wood that he'd collected since it was chillier tonight.

George had remained elusive but now he sat across from her, eating the food she had saved for him, as well as scraps of bacon for Bandito. Having gobbled down his meal, the dog came to sit beside Kate, and she looped an arm around his neck and gave him a hug.

Then she asked the most obvious question. "George, are you looking for the gold too?"

"What foolish man wouldn't?" he replied simply.

Kate wasn't so sure about that. Foolishness had no doubt become a hazard.

"And you believed we were also searching," she said as Henry dropped a pile of wood beside them and sat down. "What I don't understand is if the gold belonged to Arthur, then it doesn't matter who finds it. None of you can keep it."

"They could negotiate a cut," Henry said, then looked at George. "Is that your angle?"

"I have certain ties to Wingate," George replied. "And I would like to end them. The gold would give me the opportunity to do so."

"What kind of ties?"

"That does not concern you."

Sensing that George wouldn't elaborate, she turned to Henry. "And where did you go during all of this? Why were you with that man who seemed to know the Beckett men?"

"I was curious about Clint and the other two, and I wanted to look for them," he said. "I guess I had good reason to be suspicious after what George said. I didn't want you involved. I don't like the way Clint looks at you."

The possessive glint in Henry's gaze came and went in a flash, startling Kate with its intensity. Suddenly overheated, she scooted back from the fire. It didn't help that Henry was starting to merge with the environment, becoming as rugged and unpredictable as the wilderness they occupied. His face was shadowed with stubble, his dark hair loose and unkempt, his fingers repeatedly pushing it from his face. Kate couldn't deny that he was become more fascinating to her by the minute.

Trying to clear the air of the oppressive attraction between them, she asked, "Did they have a stash of gold somewhere?"

Henry shook his head.

"And the man?" she prompted.

"His name is Tobias Baker," Henry said. "He works for Mrs. Beckett."

She opened her mouth to ask another question, but Henry's eyes locked on her and he gave the slightest shake of his head. Fine. He didn't want to discuss this in front of George. She grudgingly bit back her words.

"Where was this gold bar found that started all of this?" Henry asked George.

"Rumor has it that it was near the spring, but it was unclear who actually discovered it. The existence of the bar only surfaced when it was sold."

"So it could all be a giant lie." Kate didn't bother to hide her exasperation.

George pressed his lips together. "It's not."

Kate suppressed the urge to roll her eyes.

Henry reached over and took her hand, giving it a squeeze. While she knew he was simply signaling her to stop talking—which in itself was annoying—she also had to contend with the way his touch ignited every nerve ending in her body. She'd already kissed him and embraced him, memories that were impossible to keep from her thoughts, and still a simple hand touch had her heartbeat doing double-time.

"Shall we join the hunt?" he asked her with a grin that did little to convince her that she hadn't fallen for him. Hard.

She needed to tell him about his father. Worry quickly replaced yearning.

Removing her hand from his, she said, "It seems to me to be a fool's chase and a dangerous one at that."

"Yes," George said. "Gilbert, you should take Sallie away from here. Take her home."

"If I go, then Bandito goes too," she said. Kate couldn't possibly leave the dog behind now. Not when the situation had degraded to gunfights over gold.

George's impassive gaze shifted from her to the dog beside her. "Perhaps that is wise."

While Kate was happy the Comanche had agreed with her, she wasn't certain she would be leaving. If Henry stayed, she stayed. It was her job.

She ran a hand along Bandito's furry back.

"Well, I'll think about it," Henry said. "I'm tired. Let's turn in, Sallie."

Her stomach flip-flopped at the prospect of being alone in the tent with her "husband." They needed to speak privately, so she couldn't deny him. But perhaps they could have a fight later, and she could kick him out.

Henry stood and reached a hand to her, pulling her to stand. They needed to stop touching one another. It was distracting, and she needed to keep her thoughts on track.

"Goodnight, George," she said.

"Sleep well, Sallie Holmes."

Bandito didn't follow her despite the look she cast at the mutt, willing him to come and sleep between her and Henry and serve as a buffer. With regret, she went to the tent and busied herself with getting settled, but finally there was nothing more to occupy her, so she lay flat on her back, her blanket tucked up around her, and stared at the canvas where it came to a point. Henry was beside her in the same position.

"Henry," she whispered. "I have something to tell you."

"I have something to tell you, too."

She glanced over at him. Although it was dark, she could see the silhouette of his face. She had never been this close to a man to whom she wasn't related. The novelty of it almost made her laugh. Her nerves were stretched to the brink.

"You first," she said.

"I did know Tobias Baker. He's my brother."

I thought so.

"What's your brother doing consorting with Jean Beckett's men? And I take it Tobias isn't his name."

"No. It's Ian. He's a U.S. Deputy Marshal but he's not here in that capacity."

"Is he also looking for the gold?" She hadn't meant to sound sarcastic, but her words did little to mask the tone.

Surprisingly, Henry chuckled quietly. They needed to keep their exchange low to avoid George overhearing.

"Maybe," he conceded. "I didn't know he was here. We have a history with the Wingates and the Becketts. One I haven't shared with you."

Kate froze. Was Henry about to confess his agenda?

He took a deep breath. "My father knew Arthur Wingate and Jean's husband, Clayton. He died here eight years ago."

"And you've come to learn more about it?" she asked cautiously.

"Something like that. Look, it doesn't change our assignment. We're still looking for evidence of counterfeiting. This thing with my father doesn't concern you, but after the gunfight, I thought you should know. I don't want you to be caught unaware again. I don't want you to get hurt."

He turned toward her, watching.

She refused to meet his eyes as her heart pounded at the confession she was about to make. "Henry, there's something you should know. Two nights ago, I awoke during the night, and you were gone. I was concerned, so I went looking for you."

She sensed the tension emanating from him. Or was she

imagining it? Did she really know him that well? It was only day ten of her assignment, that was hardly time to know her partner, and yet, it was as if it had been much longer. As if she'd always known Henry.

"I ran into someone," she continued.

"Who?"

"Dutch."

"From the livery?"

"Yes," she answered.

"What was he doing all the way out here?"

"I'm thinking now it might have something to do with this wild search for gold. Did you ever meet him?"

"Yes."

"What did you think of him?" she asked.

"I'm not sure what you mean."

"Henry, does he remind you of anyone?"

"Kate, spit it out. It's not like you to talk in circles."

She paused and swallowed her trepidation, forcing the words out in a rush. "Dutch is your father. He's Hugh Maguire."

CHAPTER 22

Henry had grown to respect Kate Ryan and to reluctantly accept her as his partner. She was smart, quick-witted, and brave, and stirred his emotions far beyond their working partnership. Sharing a tent with her had been a special form of torture for him, but in less than a second, his admiration had been doused as if a cold bucket of water had been dumped on his head.

Henry spoke slowly, his voice low. "Dutch told you that he was Hugh Maguire?"

"Yes," she replied. "Well, no. Not at first. But I guessed from the look in his eyes."

Henry's heart sank. Of all things, he'd never have pegged Ryan for being gullible. "And you believed him?" he asked.

"Yes."

"And why in the hell would you do that?"

Even in the darkness, her conflicting emotions were palpable. "Because I do. It just ... makes sense."

"How do you even know my father's name?" He sighed. "No, wait, don't answer that. It was Louise."

Even worse, Dutch knew about his father as well, knew enough to impersonate him. But why?

"My father died eight years ago in a mining accident."

"I know."

"And it was *an accident.*"

"But you don't believe that, do you?" she whispered. "Otherwise, you wouldn't be so angry right now."

"I'm angry because if what you say is true, it means my father let me and Ian believe he was dead. What kind of man would do that?"

"I can't answer that," she said. "Dutch didn't confide much to me, although he did say that he'd been in the Secret Service."

Shit.

Henry sat up, scrubbing a hand down his cheek in frustration. Dutch certainly knew enough to pull off this charade. Outrage filled him that the man would manipulate Kate in this way. That he would play with the memory of Hugh Maguire. It was beyond dishonest, bordering on unprincipled and criminal.

"Where is Dutch now?"

"I think he's been following us, but I haven't seen him since that night," Kate said, her voice filled with sympathy. "I've been meaning to tell you, but we were never alone long enough until now."

Henry gave a short nod. It wasn't her fault that she'd fallen for Dutch's lies, because even on the small chance that the man was telling the truth, then it would mean ... that Hugh Maguire had abandoned his sons. And that cut so deeply that Henry refused to acknowledge even the possibility of it.

Besides, in his line of work, people lied and manipulated all the time. Dutch had an agenda, and he obviously knew of Hugh's history in this area.

But that also meant that his and Kate's cover had been blown.

"How much does Dutch know about us?"

She paused. "He knows we're Pinkertons."

The sound of a throat being cleared outside of the tent startled them both into silence. "I think I should tell you both more of the story about the gold," George said, his voice filtering through the tent wall.

KATE SAT around the fire with Henry and George, Bandito snuggled against her feet offering her comfort. Her thoughts were a bit scattered, and she wasn't sure how to proceed. Clearly, Henry didn't believe her about Dutch, and she had to admit that doubt had been creeping in ever since. Had Dutch lied to her? Why?

"I knew your father," George began. "Hugh Maguire."

Her heart sank. She had hoped that George hadn't overheard them, but it would seem that he had.

"I need to tell you a story," George continued.

"Are you gonna tell me he's still alive too?" Henry demanded.

A frown marred George's forehead, his dark eyes contemplative. "That I do not know. Perhaps his spirit still walks here." He sat back and rested his hands on his knees. "Hugh Maguire came here in '92 to see his old friends, Arthur Wingate and Clayton Beckett. They had been in the War together. They had been spies for the North, and had spent much time routing out Confederates. And sometimes they found treasures. According to Hugh, a large stash of Confederate gold had gone missing on one of their missions. All three of them had talked about taking it, but all denied it after. It disappeared. After the War, your father went to work for the Secret Service.

"Many years later, it was believed that some of that gold surfaced, and because of Hugh's work he was able to trace it back to Arthur. So he came here to confront his old friend. By this time, Clayton and his family had moved here as well, purchasing the land adjacent to the Wingates. The friendship between Arthur and Clayton was strong, but then it seemed less so."

"Why?" Kate asked.

"I do not know. When I learned that Hugh was looking for the gold, I offered to help. I knew some of the inner workings of Arthur's home."

"Again, I must ask why?"

George took a steadying breath. "I would rather not say. I have Minnie to think of. All you need to know is that I told Hugh where the gold was. It allowed him to obtain a search warrant. But Hugh had a partner—Charlie Purcell—who I told you of earlier.

"Unfortunately, Charlie betrayed Hugh and tipped off Arthur, and somehow, he was able to convince Arthur to let him take the gold. I suppose he offered to hide it until some later time when Arthur could regain possession. But that night, Charlie disappeared and was never seen again."

"So my father raided Arthur's home and found nothing," Henry said, his tone flat and sounding somewhat defeated.

"Yes, and it was my belief that Hugh was now in grave danger."

"What about you?" Kate asked. "Didn't Wingate suspect it was you who had tipped Hugh off?"

"Hugh never revealed my connection, and for some reason Arthur and Lottie believed that someone else in their household had been the snitch." George looked into the fire, his face solemn. "I never believed that Hugh's death was an accident."

"Do you have any proof?" Henry asked with urgency. "Any leads you could give me?"

"I don't." George hung his head. "I'm afraid back then most people didn't have the guts to stand up to the Wingates, myself included. The law at the time likely didn't want to be on Arthur's bad side."

"Would you happen to know why Francis O'Malley would be claiming to be my father?"

Surprise registered on George's face. "Dutch? Where did you hear that?"

Henry glanced at Kate. "Never mind."

"Dutch is Hugh Maguire?" George muttered to himself. "I'm afraid I don't see it. He must be out here searching for the gold along with everyone else. Searching for Charlie Purcell's final resting place, for surely beside it will be a wagonload of gold bars."

While the information was welcome, Kate couldn't help but wonder one thing. Why was George out here? She liked him and wanted to believe that he had a good heart, but it would be foolish to trust him. To trust that he was being truthful out of the goodness of his heart.

And it was foolish to trust what Dutch had told her.

Clearly, the lure of the gold had become a siren's call to everyone involved.

Did that include Henry as well?

Did he know more than he was saying?

CHAPTER 23

Henry lay awake. Beside him Kate's breathing became rhythmic, indicating she was finally asleep. They'd returned to the tent after speaking with George and had spoken very little. Henry hadn't wanted to talk anyway. Kate had tossed and turned before succumbing to a fitful slumber, and while Henry had entertained the brief thought of reaching out to soothe her, what little was left of his common sense had held him in check.

He had ruminated over and over about what he'd learned—the story of Confederate gold and the falling out of three friends over it and the ridiculous notion of Dutch impersonating Hugh Maguire. As much as Henry tried to remember what Dutch looked like, nothing about him had made Henry believe he could be his father. But then, he hadn't really been thinking such a thing was possible when he'd spoken to the older blacksmith well over a week ago.

Dutch must be after the gold, and he was playing a wicked mind game to gain an advantage.

Henry thought of his father's map. Was it somehow tied to all of this?

If Dutch were truly Hugh Maguire, then he would know about the map, so had he already gone to the marked spot?

A chill went down Henry's spine.

To imagine that his own father could be so ... cunning ... it left an ache in Henry's chest.

Did Ian know any of this? He'd like to think his brother would've confided in him, but the irony wasn't lost on Henry since he'd said nothing to Ian when he'd spoken to him yesterday.

To hell with it. Henry carefully rose from his bed.

He'd narrowed down the location that had been marked on the map and he'd hoped to investigate it more today, but he decided to go now. He didn't want Kate with him anyway.

For a moment, he lingered on her face, cast in shadows. A wave of protectiveness washed over him. She was in danger because of him. The shootout earlier between Wingate and Beckett's men had made that abundantly clear.

He should send her away.

But he didn't have that authority. Only Jonesy could pull her from this assignment. When the two of them were safely back at their cabin, Henry would wire Jones and say that Kate needed to leave for her own safety. His boss would just have to abide by Henry's decision. There were certainly less dangerous cases she could work on. Henry would give her a glowing review to help her.

And with her gone, he could concentrate on both the case at hand as well as the race for Confederate gold.

He left the tent with his gun in hand and slipped into the tree line. Getting his horse would likely alert Bandito, so he went on foot. A partial moon lit the way, but Henry went into the woods for cover, following his intuition. It was the very trait that Kate had said led her to conclude that Dutch was Hugh Maguire, and one that Henry dismissed as folly at its extreme.

Had she been right?

Henry didn't want her to be right.

Although they had been traveling over several miles during the past two days, in truth they had been taking a circular route near the spring. Henry was convinced this area needed to be investigated further, so he made his way in that direction.

Movement in the distance caught his eye. Was it a man? Dutch?

Henry increased his pace, regulating his breathing to remain as quiet as possible as the ground sloped upward.

What if it really were Hugh?

Pa? Henry was a boy again, seeking the approval of a father who had never been there. A part of him was desperate to have his father back after all these years, the reason behind his disappearance be damned.

This was dangerous thinking.

Dutch was a liar and a conman. And Henry would expose him.

The ascent became more pronounced, and despite the cool evening, sweat pooled around Henry's neck. When he finally reached a flat area, he remained hidden in a cluster of trees, pausing to catch his breath while he scanned his surroundings. When he finally stepped out, he was struck from behind, the pain sharp before he lost consciousness.

Kate awoke with a start, staring into the darkness of the tent. She knew immediately that Henry was gone. She quickly donned her boots and set out to follow him.

She crept quietly away from camp not to alert George or Bandito, while inspecting the ground for Henry's tracks. She found them easily enough.

He was headed back to the spring.

After an uphill climb, she crested a plateau, but there was no one. However, there were now two sets of footprints. Someone was following Henry.

Abruptly, the second set of footprints disappeared, and evidence appeared that something—or someone—had been dragged.

She began a more vigorous search, worry for Henry's welfare propelling her, while continuously looking over her shoulder for whomever else were here.

She barely caught herself when she came to the edge of a rocky ledge, grabbing the branch of a nearby tree. Thank goodness it held, keeping her from toppling over the side

With heart pounding, she dropped to her knees and scooted slowly forward to peek below. It was a long drop, but she feared the dark shadow at the bottom of a ravine could be a body. Was it Henry? Her mind raced as she considered her options.

Whoever had done this could still be out there. She drew her gun and scanned her surroundings, listening for anything that stood out, but all that greeted her was silence.

Henry didn't have much time if he were truly down there. There was rope back at camp. And she could awaken George to help her.

With one last glance, she didn't see any movement. She wanted to yell down but feared she would alert anyone who might be in the vicinity. She quickly backtracked to camp and searched for George to awaken him, but he was gone as was Bandito. Even his gear was gone.

Dammit.

With no time to waste, she grabbed a coil of rope, her knapsack with supplies, and the reins of the mule. She began her ascent back to Henry's position, dragging the animal along on his lead. The mule was sure-footed, but it took longer than she liked to get back to the ledge.

Once she was there, a quick glance around showed her to be alone. With hope.

She debated whether to tie the rope to a tree or to the mule. She decided on the first option and set about ground tying the mule near a grazing spot. Movement caught her eye, as well as the mule's.

Without warning, a furry shadow became visible along the edge of the hillside. The mule caught its scent and in rebellion bellowed loudly, jerking his head back. The force threw Kate to the ground and the lead slipped from her hand. She scrambled to catch it, but the mule took off, back down the trail she had labored so hard to get him to ascend.

"No!" She threw down the coils of rope and tried to chase him, but he was too fast and too far ahead of her. In frustration, she stopped running. She couldn't waste any time trying to chase him. Not with Henry's life hanging in the balance.

She had almost put her knapsack and the rope onto the mule to lessen her load, but it would have taken too long to secure it. Now she was glad that she hadn't, because otherwise the damned animal would have run off with everything, especially the rope. Still, she regretted losing the mule, because she doubted whether she could haul Henry's body up by herself. She had been counting on the beast to serve as the anchor in a type of lever.

Returning to her gear, she halted suddenly. The animal that had scared the mule was still there, watching her, and from the dark outline, it was a mid-sized bear.

She took a steadying breath. Just how dangerous was this animal? Kate reached for her gun, realizing too late that she'd left it on the mule, who was probably down the hillside and back at camp by now.

Oh, to hell with it. She was wasting much needed time. She rushed forward, waving her arms and yelling like a madwoman.

The animal startled and moved back. She kept yelling and the bear moved away, looking over its shoulder at her. When she had pushed it a good distance from where she planned to descend the cliffside, she went back to the ledge. With her nerves thrumming, she decided that maybe it had been the bear who had startled Henry and not another man. It might be all right that she didn't have her gun. Or the mule. Or George to help her.

She came to the edge and looked down. Henry still lay unmoving at the bottom of the small ravine.

She quickly uncoiled the rope and after testing the stability of several tree trunks, she looped the rope and tied it securely. She kept the other coiled rope crosswise on her body and made sure the knapsack was secure on her back. With her glove-covered hands, she wrapped the rope once around her wrist. Taking a steadying breath, she faced the hillside and began to carefully walk her way backwards down the hill, holding tightly and incrementally sliding down the rope. Having it wrapped around her wrist anchored her in case she slipped, but it made it harder to rappel quickly.

She fought to keep her fears at bay, her heart pounding, keeping her focus on the descent. Had Henry not seen the edge? It seemed so unlike him to make such a miscalculation. She tried not to think about what she would find when she reached him. If he were ....

Every halted downward movement brought her closer to him, and she finally yelled at him.

"Henry! Henry, wake up!"

He moved, ever so slightly, but it was something.

Thank the Maker, as her family's foreman would say.

She quickly inched her way down, swinging to the side so that she wouldn't step right on him. Once she found solid footing for her boots, she released the rope and moved hurriedly to his side. She pulled off her gloves and with care she placed a palm against his cheek. He was cool to the touch. She was no doctor, but she knew that a lowered body temperature wasn't good.

He stirred, moaning.

"Henry, can you hear me? Can you wake up?"

She glanced down his body, searching for signs of injury. Nothing looked amiss, but he could have internal injuries from the fall. Or maybe his back was broken. She didn't want to risk moving him until she could get him to wake up so that he could tell her what hurt.

She unloaded the extra rope, her knapsack, and pulled off her coat, folding it and gently placing it beneath Henry's head. She removed the cap on her canteen and attempted to trickle a bit of water into Henry's mouth, which moved out of reflex, giving her a flare of hope.

She re-capped the canteen and looked around, making a quick investigation of the narrow pocket where Henry was lying. But her hopes sagged when she couldn't find a way out. It appeared to be completely blocked off.

She'd been hoping that somehow he would be able to walk out, or that she could get the mule down here.

Panic welled up and tears threatened as it became clear that she would need to raise him up the cliffside. She'd considered it earlier but now the futility of it settled on her. She would need to create a pulley system. She had done it once. Her pa had showed her how. But she had only the two ropes, and even if she could rig it, and in the dark no less, did she really have the strength to drag Henry up the incline?

She decided that until Henry awoke, she would take care of him. She needed to attend to their survival.

She had a box of lucifers in her knapsack and found a pile of driftwood and scattered kindling, although its presence concerned her that maybe a heavy rain had caused a flashflood and deposited the wood, and what if it happened again? She was grabbing worry from the future, as her pa would say, so she pushed her concerns aside and made a small fire beside Henry to keep him warm. It wasn't much, but it was better than nothing.

The temperature thankfully wasn't down to freezing. She managed to get water into him, but since he hadn't awakened, she was unable to get him to eat the food she had brought. She examined him more closely, and while she'd found blood at the base of his skull and on his leg beneath a tear in his trousers, she hadn't found any big gashes.

Still, the fact that he hadn't awoken concerned her more and more as the deep night went on. She retrieved a blanket from her bag and curled up against him, seeking to warm him with her body.

When she did doze, it was lightly, awaking several times to the dying fire, which she quickly restoked. Before sleep claimed her again, she found some comfort in the rise and fall of his chest.

CHAPTER 24

Henry opened his eyes, seeing only a sliver of black sky and twinkling stars, high mountain walls blocking most of it. He winced as sharp pain split his head and swallowed hard against the dryness in his throat.

What had happened?

To his left a low fire flickered. To his right was Kate, asleep and tucked close. When he shifted, she stirred.

"Henry, you're awake." The anguish in her voice tore into him. He must be worse off than he'd imagined.

"Kate." His voice was nothing more than a croak. "How did you get down here?"

"That's not important." She leaned over him. "How do you feel?"

"Water?"

She quickly had a canteen to his mouth, and blessedly cool water coated his parched throat.

"Thank you," he said, lifting a hand to his forehead, rubbing it to mute the throbbing pain.

"Does your head hurt?"

"Yes."

"Does anything else hurt?"

He tested his legs and groaned from a pain in his lower back.

"Be careful," she said.

"It's all right," he said. "I can still move." Which he did to prove his point.

"That's a good sign."

"Can you help me sit up?"

She bent toward him so he could rest an arm around her shoulders, and she helped him upright. A wave of nausea hit him, and he wavered for a moment.

Kate placed a cool hand against his cheek, then moved it to his forehead. It helped, not only in lessening his discomfort but in the fact that she was here. He saw the rope hanging nearby, and he quickly deduced what she'd done.

"Are we alone?" he asked.

"Yes. Well, I'm not sure. I came down here alone. I had the mule, but then a bear scared him off." She sighed. "I had hoped to have him pull you out. I don't think I'm strong enough to do it alone."

"George?"

She shook her head in clear frustration. "He had disappeared when I went back to our camp for rope and supplies. Bandito too. Do you remember what happened?"

"I thought I saw someone, and then ...." He gingerly touched the back of his head, wincing from the pain. "I think I was hit from behind. I must've been pushed."

"By someone?"

"Yes. Who else would it be?"

"The bear?"

"I think I would've heard that."

"Well, you should rest. I'll try to climb out at first light and get help. Your brother might still be out there. Or maybe Clint and the others."

She stopped her rush of words to take a breath, the sheer panic in her voice surprising him. Tears welled in her eyes. "You had me really worried, Henry."

He would kiss her if his head didn't hurt so damned much. Instead, he reached for her hand and squeezed it.

"I'll live," he said, not taking his gaze from her. He had always thought her beautiful—in fact, he'd been struck by her presence from the first moment he'd laid eyes on her in the foyer of the Wingate house before he had known who she was—but her grit, her dedication, and her integrity were more than he'd bargained for. He hadn't wanted a partner, but Kate was turning out to be so much more than that.

She removed her hand from his, and he could read her well enough to sense the subtle wall she was placing between them. She was struggling as much as he was with this thing between them.

She grabbed several pieces of wood and stoked the fire back to life, small as it was. But beside it was a tall upright log with flames licking it from a hollow inside.

"What is that?" he asked.

"A Comanche trick I learned from my mother. You take a piece of wood, preferably a very dry one, and split it down the center into thirds. I brought the ax, luckily. Then you shave off the inside of each piece and put them back together, so now there's a hole in the middle. I had some twine in my pack to secure it together. You stuff kindling in the hole at the bottom and then light it. It burns long and steady, eventually consuming the log. It gave me a chance to sleep a little without the fire going completely out. That way you had a bit of warmth."

"Very clever. I like it."

She reached for her knapsack. "Are you hungry?"

"A little." His stomach was settling, so maybe he should eat something.

She retrieved some dried meat and handed it to him, then laid her fingertips on the back of his head. He stilled, once again enjoying her touch—soothing and enticing.

When she shifted her hand to the back of his head, he flinched. "There's dried blood. You should let me look at that. Does your head still hurt?"

"Yes."

She grabbed a kerchief from her pack and moved behind him on her knees. "Can you turn a little so I can see from the firelight?" She poured a bit of water from the canteen onto the cloth and gently wiped away the blood crusted in his hair.

He winced a few times from her ministrations.

"You have a gash, and it's started bleeding again." She pressed the kerchief firmly against the wound.

They sat in silence with his head resting on her leg, the only sounds the gentle rush of wind from above the ravine and the lick of fire on the burning wood. Kate's nearness was both comforting and stirring up emotions he was in no shape to follow through on.

She removed the compression against his head. "I think the bleeding has stopped. Just be careful not to get it started again. Do you think there's any possibility that you could climb out?"

She scooted away from him and he immediately missed her, although the pain in his lower back was now radiating into his left ribcage, helping to take his mind off the woman beside him.

"Maybe," he hedged. He suspected he had a few cracked ribs but didn't say it. He wouldn't be climbing out on his own. "You should go alone at first light," he said.

The worry in her gaze was hard to miss.

"It's all right, Kate. I'll survive. I'm just not sure I have the strength to climb that rope." When she was about to speak, he held up a hand. "And you don't have the strength to lift me out. Even if you could find George, he probably wouldn't be much help. You'll have to find the others. Even Dutch, I suppose."

"If I can find the mule and get the horses, I can rig something to get you out."

He gave a slight smile. "That sounds like a plan."

She quieted, watching him intently, as if she had something else to say.

"Go ahead, Kate," he said.

"Why were you up here alone in the middle of the night?"

Her face was shuttered, but the hungry curiosity in her eyes revealed her dilemma. She wanted to trust him, but she was carrying doubts. Before he could think better of all the reasons not to confide in her, he plowed ahead.

"A few months ago, my aunt Lydia showed me some of my father's belongings that she'd kept. There was a cigar box and inside I found a map that had been hidden."

"A map of what?"

"This place." He indicated their surroundings with a nod of his head. "Wingate land. There was a location marked and I've been trying to find it."

"Why was it marked?"

"I don't know, but all this talk of missing gold had me wondering if it's related."

"So you tricked Mr. Jones into giving you this assignment?" she asked.

"Not tricked. Jonesy is my friend. He knows some of what's happened in my past. When the request from the bank came in, I asked him for the chance to investigate Wingate. I'm not compromised in my objectives, Kate. I came here for our assignment, but I also hoped to learn more about my father's death. There's not been much proof, but I've suspected that Arthur was behind it, and I've been searching for evidence."

Henry wanted to tell her all of it.

"Before my pa left for Trinidad the last time," he continued, "he and I had had a terrible fight. We both said things, regretful things, and I've been sitting with that remorse for the last eight years. Although Ian's never said it, I know he blames me for driving Pa away that day."

"I'm sure that's not true," she replied quietly. "He's here now as well. He must be thinking the same as you."

"Maybe. I'm not sure why my father was here back then. Had he come to put Arthur away for stealing the gold, or was he here to take it for himself? I'm not sure I really want to know. I always idolized my father, and I'd hate to think he was a thief."

"Dutch ...."

"Yeah, Dutch." Henry huffed in disgust.

"What if he *is* Hugh?" she asked in earnest.

"Then my father really was the worst father." His voice sounded hollow even to him.

"We need to find him to know for sure. Thank you for being honest with me, Henry."

In the soft glow of the firelight, Henry watched her. "I never expected you, Kate Ryan."

"I thought as much," she said quietly.

"You've been a very devoted wife. I should've said so sooner."

"Just doing my job," she teased, but he didn't miss the yearning in her gaze.

She'd said she had no husband, but was there a man she fancied?

"Is there someone ...?" he asked before he thought better of it.

"No," she said. "And you? I know you said you and Louise weren't .... But is there another woman?"

"No."

"Henry—"

"Kate—"

They both spoke at the same time.

"Go ahead," he said.

"No, you go." She glanced at him then looked back at the fire.

"You are ...." He paused. "You've been an unexpected addition to my life and not just on this job. I guess what I'm trying to say is I didn't expect to feel this way about you." So much for keeping it professional, but if he really thought about it, they'd been headed in this direction from the moment they'd met.

She worried her lower lip, distracting him, and said, "I feel the same." But there was a hint of a shadow in her eyes.

He wanted to kiss her, but he couldn't refute the inherent selfishness of it. It was entirely unfair to her.

"Don't worry," he said. "I'll stay on my side of the fence."

"Why?"

He frowned, watching her. "This isn't a good idea."

"I know." She held his gaze. "But I've never felt as bad as I did when I saw you lying at the bottom of this ravine. And my sister was attacked by a mountain lion when she was a girl."

"That's terrible. Was she all right?"

"Thankfully, yes. But nothing is guaranteed, Henry."

"Believe me, I know that more than most."

"So maybe, if you're feeling up to it, you might want to kiss me."

There was defiance in her eyes as well as longing. Damn, she was something.

"You'll have to come closer," he said, indicating his injured ribs, not taking his eyes from her.

She moved toward him on her hands and knees until her face hovered near his, her features soft in the glowing firelight. He reached a hand to cup her cheek as she brought her mouth to his.

Sweet. Innocent. Provocative.

He framed her face with both hands and kissed her, deeply, the way he'd wanted to from the beginning. She didn't retreat, and he unleashed the hunger he'd kept clamped down during all the playacting of their fake marriage.

He ignored the discomfort of his injuries, wanting to savor the moment. This might be the only time he could touch her with no barriers between them.

It would seem he was selfish after all.

HENRY'S MOUTH slanted over Kate's and her body ignited with desire, leaving her lightheaded. She reached for his shoulders, then slid a hand up to his neck, an anchor to hold her steady. He explored her lips with his, and emboldened, she did the same. He tasted of the dried meat and cheese he'd just eaten, his whiskers rubbing against her skin, a friction so intimate that she yearned for more.

Knowing he was still in pain, she angled her body to face him, sinking to her knees as she gave in to her hunger for him, feeling a delicious tug deep in her abdomen.

He braced a hand on the ground and with the other held her head, his mouth capturing hers more fully. It was heady kissing Henry, heady that he wanted her as much as she wanted him. He was no girlhood flirtation. She hadn't been certain he'd felt the same for her, and now it filled with her excitement and anticipation.

She wanted him, a longing reserved for that between a man and a woman, and while she didn't fully comprehend what that would mean, she surrendered to the desires of her body.

Henry's hands moved down her arms and then his palms cupped her hips. As his mouth devoured hers—thoroughly and with carnal intentions that lit a fire in her belly—her breasts felt heavy, and her lower body sought more contact with his.

He winced and she stopped, her breathing heavy and rapid. But just as she was about to ask if he could continue, he kissed her again. Despite his injured state, he exuded strength, and she clung to him. She wanted nothing more than to remove the clothing between them and feel him against her skin.

"Henry," she whispered, letting the invitation bleed into her voice.

Shifting onto her back, she urged him to follow. He came to rest on an elbow, his face above hers.

"Don't hurt yourself," she whispered.

"It's too late for that."

He consumed her mouth in a kiss that took her breath away, his tongue tangling with hers, every nerve in her body vibrating, anticipating the pleasure that was building. His arousal pushed against her hip, hard and ready, and his hand, cool against her skin, crept under her shirt and camisole and rested against her bare ribcage. She arched her body into his, her fingers clawing at his biceps, reveling in the strength and power of him.

His hand went lower, sliding beneath her bloomers, and she gasped when he touched the cleft between her legs. He captured her mouth with his and an arousing pressure began building in her body. When he slipped a finger inside her, she bucked, blind with want, clinging to him as the tension released into a thousand pinpoints of light.

Henry held her close, her body shuddering beneath him, her breath hard and fast, and she found his mouth again for a long, lingering kiss. Finally, the waves of gratification eased, and she opened her eyes.

"I had no idea," she whispered.

"That went a lot faster than I expected." He buried his face in her neck, his hand still between her legs.

"What about you?" she asked. His erection was still prominent between them.

"I'll be fine," he said, his voice a bit strangled. "Just give me a minute."

"Henry." She tugged his face up to look at her. "We can finish this properly. Let's take off our clothes."

He groaned. "I want to, believe me, but an affair is dangerous for you. This way is better."

Her body was still humming from what he'd given her. "Better for me, but not you."

"I don't want to get you with child, Kate."

"There are ways to avoid that."

His breath was hot on her neck as he said, "Would you happen to have one of those ways with you at the moment?"

"Unfortunately no."

She shifted beneath him, and he removed his hand from her. Rolling toward him, she tugged his shirt free from his trousers. He caught her fingers and stilled them.

"Let me," she said.

"I don't expect you to."

"Just tell me what to do."

He moaned in frustration, and she folded herself into his arms, kissing him with abandon. It felt so good to touch him, to be close to him.

After much coaxing and cajoling and care with his injuries, Kate had her palm wrapped around him. She expected more instruction than she actually received, but Henry seemed unable to talk, so she did her best to give him the same bliss he'd given her.

It was dark and erotic and more intense than she'd ever imagined such an encounter could be. Henry said her name during his release, and it filled her with satisfaction.

After, as they lay together, she basked in contentment. They'd never completely disrobed, however, and she was curious to see him.

Kate's mother had had a frank discussion with her before she'd left for Chicago—about men and the possibility of getting with child outside of marriage. And while Kate had decided that matrimony was very possibly not in her future, she hadn't wanted to believe she would live a life of solitude in the meantime, so she had sought out her aunt Claire about ways to be with a man and not become pregnant.

Aunt Claire had reluctantly agreed to educate her. There were condoms that men could wear. A woman could track her monthly cycle and avoid intercourse on certain days. Or the man could stop penetration before his completion, thereby not spilling his seed inside her. And while there were herbs that could end an unwanted pregnancy, Kate had agreed with Claire that she would never do such a thing.

These methods weren't foolproof, her aunt had cautioned, and truly the best and only method of protection was abstinence.

But Kate already concluded in her early days with the agency that if she wanted a career as a detective, then marriage was not likely on the table for her. Liaisons would be the course of her love life. If Henry was amenable, then she would very much like him as a lover, but there could be no child.

She lifted her head. "Henry, next time can we do it proper?"

He opened his eyes and slid a glance at her, hot and heavy and wanting. He released a frustrated moan, then said, "You're not a whimsical woman."

Kate frowned. "No."

"If we engaged in an affair, the ramifications could be far-reaching for you."

"I understand," she said.

He looked at her. "Do you? It wouldn't be fair to you."

"Isn't that for me to decide?"

He buried his hand in her hair. "You're not what I expected, I'll give you that."

She liked the awe in his tone, that she had managed to unsettle the unflappable Henry Maguire.

"I hope I didn't hurt you," she said.

"Just looking at you hurts."

The yearning in his voice sent a shiver of pleasure through her.

"We may have to agree to address this at a later point in time," he added.

"Are you always so practical?"

"I try to be."

"Should I be impressed by that?"

"I don't know, are you?" he asked.

"Of course I'm impressed by you, Henry. But I feel I must say that I didn't join the agency looking for a husband."

"But you got one anyway," he added, his tone teasing. "Try to get some sleep. I'll watch over you this time."

With the fire crackling and the steady light from her Comanche log, they settled into a companionable silence and Kate soon dozed.

"Ahoy down there!"

The male voice from above startled her awake. She sprang to her feet, craning her neck to see who it was.

"Hello!" she responded. "We need help!"

"Is anyone injured?"

"Yes!" She caught herself as she was about to say *Henry*. "It's my husband, Gilbert! Who is this?"

"Tobias Baker."

She met Henry's eyes, hope filling her over the man's identity. "Your brother?" she whispered.

He nodded.

"Can you rig a pulley?" she yelled back up to the man.

"Yeah. I can do that."

CHAPTER 25

Henry sat against a tree, catching his breath after the ordeal of Ian and Kate hauling him up the steep cliffside. Kate had worked with Ian to rig a pulley, and Ian's horse had done much of the exertion.

Ian knelt before him and did a quick examination. When Henry winced a few times, he said, "Can you take off your shirt? Those ribs need to be wrapped."

Kate helped, and once Henry was bare-chested the purple bruising on his ribs was visible. She laid a hand on his shoulder, the touch both comforting and inflaming after their encounter a few hours earlier.

"That doesn't look good," she said.

"He'll survive." Ian's tone bordered on sarcasm. "When he was younger, he took more than one pummeling by the town bullies."

"I think you mean you," he hissed as he lifted an arm to give Ian more access.

"I was toughening you up, Henry."

Kate and Ian exchanged a smile.

Henry frowned. They'd had a quick introduction only *after* raising him up the cliffside, and she'd been warmer and more welcoming to his brother than she'd been with Henry in the beginning.

When Ian had finished his ministrations, he stood and Kate asked, "By the way, how did you find us?"

"I decided to scout the springs again. This boundary dispute has me thinking there's more to this place than water. I came across tracks and found you both."

"We're grateful," she replied.

"Besides, I wanted to meet Henry's partner."

Kate's face beamed and jealousy shot through Henry. He'd thought to keep the existence of the map from Ian, but then decided it was just the distraction that would keep his brother's focus off Kate Ryan.

"I have something that belonged to Pa." Henry reached inside his jacket lying nearby and retrieved the map. He handed it to Ian.

His brother unfolded the paper and examined it. "Where did you get this?"

"An old cigar box that Aunt Lydia had. She only recently gave it to me."

"Why didn't you tell me about this yesterday?"

"You think one conversation erases the last few years of no contact from you?" Henry threw back.

Ian cast him a dark look. "That no contact goes both ways, Henry."

"Fine," Henry replied with a huff. "Well, I'm showing you now."

"So you think Pa had a hiding place out here?" Ian asked, his attention on the map.

"I've been looking." Should he also tell Ian about the ridiculous claim by Dutch to be their father? Well, considering that Henry didn't believe it, there was no reason to give it credence by talking about it.

Ian glanced around their surroundings.

"What?" Henry said, his senses on alert again.

"This marker on the map." Ian knelt again beside Henry and pointed to a spot on the map where three trees were drawn. "I think I know where this is."

Henry was skeptical. "It's trees, Ian. They're everywhere."

Ian shook his head, dropped the map into Henry's lap, and stood. "Still stubborn. It's nice to see some things never change." He retrieved his hat and settled it on his head. "It's not three trees. It's three in one."

"A deformation?" Kate asked.

"Exactly." Ian's eyes glittered. "And I know where it is."

Kate trailed after both Maguire brothers. Only Ian had a horse, since neither Kate nor Henry had brought theirs, and the mule she'd led last night had run off. Once they were done here, she would need to look for him, as well as get back to their animals and make sure they were safe.

Henry had donned his shirt once again, but Kate admired the torso beneath, having had her desire to see some of him bare come true. Not that she was happy about his bruised ribs, but he seemed to be functioning despite the injury, so it must not be too extreme thankfully.

She itched to touch more of him than just a hand on his shoulder, but she doubted that Henry wanted his brother to know about their romantic entanglement. She was also aware of her own reluctance to advertise her feelings about him. In truth, it jeopardized both of their jobs.

Perhaps that explained Henry's surly mood since he'd been rescued, although she was sure he was in discomfort from his fall and the subsequent injuries. It had been easier to talk with Ian, who to Kate's thinking, was a less suspicious version of Henry, although not nearly as compelling to her as her fake husband.

With his horse's lead in hand, Ian led them behind the spring. At one point, he tied off his animal and they continued on foot, the path rocky and uneven, but then an opening in the foliage appeared and a very distinctive tree stood vigil—three trunks growing from one, each one having grown tall and arched over, as if protecting something.

A quick search and they found an opening in the hillside. Not a cave exactly, more like a covered niche. As Ian searched inside, Henry beside him, Kate noted the ground.

"It's empty," Ian said.

Kate pointed around them. "There are recent footprints. They go down that path." It was opposite to where they'd entered the clearing. She went to the niche, wanting to inspect it. When her eye caught on something shiny, she removed her hat and carefully brushed some dirt onto the brim, and then carried it to Ian and Henry.

"What did you find?" Henry said.

She held the hat so they could inspect it.

Ian looked closely. "Is that what I think it is?"

Kate nodded. "It's gold."

Henry sat atop his horse and faced Ian, also ready to ride. Kate was settled on her mare, the mule's lead attached to her saddle. They'd found the contrary animal back at their camp upon returning from their little adventure at the spring.

"What now?" Ian asked.

"Kate and I continue our investigation. We have the cipher, so we'll translate the message we found as soon as we get back to the cabin." And what about George? Perhaps he was in collusion with Dutch. He'd claimed to have been Hugh Maguire's friend eight years ago, and if he believed Dutch to be Hugh then maybe he had decided to help him again.

"Someone had that gold, or at least some of it, in Pa's secret hideaway," Ian said. "And fairly recently."

"And the conclusion of that discovery is to trust no one."

"I'm glad you've learned to be so discerning, Henry," Ian said, then shifted his gaze past Henry's shoulder. "It was a pleasure, Kate." He gave a slight tip to his hat.

"Likewise," she said. "I hope we'll see you again."

"We'd better get going," Henry said, turning his horse and not looking back. He wasn't sure exactly what he and Kate were now after their rather steamy interlude in the ravine, but he didn't need Ian distracting her.

If Kate's discovery was correct, and there had been gold hidden in his pa's secret little cave, then someone had found it. Was it Beckett's men? Ian didn't think so, as they seemed to be loyal to Jean, and by association would have informed Ian. Was it Clint, Jim, or Fred? Henry didn't think the three of them were that smart.

He, Ian, and Kate had followed the opposite trail and found hoofprints. Whoever had moved it had a horse or horses. Henry's money was on George or Dutch.

And speaking of Dutch—Henry planned to pay him a visit tomorrow, if the man was even in town.

The ride wasn't nearly as tiring as Henry had anticipated, despite the dull ache of his ribs and a mild headache, the journey to the cabin taking all day. At least his appetite and thirst were present, in more ways than just water and food. His hunger for Kate was sharp and fully present, but he kept the rest stops short to keep from doing something foolish such as seducing her in the shade of a pine tree.

In late afternoon, they arrived at the cabin.

"You get inside," Kate said. "I'll see to the animals."

He would have argued but he was sore from a day in the saddle.

He gave her a quick kiss of thanks, rewarded by a smile that almost had him reaching for her again.

Once she returned, she stoked the fire in the kitchen stove, and said, "I'll make you some supper and then I'll decipher that note."

Henry allowed himself to relax on the sofa, enjoying the natural ease of the moment, as if they *were* a real married couple. It felt ... nice.

Kate kept the meal simple—a ham sandwich and hot coffee.

"If you want something stronger for your injuries, I found a bottle of rum in the pantry," she said as she sat at the small dining table across from him.

"Charlie Purcell's?" he asked as he dug into the food.

"Perhaps." She placed a napkin on her lap. "But he disappeared eight years ago. I would think this cabin has been occupied since then." After a bite of food, she said, "Do you think Charlie Purcell really disappeared? Maybe he was the one who stashed the gold and then recently returned."

"Doubtful. Why would he wait eight years to do it? And surely someone would have seen him."

"So it's George or Dutch," she said, echoing Henry's own conclusion.

"What about Clint?" he asked.

She smirked. "Doubtful."

He laughed. "Yeah. I agree." He made fast work of the meal. "That was delicious. I was starving."

She reached for his plate, her fingers brushing against his. "Me as well."

Her voice sounded huskier. Or was it his own wishful thinking?

After depositing the dirty dishes, she returned with a glass and the bottle of rum, pouring him a finger. Silently, he downed it in one swallow. It burned a path down his throat but quickly warmed his belly.

"I don't usually drink on the job," he said, sitting back in his chair, his gaze lingering on her. Thoughts of what the night might bring hung heavy in the air.

"You drank at the party when I met you. And the next evening, too, in fact."

A testament to how much Kate Ryan had turned his world upside down. "Both had one thing in common. You."

Her nose and cheeks were slightly sunburned from the day's ride, her braided hair a bit unkempt, and her green eyes blazed with mischief and what Henry hoped was need. For him.

She shifted into a serious countenance. "Henry, about last night. I want you to know that work comes first. I've never lost sight of that."

Her gaze carried a shadow of worry. He wanted to kiss away her concerns. He wanted to keep her close, long after this assignment was over. Damn. He was beginning to suspect that Kate was a once-in-a-lifetime occurrence.

"I want a career," she said. "Not simply a job until I marry and have children. In fact, I've concluded that I won't marry. So, on that note, I wanted to let you know that I'm open to a relationship, discreet of course. But I plan to be an independent woman."

While he hadn't completely thought through the ramifications of his feelings for her, his aunt and uncle had raised him to be a gentleman. If he gave in to the temptation she presented, there would be no walking away from her. He was fairly certain he would be *unable* to walk away from her. And if that were the case, then he would most assuredly marry her.

But it would seem she didn't want or need a husband.

His disappointment was sharp, which confounded him. He wasn't in search of a wife.

The irony of the situation wasn't lost on him. Despite their best intentions, he was her "husband" and she his "wife."

He stood and reached for her, pulling her from her chair and into his arms. She met his mouth with the same urgency pounding in his veins, supple and willing, her lips as hungry as his as he ignored the pain of his injuries.

Their time was limited. He felt it as surely as if a clock were ticking down the minutes.

His need was sharp, and the breathless gasp that escaped Kate's lips only inflamed him more. He shifted her toward the sofa and pressed her down onto the soft cushions, his body fully covering hers. A moan escaped him, the throbbing in his groin feeding into the urgency of his desire. He wasn't inexperienced with women, but his body was acting like a youth that had just caught a glimpse of his first bared breast.

Kate's hands twisted into his hair and her back arched, bringing her breasts against his chest, and he wondered how far he could push his body without compromising her. He didn't want to pleasure her with his hand this time ... he wanted her stripped down to nothing, and him inside her.

A knock on the door startled them both. They locked eyes, her lips red and swollen from his kisses.

Damn. With great reluctance he removed himself from the sofa. She pushed to her feet, a little unsteady, so he reached out to clasp her elbow.

"I'll get it," Kate said, still trying to catch her breath. She adjusted her dress and patted her hair.

When she opened the door, a wide-eyed Nell stood at the threshold, her chest heaving as she took big gulps of air.

"What's wrong?" Kate pulled the girl inside and shut the door.

"It's George. He's not well. Will you come?"

"Of course," Kate replied quickly.

CHAPTER 26

Kate looped the reins of her horse to the hitching post outside of Minnie's house as Nell slid to the ground. They had ridden together since the girl had run all the way to Kate and Henry's cabin.

Henry had insisted he would ride to town and get the doctor, despite Kate offering. She thought he should stay and rest, despite that he'd been doing anything but that with her. Her body was still reeling from what had almost happened on the sofa. Since he'd hadn't refused her offer to have a love affair outside of marriage, she had to assume he was onboard, the thought giving her a secret thrill.

She would need to acquire some sort of pregnancy prevention per Aunt Claire's instructions, since she doubted abstinence would work between her and Henry, and while what had occurred the previous night between them had been unexpected and gratifying in a wickedly sensual way, Kate knew she wanted to be true lovers with Henry.

Nell led her through the front door and into the first bedroom down the hallway where Minnie sat vigil at the bedside, George tucked into bed, his darker skin showing a pallor as he labored to breath, his eyes closed.

"Sallie's here," Nell announced, worry in her voice.

Minnie turned and offered a wan smile.

"Gilbert has gone for the doctor in town," Kate said, coming to George's bedside and resting the back of her hand against his forehead. He was burning up. "What happened?"

"He came home late last night, saying he wasn't feeling well," Minnie said. "This morning he awoke in great pain in his abdomen. I thought it was a stomach ailment and have been giving him broth and willow bark tea, but he's not getting better. I didn't want to leave him, so I sent Nell to find you. Will the doctor come out here?"

"Yes," Kate replied. "Why wouldn't he?"

"Because George and I are Comanche."

"Oh." Kate didn't know what to say, but she was sure that Henry would make the man or woman come. "Don't worry. Let me have a look at George."

"Are you a doctor?" Minnie asked, stepping aside.

"No. But my aunt is. When I was younger, I would sometimes assist her when she made house calls."

Kate had watched and learned from Aunt Claire, and while she had at one time considered becoming a doctor herself, she had later realized she liked helping people, and that's exactly what she could do as a Pinkerton.

Minnie turned to her granddaughter. "Nell, fetch some water." The girl nodded and left the room.

Kate gently pulled the covers back and loosened the ties on the night shirt George wore so that she could look at his skin for any signs of injury. He had disappeared after being with them and perhaps he'd been hurt in much the same way Henry had. She began to lightly press her fingers in different spots on his chest and abdomen. When she was on the lower right side, he screamed in pain, his eyes flying open.

"I'm so sorry," Kate said. She quickly righted his shirt and pulled the covers back up.

Minnie came around her and applied a wet cloth to his forehead. "What do you think it is?"

"If I were to guess I'd say his appendix is infected."

Minnie cast a confused look her way.

"It's located here." Kate indicated the place where she had caused him pain, although this time she didn't touch him. "It will require surgery, but I'm sure the doctor in town can handle it."

Minnie shook her head. "Oh, this is very bad."

Kate clasped her arm. "It'll be all right. My aunt has performed this procedure. Henry and I will make sure the doctor will treat him."

Minnie froze. "Henry?"

"Oh, I meant Gilbert." Damn, Kate was tired. She quickly added, "Henry is his middle name."

Suspicion clouded Minnie's gaze. "You're not Sallie, are you?"

Kate let her shoulders sag. George knew who they were, it was only a matter of time before Minnie learned the truth. "No."

"Then who are you?"

"Henry—Gilbert—and I are Pinkerton agents. My name is Kate Ryan. We were assigned to investigate Arthur and his possible connection to a counterfeiting ring."

Minnie accepted the statement with little fanfare, a ghost of a smile tugging her mouth. "It's about time. Don't worry, your secret is safe with me."

Nell returned with a pitcher of water and more cloths to keep George cooled down, which Kate applied to his forehead while Minnie returned to the kitchen for a bowl of broth. They were able to get a few spoonfuls into him.

Time passed slowly, and Kate worried over George's predicament. If he didn't get help soon—which meant surgery—he could die from infection. She also hoped that Henry wouldn't be angry that Minnie knew their identity.

But what was done was done. There was nothing she could do

now except say a prayer that George would survive and offer her support to Minnie and Nell.

Close to dawn, Henry arrived with the doctor, who asked everyone to leave the room except Minnie.

In the hallway, Kate stepped close to Henry so that Nell wouldn't overhear and asked quietly, "Will he treat George?"

Henry took her hand, his warmth taking the chill from her fingers, and didn't pretend to misunderstand. "It took some arm twisting," he murmured, "but then I told him that George was Minnie Wingate's brother. Not sure if the Wingate name invokes pride or fear, but the doc agreed."

She leaned into Henry, unable to stay away from him, seeking comfort in his strength. "I think it's his appendix."

"That sounds serious." His lips brushed her temple, setting off a wave of yearning.

"It can be," she replied.

The doctor reappeared. "I need to take him to my office to treat him. He'll need surgery."

"We have a buckboard," Minnie offered.

"I'll go with them," Henry said.

Kate nodded. "I'll stay with Nell."

"But I wanna go," the girl demanded.

"No," Minnie said. "You'll remain here with Kate."

Henry flicked his gaze to Kate and his jaw flexed. His censure couldn't be any clearer.

"Who's Kate?" Nell asked.

"Oh, I mean Sallie," Minnie corrected. "I'm just tired and worried about George."

Nell crossed her arms but accepted her fate. Everyone got busy getting George settled into the buckboard.

Just before they left, Henry pulled Kate aside. "Minnie?" he asked, his breath hot against her cheek.

"Yes, she knows. I slipped up. I'm sorry."

"Watch your back. We've been compromised. In more ways than one." His eyes met hers, dark and hungry. For her. It filled the space between them, taking her breath.

"The message," she whispered. "I never had a chance to decipher it, but I brought it with me. I'll try to work on it as soon as I have a free moment."

She should've done it before now, but clearly she'd been too distracted by Henry, her willpower steadily dissolving the longer she was alone with him.

Without warning, Henry's mouth was on hers, gentle and warm, a quiet and undemanding gesture, tame enough to be witnessed by Nell. As he released her and walked out of the house, Kate swayed slightly.

On the surface, the kiss had been kind and supportive, something sweet a husband would gift a wife. But the undercurrent was something else entirely as possession and desire pounded in her veins. For a brief wild moment all she wanted to do was run from the house, chase Henry down, and demand more.

Kate brought the fingertips of her right hand to her lips, a bit stunned.

Is this love? Is this why her pa still looked at her ma as if the sunrise depended on her? Why her ma ran like a young girl in the first flush of love to her pa whenever he'd return from the seasonal roundups after being gone for days? Kate had never quite understood it. This year they were celebrating twenty-two years of marriage. Surely such passions ebbed over time.

But there was no denying that Henry's kiss had effectively knocked the wind from her.

She walked to the porch in time to watch the buckboard depart as the sky began turning to gold from the impending sunrise. Henry drove while his horse trailed behind on a lead, the doctor rode his own horse, and Minnie was in the back of the wagon keeping vigil over George.

Feeling Henry's absence acutely, a shadow hung over Kate as she went back into the house with Nell. "Have you eaten?" she asked the girl.

Nell shook her head, but she looked exhausted. Kate's body responded with a similar weariness. Neither she nor Henry had had any sleep during the night.

"Why don't you rest for a bit, and then I'll fix you something."

Nell nodded, sagging against Kate.

"Show me where your room is."

Nell took her to the end of the hallway. Soon Kate had the girl tucked into bed. Craving a bed and a soft pillow herself, she stepped out of Nell's room and quietly closed the door, wondering if she could find a place to rest.

But first, the encoded message. She pulled the note she and Henry believed to belong to Clint along with the cipher she had recorded in Walter Beckett's office at the warehouse.

As she passed a room on the opposite side of the hallway, she pushed open the door, hoping for a desk to work and a bed to sleep. Instead, canvases filled the room, some finished, some still in the early stages of creation. Paint and paintbrushes crowded two tables, and a stool was perched before an easel with an outline of an outdoor scene sketched on a large strip of paper.

Kate stepped inside, mesmerized. Minnie was an artist?

With the early morning light illuminating the room, the scene had an ethereal quality as if Kate had walked into a magical wonderland.

She inspected several smaller paintings on parchment, the edges curled up. They were landscapes, some quite simple consisting of pine trees and mountains, similar to the terrain here in Colorado, but others were of the plains. She moved several aside to see the ones behind them. Faces greeted her, and if she weren't mistaken, they were Comanche, both men and women.

Wait a minute ....

Kate searched for a finished piece among the artwork, but everything was either a sketch or a painting in process. Then she spied a framed work tucked into the corner of the room, the painting faced toward the wall. Replacing the note and cipher back into her skirt pocket, she lifted the piece and turned it around, setting it back against the others.

She gasped.

J. Montgomery was signed in the corner. The style of the unfinished pieces was so similar to this one that there could be no mistake that whoever had painted those had painted this. It was a breathtaking rendition of a Comanche warrior atop a horse, his piercing eyes looking straight at Kate as if he were in the room with her. Her grandmother would love to own this.

Kate glanced around the makeshift art studio.

Were these Minnie's creations? Why did she sign her work under a pseudonym? Why did she keep it a secret?

Kate suspected that Nell might know something. As soon as the girl awoke, Kate would ask her.

Having gained a jolt of energy from her discovery, she made a pot of coffee in the kitchen and sat at the table with Clint's note. It took her only thirty minutes to learn the contents within.

HAVING FALLEN asleep on the sofa in the parlor, Kate awoke with a start as Minnie entered the room.

"What time is it?" she asked, sitting upright and pushing errant strands of hair behind an ear. She'd been in the same split skirt and blouse for two days now and hoped she would have a chance to get back to the cabin today and change.

"It's midday," Minnie replied, slumping into a nearby stuffed chair.

Shocked that she'd slept all morning, Kate asked, "Did you just get here?"

"A few minutes ago. I checked on Nell. She's sleeping."

Kate rubbed her face, shaking the last vestiges of sleep from her. "How's George?"

"The doctor performed the surgery and he's resting now. He should be fine and will be able to come home in a few days."

"That's good. What about Bandito?"

Minnie looked surprised. "You know of George's dog?"

"We met when Henry and I were scouting the spring."

"Why was George out there?"

Kate wasn't sure what to say. Minnie already knew too much about her and Henry. It seemed prudent to keep the revelations to a minimum.

She shrugged. "I'm not sure, but the dog was injured."

Minnie nodded. "He's doing better. I applied a poultice when George returned with him, and then I put him in the barn with food and water. I just checked on him. He's still sleeping."

"I'll go and see him," Kate said. "But first let me make you a cup of tea. You look like you could use it."

Minnie didn't argue and they silently walked to the kitchen. While Kate busied herself with stoking the stove and getting water into the kettle, she debated whether to inquire about the art room at the back of Minnie's house. She found a loaf of bread in the pantry and brought several slices as well as butter and jam to the table where a tired Minnie sat, her chin in her hand.

Once they had both sipped some tea and eaten, regaining their strength, Kate said, "Minnie, may I ask about the artwork?" She nodded toward the back of the house. "I saw it when I put Nell to bed. J. Montgomery is famous among collectors. Is it you?"

Minnie set her teacup down, and for a moment was silent. "No," she finally replied. "It's George."

Was this what George had alluded to when he'd said he was tied to Wingate? That would explain why one of his paintings was hanging in Wallace Wingate's office at the warehouse in town.

"He's very talented," Kate said. "My grandmother has one of his pieces. I sense there's a story here. Would you tell me?"

Minnie's shoulders sagged, and she took another sip of her tea. "Yes, I suppose I will, since you confessed your true identity to me.

"Over thirty years ago I married Ellis, Arthur's father. We met here in my homeland, but he took me back to Ohio." Minnie became pensive. "I wasn't very happy, so a few years later he brought me back and built me this home. He worked in the coal mines, and I raised our little Oliver. He's Nell's father. Arthur never really liked me, but Wallace, the older one, was friendly and he came with us. Ellis worked hard. We never had much but it was enough, and we were happy.

"About six years later, Arthur, and his wife, Lottie, decided to move here as well. Arthur was gaining considerable wealth investing in ore deposits in Minnesota, but I suppose he wanted to be near his father. He and Lottie liked to flaunt their wealth, and very quickly bought most of the surrounding land here. But my husband was happy to have Arthur near and they reconciled their relationship a bit. Wallace never married but soon after Delia was born to a woman he knew in town. The woman passed away at the birth and Wallace didn't know what to do, so Delia was raised by Arthur and Lottie. I had offered to help, but I was rebuffed.

"My brother, George, came to visit from time to time and would stay with us, but I hadn't realized how much he liked to paint. He'd kept that part of himself hidden. In 1885, the Becketts came to Trinidad. Clayton was an old friend of Arthur's, and he and his wife, Jean, bought land to the east from Arthur and began building a life. But Lottie and Jean never got along, and to be honest Arthur's relationship with Clayton felt strained. Ellis chose to stay out of it, and we didn't much concern ourselves with whatever was going on with them."

She cleared her throat and continued. "Five years later I lost Ellis. Around that time, our son, Oliver, and his wife were due with their second child. It was Nell. I was barely coping with the loss of my husband, so I went to California for a time to help them. While I was gone, George stayed and watched the place for me. When I returned a few months later, I learned that Arthur had made a move for my land. I had assumed that it would be entailed to Oliver, and I know he would've let me stay, but Arthur managed to gain control of Ellis's estate, modest as it was, and used dirty tactics to evict me. I'd known he could be cruel, but still ... I was unprepared for it."

She took a deep breath. "But George saved the day. He gave several paintings to Arthur, and Lottie was convinced they were worth something. And they were. George has unfortunately seen very little money from the fame his work has brought, and he did it all for me. I know it's a devil's pact, although he's never shared the specifics of his deal with the Wingates. I've told George to walk away from it, but he refuses. He knows how much I love this land. Our mother and father raised us here. We have much history. I suppose in his mind it's a small price to pay to stay and be left alone. But George has been forever tied to Arthur and Lottie, and I'm guessing to Wallace and Delia as well.

"And then Hugh Maguire arrived, and that odd Charlie Purcell moved into the cabin where you now stay. Hugh and Clayton and Arthur all had known each other during the War. I know most of this only because George told me. Hugh was looking for gold that had been stolen back then, and he believed that Arthur had it.

"Somehow George had seen the gold in Arthur's home and knew where it was hidden, so he told Hugh. Hugh was some kind of law enforcement, and he was undercover, much like you and Henry it would seem. George was weary of being tied to Arthur and was seeking a way out. He told me later that Lottie had been having him do forgeries along with his own paintings, and he didn't want to do them anymore."

Kate reached for the pot of tea and topped off Minnie's cup but remained silent so that the woman could continue.

"Charlie Purcell was Hugh's partner," Minnie said after taking a sip, "and betrayed Hugh by alerting Arthur ahead of time that they were coming for the gold, so Arthur was able to remove it. For some reason, Arthur struck a deal with Charlie and let him take it, at least that's the story I heard. Charlie escaped into the hills and was never seen again, and then Hugh was killed. They said it was an accident, but George was certain Hugh had been murdered. It scared him. He worried for his own life and for mine, but Hugh had never divulged that George had told him of the gold, not even to Charlie.

"So life went back to the way it was, until earlier this year. A bar of gold was found in the mountains and suddenly both the Wingates and Jean Beckett were combing the area, both using their own men to police the region where their properties meet."

Everything Minnie was saying corroborated what George and Dutch had told Kate. "Near the spring?" she asked.

"Yes. They all seem to think the gold is there somewhere, that Charlie hid it thinking he'd come back for it later. But perhaps there's no gold at all. Maybe Charlie managed to run off with it and now everyone is chasing their tails." Minnie shook her head, clearly tired of it all. "And now you and Henry are here." She took another drink of tea and then raised her gaze to Kate. "What is Henry's last name?"

It was clear that Minnie already knew. "Maguire," Kate said quietly.

"Hugh's son," Minnie said matter-of-factly. "It hardly seems a coincidence that he's here then."

"I suppose not."

"I can't help but feel," Minnie said, "that you should take care poking around the Wingates. I should know." A wan smile spread across her lips. "I'm one of them."

Why would Minnie group herself with the likes of Arthur and Lottie, and probably Delia and her father, Wallace, as well?

"It sounds like you've done the best you can," Kate offered. "And it would seem that George has been trying to protect you."

"Yes. He has been a good brother, but I wonder if I should simply have left when Ellis died. I could have stayed with Oliver and his family in California."

"You can still go."

Minnie finished her tea and became contemplative. "I won't leave George, at least not until he's better. I can't deny it would be nice to see Arthur and Lottie get their comeuppance." She raised her eyes to the ceiling. "Please forgive me, Ellis." Then she returned her focus to Kate. "Do you have enough evidence to put them in jail?"

"We're working on it."

"So was Hugh. And in the end it couldn't save him."

But what if Hugh was still alive? A chill ran down Kate's back.

"Please be careful," Minnie added.

"I will."

CHAPTER 27

Henry had stayed with Minnie all morning while the doctor performed surgery on George. Once they knew that George had come through it, Henry had sent Minnie home to rest, and he'd set out to attend to a few matters while he was in town. He'd debated whether to ask the doctor to look at his ribs, but he was feeling better so decided he could get through it on his own. All the better to avoid questions about how he'd gotten the injury.

The first item on his list, and most important, was a visit to Dutch. With the sun high in the sky, Henry walked to the blacksmith shop, his outrage building with every step. How dare Dutch claim to be Hugh Maguire.

Even worse, what if he was?

Both outcomes had Henry's head spinning, so he latched onto his anger. It helped to keep him from becoming so unmoored that he'd be unable to do his job. And that job had now shifted to include not only locating the counterfeiting equipment and connecting it to Arthur, but also finding Confederate gold that had been lost for over thirty years. One way or another, Arthur Wingate was going to jail.

When Henry reached the blacksmith shop, it was closed up. He knocked but no one came. He peered through the window, but Dutch wasn't there.

Reluctantly, Henry headed to his contact's house. There were two letters for him. The first was from Jonesy regarding Wallace Wingate and Charlie Purcell.

Wallace's company—Wingate & Wingate Ltd., purveyor of foreign and American paintings—dealt with many artists but appeared to have a special relationship with J. Montgomery. Wallace maintained a gallery in San Francisco and had been investigated three different times for dealing in forgeries, although nothing had ultimately come of it, and the charges eventually had been dropped.

The information regarding Purcell was more disconcerting. Jonesy was able to dig up a bank account that Purcell shared with another account holder, and it was none other than Hugh Maguire. *Did you know about this?* Jonesy wrote.

No, Jones, I didn't.

The account, opened eight years ago, was still in existence, although the last withdrawal had been three days after the most important date in Henry's life—Hugh Maguire's death. Jonesy said the withdrawal had been made by Purcell, but considering that both men were presumed dead, it was hard to know who had executed the transaction.

Henry frowned. Why would Charlie Purcell and his father share a bank account? Was this why Purcell betrayed Hugh and took the gold for himself?

With more questions than answers, Henry turned his attention to the second letter. It was from Louise.

She was well and mostly recovered, and she was coming to Trinidad. She would come directly to the Purcell cabin, so there was no need for Henry to meet her. Reading between the lines what that really meant was that her arrival was variable. Hell, she might already be here.

He was running out of time to resolve the case, and he didn't need Louise having a front row seat to his improper relationship with Kate.

With his mind on the information he'd just received, he walked to the main street of town intending to retrieve his horse from the livery when he bumped into Delia.

"Good afternoon, Gilbert," she said with a bright smile.

"Delia." He gave a cordial nod.

"Where are you off to?"

"I had some business in town but now I'm heading home."

He tried to step around her, but she moved closer, resting a hand against his abdomen. Her flowery scent filled his nostrils, and while not altogether unpleasant, he wasn't of a mind to engage in this flirtation any longer. It felt like a betrayal to his "wife." To Kate.

"Won't you have tea with me?" she asked, her blue eyes earnest and filled with desire.

"Delia, I'm a married man."

"Of course you are." She released a bemused laugh, but she still stood too close to him.

He took a step back, putting distance between them.

Frustration pinched her face for a moment. "Uncle Arthur says you'll be leaving soon."

"Oh?" Henry wondered what that meant. He and Arthur hadn't discussed the end of his employment as the man's ghostwriter.

"He said you'd be gone in a few days," she added, then hesitated before saying. "I just ... I'd like to get to know you better, Gilbert."

Why was Arthur dismissing him? "I'm afraid that's not possible," he said.

Delia extended her parasol to block the sun, and Henry realized to also shield them from anyone who might pass by.

"Sallie told me," Delia said, the calculating gaze returning, the one he'd come to expect from her.

"Told you what?"

"About your marital problems."

So that's where that rumor had started.

He was uncertain how to respond, not wanting to give the impression that he didn't know what Delia was talking about and possibly ruining some covert angle that Kate was using. The bigger question was why was Kate using this approach at all? And why the hell did it bother him so much?

"If it's not going well between you two," Delia continued, "then I'm truly sorry, but perhaps you and she just aren't suited."

The memory of Kate in his arms said otherwise.

"Is that what happened between you and Walter Beckett?" he asked, trying to turn the attention away from the "state" of his marriage.

Delia's eyes widened. "Walt? We were never married."

"But you were engaged."

"Yes, but it was some time ago. I can assure you I have no feelings for the man."

"I'm not sure he feels the same," Henry said.

Delia shifted the parasol to rest on her shoulder. "Walter has always wanted to be near the Wingate fortune. I was just a means to an end, so I ended it. I won't be used by a man."

"Haven't you ever wondered why he continues to work for your uncle?"

"Oh," she said with a laugh. "You think it's for me? I can assure you it's not. Walt has always liked working for my uncle more than the bank. That's all it is."

"Beckett worked for the bank?"

"Yes, First National here in town. Before he left, he was the engraver."

That caught Henry off-guard.

Banks frequently printed their own money, and skilled artisans were often sought for the job, possessing a knowledge of paper, dyes, and expertise with printing machinery. They also made excellent counterfeiters for producing illegal banknotes.

"How long has Walter worked for your uncle?"

"I'm not certain. I've known him since we were young, but he left for several years after a terrible accident here that involved a friend of my uncle's."

"Hugh Maguire?" Henry asked.

Delia nodded. "Yes. I see you've heard about it. I think Walter worked for Uncle before that, but when he returned after being away for several years, he courted me and took a job at the bank. It wasn't until I broke off the engagement that he took a more permanent position with Uncle." Delia paused, watching him, her eyes glittering. "Why are you so interested in Walter Beckett?"

Henry sighed inwardly. The only way to salvage this was to stoke Delia's affection for him. Dammit.

"Just curious about the competition," he said quietly, keeping his eyes locked onto hers.

Delia's face all but glowed as she smiled at her victory.

Kate didn't know where Henry had gotten to. Minnie said he'd left the doctor's office when she had, saying he had some business to attend to in town. After checking in on Bandito, Kate left Minnie's house and returned to her cabin in the early afternoon.

A knock on the door revealed a Wingate ranch hand—a young man with curly brown hair—who handed her a note. It was from Lottie, inviting Sallie to tea now that she was returned from her adventure with Gilbert. While Kate debated about whether to decline, the young man said he would accompany her back to the main house.

"I'll need a few minutes to freshen up," Kate said. She closed the door.

She quickly wrote a note for Henry telling him where she was going and left it on the kitchen table.

She was soon on her horse, accompanied by the man, and they rode in silence the short distance to the Wingate mansion. When they arrived, he tended to her horse, and Kate was greeted by a housekeeper at the front door. She led Kate to a parlor and left her alone.

Sunlight slanted through the west-facing windows, warming the room. Kate walked to the fireplace mantel, her calico skirt rustling around her feet, and she wondered if she should have changed her gown to something nicer.

The door closed behind her. She turned, expecting Lottie, but instead a man she didn't recognize greeted her. The look in his eyes immediately put her on alert.

"I'm waiting for Mrs. Wingate," Kate said.

He narrowed his eyes, his dark hair brushed away from his face. He appeared to be about the same age as Henry and Ian.

"And you are?" Kate asked.

"Walter Beckett."

Jean's son, who also worked for Arthur.

"Pleased to meet you." She plastered a fake smile on her lips. "I'm Sallie Holmes."

Walter chuckled and moved toward her. She backed away toward the sofa sitting in the center of the room. Tea had already been laid out on the coffee table so she used that as her excuse to avoid him.

Sitting, she reached for the pot. "Would you like something while we wait?" She poured a cup.

"No." Walter's tone sent a shiver down her back. "I know who you are."

Kate stirred a dollop of cream into her tea, trying to keep her expression impassive although he had moved behind her.

Kate schooled her features. "I'm not sure what you mean," she said, striving to keep her voice calm and casual. "I don't believe we've ever met."

"You and *Gilbert* are undercover."

Kate cleared her throat. "What a silly notion. My husband and I aren't undercover. Wherever did you hear such a thing?" She brought the cup to her mouth and was glad her hand didn't shake as she took a sip.

"Well, Arthur told me."

Arthur? Oh no. A frown marred her forehead, and she was glad she was faced away from the man.

Kate set her tea on the coffee table and glanced up, catching a glimpse of Beckett in the reflection of a vase.

His arms were raised holding a fireplace poker!

Kate bolted forward but the metal grazed the side of her head. She landed face down on the carpeted floor, the material scratching her cheek. Remaining motionless, she kept her eyes closed, praying that Beckett would leave her alone if he thought he'd succeeded in knocking her out.

Please don't kill me.

Every cell in Kate's body screamed to stand and fight back, and it took everything she had to lie still and ignore the impulse.

Walter expelled fast breaths, so at least Kate could locate him in the room. He didn't move from behind the sofa for at least a full minute, then a clanking indicated that he'd replaced the metal poker into its holder near the fireplace.

A knock preceded the opening of the parlor door.

"Sallie, I'm sorry I'm late," Lottie said, her skirt and petticoats whooshing as she entered. Then she gasped. "Walter, what's going on?" Lottie demanded in a low and fierce whisper. The door slammed shut.

"Arthur told me about them," Walter said. "About her and her husband's true identities."

Kate felt the brush of Lottie's skirt against her feet. "Is she ... is she dead?" Lottie asked, fear in her voice.

Walter came around the sofa and knelt beside Kate. "No. She's breathing."

"You could've killed her." Lottie's voice vibrated with anger. "What has gotten into you?"

"I wasn't trying to hurt her."

"Obviously you were."

"Look," Walter whispered, "I'm trying to help you and Arthur. He told me about the gold. About how he was betting on the fact that Henry knew the location of it. Henry and Kate Ryan have just returned from the wilderness, and if he knows where the gold is, then he'll talk when he finds out that we have her."

"You plan to kidnap her?" Lottie released a loud huff. "For God's sake, Walter. We had this under control. If something happens to a Pinkerton detective, we'll have more trouble than we need. The plan was to keep this out of the limelight. We don't need the sheriff around here again. It was bad enough when you killed Hugh Maguire."

Kate kept her breathing even.

"I told Arthur that Henry never located any stash of gold while he was in the wilderness," Walter said. "I should know since I was assigned to follow him. But what if he had?"

"You're saying he does know where it is?"

"He could've slipped it past me. We'll use her as leverage."

"What makes you so certain that Henry even cares about this girl?"

Kate could feel Lottie's eyes on her.

"He cares. It must be driving Delia insane. Does she know they're not really married?"

"No," Lottie admonished him. "She knows nothing, and it's better that way. You're not to say anything, you hear me?"

"You're okay with her throwing herself at him?" Walter was

jealous. It would seem he'd never gotten over Delia ending their engagement.

"It doesn't matter, Walter."

"Fine," he replied. "Henry Maguire won't leave this girl here."

The movement of her skirts indicated Lottie's pacing. "I don't know. Does Arthur know about this?"

"No. Not yet."

"All right, don't tell him. We'll handle this ourselves. I need you to go to the secret room and get a pair of handcuffs."

"I haven't been there in a while. Which book is it?"

"Jane Eyre."

The opening and closing of the parlor door indicated Beckett's departure.

The sound of liquid poured into a glass told Kate that Lottie had skipped the tea on the coffee table and instead found something stronger hidden in a side cupboard. She slurped down the drink and then came back to Kate.

She roughly grabbed a hold of Kate's arm and rolled her over.

Kate maintained her catatonic state, not wanting to alert Lottie that she was fully awake. Lottie's cool hand rested against Kate's forehead and in any other circumstance Kate might concede that Lottie wasn't such a terrible woman. Except for the fact that she and Walter Beckett planned to keep Kate prisoner and lure Henry here. Did he really know where the gold was? Was he keeping this from Kate?

Maybe Henry wouldn't come for her. She hadn't seen him since he'd fetched the doctor for George. If he had somehow located what remained of the gold, perhaps he'd fled.

Could she have been completely wrong about him?

The thought left her sick to her stomach.

The parlor door opened and closed, and the smell of nervous sweat permeated the air, signaling the return of Beckett. "What now?" he asked.

Lottie pulled Kate's hands together and affixed the handcuffs. "We can put her in the empty study at the end of the hall. No one uses it. It shouldn't be a problem to lock her in. And then you'll need to get a message to Henry."

"When is the next Wells Fargo shipment?"

"I told you before, Walter, I have it taken care of."

"By who? Clint?"

Lottie sighed. "You should be happy about this. We're keeping you out of it. We've got a plan to pin it on Clint and the boys. And we've got William Phelps in our back pocket, so he's taken the money we deposited, no questions asked. The robbery will happen Thursday night, during the art auction. It's the perfect cover. But good Lord, Walter." Lottie let out a frustrated groan. "I wish you hadn't gone and saddled us with *her*."

"Did your psychic come up with anything else?"

Kate sensed that Walter had pointed at her.

"Actually no," Lottie replied. "I thought it would be an interesting test for Roberta to see if she could rout it out, but she didn't. All she said was that Sallie Holmes had protection from the spirit world, and she couldn't see past it. But she did give me a juicy tidbit about Laura Phelps, which helped to secure William's cooperation at the bank."

"What was that?"

"Laura Phelps was underage when William married her. I didn't have proof of course, but when I brought it up to William, he paled considerably. It was easy enough after that to get him to cooperate. It was frustrating to have to do it again so soon with a new bank manager after everything we'd done to manipulate that Rogers fellow who held the position before William. I still think Arthur needs to send someone after that slimy weasel. I think he'll talk, but Arthur thinks he's too afraid. Arthur has never liked the dirty work."

Walter released a huff. "Yeah, that's what I'm for."

"Maybe we should send you after Rogers."

"Like you made me chase Charlie Purcell? I wasted three years doing that. I ain't doin' it again."

"Fine. Stay here. I'll get the room ready." Lottie's voice trailed away as she left.

Had Lottie and Beckett truly confessed so much?

Kate had to hope that she would survive this because she'd just cracked the case.

CHAPTER 28

Kate allowed a good ten minutes to pass before she opened her eyes. Lottie and Beckett had unceremoniously dumped her onto the study floor, although a rug had cushioned some of the jostling. Kate had been forced to empty her mind in order to allow her body to be completely limp, since the urge to press back against the inelegant handling of these two had been strong.

She took in her surroundings. The shades and curtains were drawn so the room was cast in a murky grayness. Slowly Kate pushed to a sitting position, her hands bound together before her with the handcuffs. Thankfully, it was the only restraint that had been placed on her. Her feet were free, and she could move about the room at will.

It was clear that Lottie and Walter hadn't thought this through since there was much Kate could do here to help herself. And help herself she would.

The first order of business was to remove the cuffs. She stood and moved closer to the window, a sliver of sunlight peeking past the blind. She used the light to inspect the manacles. They were the Tower model, exactly what the Pinkerton Agencies used. Kate looked around the ornate wooden desk for something to pick the lock, but then remembered her hairpins. She pulled one free and bent it lengthwise.

Tower cuffs were lightweight, which compromised security because the usual double locking mechanism had been eliminated, so the good news was that they were easy to escape from. A negative, of course, when dealing with a detained criminal, but Kate had practiced with these, so she knew the trick. Trying to pick the lock while the cuffs were on proved to be a bit challenging, but she eventually freed herself. She placed the cuffs into one of the desk drawers and quietly moved to the door, carefully cracking it open.

The back of her head where Beckett had managed to get a partial swipe still throbbed, but Kate did her best to ignore it. She had a limited timeframe to explore the house before Lottie or Walter decided to check on her. Henry had been unable to do much sleuthing inside the main house, and now Kate had the perfect opportunity. She couldn't waste it.

As distant voices drifted to her, Kate went to the main room with an extensive bookshelf, hoping this was the one that Beckett had gone off to when he'd left the parlor. A maid hustled down the hallway and Kate darted behind a wall hanging. After a long moment, she chanced a glance around the room. Empty.

She moved quietly to the bookcase and began quickly skimming the titles. When she located Jane Eyre, it was eye level and to her right. She fiddled with it for a second, wiggling it then pulling on it. Only when she pushed did she hear a soft click as a panel released behind the shelf. Kate slipped inside, tugging it closed behind her. She could only hope she wasn't trapping herself inside with anyone who might already be there.

As the darkness enveloped her before she shut the panel, she'd caught sight of a table with a candle and a box of matches beside it. She fumbled in the dark, but soon had a small flame going. She picked up the dish holding the light and proceeded deeper into the secret passage, walking slowly in case she met up with someone. After ten feet, it opened into a room opened and she stopped.

She'd struck her own version of gold.

A rolling printing press sat at the center of the room. A table held bottles of dye and stacks of paper. And if that hadn't convinced her she'd found the counterfeiting equipment, then the one-hundred dollar bill lying on the floor did. Louise had briefed her on ways to tell the difference between legitimate currency and fakes. Kate tucked the bill into her skirt pocket so she could inspect it in fine detail later.

Unwilling to spend any more time here than was necessary, she crept back to the entrance but hesitated since she had no way of knowing if the outer room was occupied. Taking a deep breath, she pulled on the latch near the exit and extinguished the candle, placing it back on the side table.

She peeked into the room and froze when the flash of a maid's backside exited the room, but thankfully the young woman hadn't noticed Kate.

She scurried from her hiding position and quickly put the bookshelf back into position. To calm her pounding heart, she hid behind the curtains, debating her next move. She wasn't going back to her imprisonment in the study. Lottie or Beckett would find out soon enough, so she needed to get out of there with haste.

It would be too difficult to leave out the front door. Her best option was to find the kitchen and use a back door.

She left the room and moved quietly down the hallway, but as she rounded a corner, she ran straight into one of the maids. With no time to think, she squared her shoulders and faced the girl head on.

"I'm visiting with Mrs. Wingate," Kate said, "and I've forgotten something in my saddlebags. Could you show me to the back entrance, please?"

The girl, clearly startled to see Kate, nevertheless nodded. "This way, ma'am."

The maid turned and Kate followed, praying she wouldn't run into Lottie or Beckett.

Instead it was worse. Just before Kate made it to the kitchen, Arthur Wingate appeared in a doorway.

"Sallie," he beamed. "I didn't know you were here."

Kate stopped abruptly, pasting a smile on her face. "Yes. I'm helping Lottie with preparations for the auction."

She prayed that Lottie hadn't told her husband that she'd locked Kate up in the study with a plan to extort Henry for the gold. Also, hadn't Walter Beckett said that it was Arthur who had alerted him to Henry's true identity? If that were true, then the man knew that Kate was an agent.

Nerves gripped her.

The maid had stopped, hesitating, the confusion on her face all too clear. She didn't know whether to leave or stay.

"Well, I best be getting back to the preparations," Kate said, keeping up the façade of her alias. "Your maid was about to help me." Kate glanced at her, willing her to stay.

"Hold on," Arthur said. "I want to get your opinion of something." With a nod he dismissed the help.

Kate's heart sank.

He clasped her elbow and stood much too close as he guided her away from the kitchen and her hope for escape. She was so distracted by losing her chance to flee that it didn't register that Arthur had brought her to his private study and shut the door until it was too late.

"Did you and Gilbert have a nice excursion into the wilderness?" he asked, moving to his desk. "I've not seen him since you returned." Still standing, he picked up a stack of papers and tapped them together to organize them. "Did you find anything special while you were out there?" He raised his gaze and locked onto her with a pointed stare.

She fought the urge to squirm. "No," she replied. "Nothing

special. Just the great outdoors and plenty of fresh air. I'm sure Gilbert will get back to work tomorrow."

"Please sit." He indicated the chair opposite his desk.

Reluctantly she did so.

He took his seat, leaning back in his chair and giving her his full attention. "I'm glad we have a chance to talk."

"As am I."

"Look, Miss Ryan ...."

So much for keeping up the charade. She fought to keep her breathing steady as a rivulet of sweat slid between her breasts.

"I know who you are," he continued. "And I know who Henry is. I've known all along, so there's no reason to deny it. In fact, I was the one who made sure Henry was assigned to me. I know of his history."

The cold calculation in the man's eyes sent a frisson of fear along Kate's spine.

"I'll admit I didn't know much about *you*, however. Your appearance was somewhat of a surprise. My contacts had said a woman named Louise Foster would be joining Henry as his 'wife,' but then you showed up. But no matter. Enough money can buy any information one could need. You're Katharine Rosemary Ryan. Your parents are Matthew and Molly Ryan. Your mother was a captive of the Comanche for nearly ten years when she was a child, and her return from the dead was quite the scandal at the time."

Kate's blood ran cold, and she felt the color drain from her face.

"You have an older brother—Elijah Robert Ryan—as well as a younger sister, Josephine Elizabeth. Shall I continue?"

Kate paused, swallowing against the dryness in her throat. "What do you want?"

He leaned forward. "Let's not pretend you don't know what I want."

"The gold."

"Yes. Did you find it?"

"No."

Arthur sighed. "I'm not a fool. And that much gold can sway the conscience of even the most stalwart and moral person, so I'll be needing your help."

"I don't understand."

"I need *you* to make sure that *Henry* doesn't run off with it."

Apparently, Arthur shared the same conclusion as Walter Beckett—Henry secretly had the gold.

"I told you we didn't find it," she said.

"Were you always with him?" Arthur shot back.

"I ...." She stumbled over her words. "Um ... no."

He looked upon her like a naïve child. "I need you to keep tabs on him. I need you to report back to me. I need you to get me that gold."

"You're insane," she whispered. "You're a criminal."

"Such accusations." His eyes were defiant. "You seem to have misunderstood why I know so much about your family. Their safety, well ...." He raised his hands in supplication.

The gravity of his insinuation horrified her.

"I can't guarantee it if you decide to stay on this course you've set yourself on," he said. "And how do you know that Henry is still your true partner? How do you know that he hasn't found the gold and is already making plans to retrieve it right out from under all of us? Would you risk your family for a man you hardly know?"

Rage flooded her.

Bastard.

How dare this man threaten her family. He was a dirty, underhanded ass who couldn't hold a candle to her pa. Matt Ryan had been in the U.S. Army and the Texas Rangers. Her pa could handle a man like Arthur Wingate with little effort, of that Kate was certain. Not to mention her uncles, all of them ex-lawmen. Arthur had no idea who he was threatening.

But she wouldn't say it aloud, despite the words heavy on her lips. What she needed was to escape this house.

"Fine," she said. "I'll do some spying for you."

"Good girl. You have until the auction tomorrow evening. And don't even think about running."

"May I go now? I clearly need to find Henry." She didn't have much time before Lottie ruined her credibility.

He inclined his head toward the door. "You're free to go."

She stood with an air of confidence she didn't feel. With great restraint, she moved as normally as she could considering she really wanted to bolt from the study and not stop until she was back at the Purcell cabin. Maybe she wouldn't stop there. She'd keep running until she made it back to Texas, to her family. She'd tell her pa and uncles everything, and they'd keep her protected; she'd never leave the safety of home again.

She didn't look back as she exited Arthur's study. With anxiety heavy in her chest, she returned to the spot near the kitchen where Arthur had intercepted her. Ignoring the staff who were present, she went straight to the back door.

Once outside, she let herself scurry, and then she ran. Her horse was still tied to a rail near the front porch. She forced herself to a walk in the event anyone was watching. As soon as she reached her horse, she grabbed the reins and climbed atop her, spinning the mare around and kicking her into a gallop. She didn't stop until she reached her and Henry's cabin.

She hastily got her horse settled into the small barn and then burst into the cabin, finding Henry seated at the kitchen table reading a piece of paper. His surprise at seeing her was obvious.

"What's wrong?" she asked.

He stood. "I could ask the same thing. This was just delivered." He held it out. "It's a ransom note from Walter Beckett. For you."

She took the paper and almost laughed at the absurdity of her afternoon.

Henry closed the distance between them, concern etched on his face. "Are you all right?" He reached up and pushed her hair from her cheek; it had been freed from her hair pins hours ago. "There's blood."

The day's events caught up to her and she fell into his embrace, relieved he was here. He hadn't left her. Yet.

He returned the hug with equal possession when a knock at the door interrupted them. Reluctantly, Henry broke the contact and Kate felt immediately bereft.

He motioned for her to move away so she wouldn't be seen by their visitor, and she pressed against the wall near the door. Henry cracked it open, and then he opened it wide.

It was Louise.

CHAPTER 29

Henry sat at the kitchen table, Kate and Louise on either side of him, as Kate recounted her day, his anger rising with every detail she shared. Walter Beckett assaulted her, Lottie Wingate imprisoned her, and finally Arthur threatened her, demanding that she spy on Henry.

"This certainly complicates things," Louise said. She was well-groomed in contrast to Kate's disheveled appearance, her auburn hair tucked back in a practical bun, and a coffee-colored day dress and jacket that set off the freckles across her nose and matched the brown of her eyes.

Louise was all business. She turned to Henry and said rather pointedly, "Do you know where this gold is?"

Her forthright gaze triggered a suspicion he hadn't quite realized he'd had until this moment. There had been times he'd sensed that Kate was hiding something from him, but as it all clicked into place, dread pooled in his stomach.

"You sent Kate to spy on me, didn't you?" he asked.

Louise sat back in her chair, nonplussed by his question. "I assigned her an extra task. Off the books, of course." She released a sigh, one that a mother might bequeath an errant child, except that she was the same age as Henry. "I know you, Henry. And this job was going to be emotional for you."

"I don't get emotional," he countered.

"No, not usually." She shifted her attention to Kate. "Has he been?"

"Has he been what?" Kate asked, her lips hardly moving and her face suddenly pale, as if she'd been caught doing something she shouldn't.

Disappointment landed hard in his gut, taking his breath.

Kate Ryan had played him? It wasn't possible. He was a better agent than that. And he wasn't so enamored of her that his romantic entanglement with her could hurt him.

Another glance at her face, however, said differently.

He'd fallen for her.

He'd fallen hard.

"Has Henry been emotional?" Louise asked.

Kate licked her lips. "He's been ... distracted."

"It's the same thing. It's good that I've come and just in time. Kate has located the counterfeiting equipment, so I'll go into town and get an arrest warrant from the sheriff. We can serve it tomorrow morning, first thing."

"No," Henry replied. "The art auction is tomorrow at their home. Do it then. There'll be more people. It'll be safer."

Louise raised an eyebrow. "Not planning to join us, Henry?"

"Actually," Kate cut in. "There's something else you both should know. Henry and I intercepted a message a few days ago, and I was able to decipher it earlier. I believe that Clint, a man who works for Arthur Wingate, will be robbing the Wells Fargo shipment tomorrow evening at the same time as the auction. When I was pretending to be unconscious, Lottie said something about Clint and his men taking the blame. Shouldn't we try to stop that as well?"

The snort of a horse sounded from outside the house. Henry rose and peeked through a curtain, then he opened the door.

"We need to talk," his brother Ian said.

Henry stood back, ushered him inside, then shut the door. "You've met Kate," he said. "This is Louise Foster."

She stood. "You must be Ian Maguire. I've always wondered if I'd make your acquaintance."

Ian removed his hat and shook her hand. "It's a pleasure, Miss Foster. I'm a fan."

For the first time since she'd arrived on Henry's doorstep, Louise smiled. Well, it was almost a smile, maybe more like a passing moment of amusement. Louise wasn't always so serious, but she'd been all business during the last hour of debriefing about the case. Perhaps it was for Kate's benefit.

Ian shifted his attention to Kate, and his face took on a look of concern upon seeing the disarray of her clothing and hair. "Did something happen?"

"Let's sit in here," Henry said, indicating the living room.

Louise brought coffee and was soon situated beside his brother on the sofa; Kate sat across from Henry in a stuffed chair. Still feeling bruised by Kate's "supposed" interest in him, he sought to put as much distance between them as possible.

"What's your news?" Henry asked Ian.

"I have reason to believe that my cover's been blown. Jean Beckett made a comment about our father and that he had two sons. She didn't come out and say it, but I've a feeling she's known who I am all along. I wanted to warn you."

Henry sighed. "Join the club."

"What do you mean?"

"Wingate knows who I am. He's known from the beginning." Henry indicated that Kate should recount her day again.

As Kate spoke, Ian's face became more impassive by the moment. Henry may not have been around his brother for the last few years, but he knew that look. Ian would need to right this wrong.

"Have we been played?" Ian muttered.

Henry was beginning to think he had, by both the Wingates and Kate Ryan.

Ian frowned. "But why?"

"It's the gold," Henry replied. "Both sides seem to think either you or I know the location. They've been waiting to see which one of us would lead them there first."

Ian's face hardened. "I know nothing. Do you?"

Perfect. No one seemed to trust him. Henry almost laughed. "No," he answered begrudgingly.

"Kate and I will handle Arthur Wingate," Louise said. "You and Henry can intercept Clint and the Wells Fargo stage."

"I don't think you both should face Wingate on your own," Ian said.

"We can handle ourselves," Louise replied. "Henry can contact the agent at the Wells Fargo office and request that you both be placed on security detail on the stage itself. That should make it easy enough to apprehend the thieves."

"But it won't resolve the insurance fraud," Henry said. "All it will do is prove that Clint and any men with him are criminals. That doesn't link them back to Wingate."

"That's what Lottie and Arthur want," Kate said. "When the money was stolen before, Clint must've hidden it somewhere."

"You never found it?" Ian asked.

"No."

"I think I know how we can handle this." Ian leaned forward, his elbows on his knees. "Henry and I can sneak away from the stage as the robbery is occurring, hide, and then follow Clint. With hope it will lead to incriminating evidence against Wingate."

"That sounds dangerous," Kate said quietly, shifting her gaze to Henry. He looked away.

"If we want all of this to stick, then it's the only way." Ian flexed his right hand and rolled his shoulder. "I should go." He stood.

"Wait!" Kate's voice startled everyone. "There's something else I should tell you. While I was pretending to be unconscious, Lottie and Beckett discussed Hugh Maguire."

"And?" Henry said, wondering why she hadn't spoken of it earlier. More reason for his foolishness in trusting her.

"Walter Beckett was the one who killed him."

"That son-of-a-bitch," Ian ground out.

Henry rose to his feet. "Why didn't you say something sooner?"

The look she gave told him why. She still didn't believe that Hugh was dead.

Henry swore under his breath and ushered Ian to the door. "I'll see you out."

Once they were alone, Henry ran a hand through his hair, his frustration reaching a boiling point. "I have something else to tell you. Francis O'Malley, the blacksmith in town, has declared himself to be none other than Hugh Maguire."

Ian stopped at the bottom of the porch steps and swung his gaze back to Henry. "What?"

"So Walter Beckett might not be guilty after all." Henry didn't scale back his sarcasm. Then he asked, "Do you know O'Malley?"

"No." Ian's face was frozen in surprise.

"Look, I don't believe him. It can't be true. Somehow, he knows enough of our pa to convince others."

"Convince who?"

"Kate."

"And you don't believe her?" Ian asked.

"I don't."

"Have you met him?"

"Once." Henry paused. "It's not him." Then lower, he uttered, "It can't be him." He braced a hand on the railing. "Do you know the whole story about Arthur, Clayton, and Pa?"

"Tell me."

Some Ian already knew but Henry rehashed it—their time in the

War, the missing Confederate gold, and the betrayal of Charlie Purcell.

"There's something else," Henry added. "My boss, Jonesy, sent me information about a bank account that was in the name of both Purcell and Pa. There were deposits and withdrawals around the time of Pa's death."

Ian went quiet, as did Henry.

"There was no betrayal," Ian finally said. "Purcell and Pa were working together to get the gold from Wingate."

"Maybe." Probably. The evidence was telling.

"Why would Francis O'Malley impersonate Pa?" Ian asked.

"I haven't figured that one out yet, but it must have to do with the gold."

"I take it Kate and Louise know nothing of this?"

"I've been trying to keep this part of my investigation to myself," Henry said.

"And what made you decide to finally share it with me?" There was censure in Ian's voice.

Henry released a humorless chuckle. "Because you never believed me before. I had no reason to think you would now." He sighed, drained from it all. "But it's become dangerous, and you deserve to know who all the players are."

"Someone has that gold," Ian said. "The question is—who?"

"I'll meet you at the Wells Fargo office tomorrow morning. Afterward we can look for O'Malley."

"Unless he's the one who found it. Then he's long gone."

Ian was probably right.

"Ian," Henry said as his brother mounted his horse. "Don't do anything reckless with Beckett. I'll get a warrant for his arrest. Kate's testimony should be enough to put him away."

Ian's barely contained anger was evident from the dark slant of his face. "And if it's not, then I reserve every right to become reckless."

He turned his horse and disappeared into the night.

THE NEXT MORNING Kate awoke with a start. She'd slept deeply, a surprise considering everything that had happened the day before. She felt under her pillow and found the derringer she'd placed there, in case Beckett or Lottie had decided to come for her. Surely they knew by now that she'd escaped, that Arthur had cornered her and sent her on her way. Did they believe she was sufficiently frightened to keep the abduction to herself? Would they try to nab her again?

Louise had shared the bed with her since Henry was on the sofa, but Kate was now alone. With a steady thrum of anxiety gripping her, she donned a robe and went to the kitchen, taking a quick scan of the home she'd been sharing with Henry for anything amiss. Louise was at the table with a pot of coffee. Henry was gone, although the Winchester he'd placed by the front door remained. Protection from the Wingates.

"Good morning," Louise said. "Come and sit."

"Where's Henry?" Kate asked as she took a seat, disappointment mixing with her apprehension.

"He went into town to meet Ian."

Louise poured her a cup of coffee and Kate took a sip, wincing when it burned her tongue. She set it aside, not wanting it. Her nerves had locked down her stomach.

"I'm glad we're alone." Louise's brown eyes conveyed concern. Her mentor appeared well-rested and recovered from her injury, her auburn hair again tucked into a practical bun and her face scrubbed clean. Louise wasn't pretty by conventional standards, but she was striking. And Kate had always been impressed by her ability to don a disguise, although today she was in a crisp white blouse and a navy-blue skirt.

Louise was in work mode.

Kate simply felt spent. "How are you?" she asked.

When Louise's brows pinched in confusion, Kate added, "The bullet wound."

"Oh, I'm fine. Everything is healing. It was just a graze along my rib cage. The doctors made more of it than it really was." Louise moved her saucer and cup to the side and folded her arms on the table. "How is the assignment going? Are you and Henry getting along?"

"Yes."

"I spoke with him briefly this morning. He said you've been doing well, but he seemed a bit ..."

"What?"

"Guarded. Is everything all right between you two?"

Kate considered telling Louise everything, but something held her back. As much as she liked the woman and respected her, Louise was still her boss, and the fact that Henry and Kate had allowed their marriage to veer into "real" territory probably wouldn't sit well with her.

"Yes," Kate repeated, pushing a clump of hair away from her face and taking another sip of her coffee. She needed to get herself together. "I should fill you in on the secondary assignment you gave me." Louise knew bits and pieces, but now it was time to tell the complete story.

Louise waited with quiet attention.

Starting at the beginning, Kate described Dutch driving her to the Wingate party on the day of her arrival to Trinidad. She continued with meeting Minnie Wingate and the details of her estrangement from her stepson Arthur. She revealed the reconnaissance of the warehouse that she and Henry performed, discovering the cipher as well as a never-before-seen J. Montgomery painting, adding that Minnie's brother, George, was the true artist. She described the séance with Lottie and how she used it to learn intimate secrets from the guests to blackmail them later, using it to manipulate the bank manager through his wife.

Kate confided the details around Henry's father, about the missing Confederate gold, about the map that Henry possessed from his pa. She spoke of their encounter in the wilderness with Clint and his men, and that she, Henry, and Ian had found a small cave that had very likely been storing the gold bars that both the Wingates and the Becketts were searching for.

Then she told her about Dutch, and his claim to be Hugh Maguire.

Louise was stunned. "Henry's father is alive?"

"If what Dutch is saying, then yes. But Henry is skeptical."

"Has he seen the man?"

"Yes, once. But it was before we knew this. Henry believes that Dutch is lying, that he's also after the gold."

"And no one has seen this gold?"

"No," Kate answered.

"So someone has found it, based on what you found at that cave."

Kate nodded. "We believe so."

"Well, I have some information about Hugh Maguire that might be pertinent."

CHAPTER 30

Horses and buggies crammed the area in front of the Wingate house, lanterns lighting the way along the roadway as well as at the house. The Wingate Art Auction was turning out to be the event of the year. It was even more crowded than the soiree that Kate had attended previously when she had first arrived. But this time she wasn't accompanied by Dutch, Henry's father if the man was to be believed, but instead Louise was at her side as Kate stepped into the foyer of the Wingate house.

She wore a peach-colored gown she'd purchased that day she'd gone shopping with Delia, which seemed so long ago now. Louise was in the extra gown Kate had bought, a royal blue that offset her auburn hair with a striking contrast. Kate had never worked with Louise, she'd only been trained by her, and as they entered the lion's den she was struck by the confidence and focus her mentor projected. It buoyed Kate's own determination, which admittedly had been floundering as the day had worn on. Fearful that Lottie would send Beckett after her, she'd been skittish for the better part of the day, and it hadn't helped that Henry had all but avoided her earlier except to discuss the case with her and Louise after returning from the Wells Fargo office.

Something had changed between them, and she feared it had something to do with her assignment to spy on him, but they were not alone long enough for her to broach the subject.

Kate's nerves were taut, reminding her of her first night as a new agent, at a Wingate party much like this one. The night she'd first met Henry.

She and Louise both had two weapons at hand—a derringer in a deep pocket that Louise had modified on both dresses, and a knife strapped to their right thigh. Louise also had the arrest warrant folded into her reticule, ready to present once Kate exposed the secret room. It should go like clockwork, but Kate was anything but calm. The last time she'd been in this house, she'd been assaulted and imprisoned. There was also a knot of worry in her stomach over Henry and Ian intercepting Clint and his men as they robbed the Wells Fargo stage.

So many things could go wrong.

Caught up in a group of several couples, Kate and Louise were able to skim past the foyer where Lottie Wingate was greeting guests by hiding against the tall figures of two men whose wives were on the opposite side, chatting up the woman.

Once inside, Kate guided Louise toward the main room. The hum of chatter filled the air, the ladies wearing their finest gowns and the men in suits. If Kate didn't know how rotten the Wingates were at the core, she would allow herself to be impressed by the display of finery and opulence. The Wingates hadn't held back with this event.

The furniture had been removed from the space, allowing for artwork to be on display along three of the walls, with a bar along the fourth. Kate recognized some of the pieces, having learned of the artists from her grandmother. A large painting stood out in one corner because it was covered with a black cloth, and Kate knew without a doubt it had to be a J. Montgomery, maybe the very one that had been hanging in Wallace Wingate's warehouse office.

Kate and Louise accepted glasses of sherry from a tray held by a housekeeper, and Kate took a fortifying gulp, remembering the night Henry had become quite inebriated after Sunday supper. Had he been anxious that night? He had said it was because of her. But everything she had come to know about him showed him to be calm and organized, far from the type to engage in reckless behavior.

"Have you ever seen Henry drink too much?" she said quietly to Louise at her side, her eyes darting around the room for Walter Beckett. She was determined not to let the man have the advantage again.

Surprise registered on Louise's face. She seemed to consider her words before saying, "Only once. It was after a particularly trying case that had involved child abuse, and several of us were unwinding in the office with a bottle of bourbon. We needed it." Louise glanced around to make certain no one was listening. "It was the only time he spoke of his father to me. The more he drank, the more the grief he carried spilled out. He usually keeps it tightly bottled-up, but that night I became aware that Henry was not okay with what had happened to Hugh Maguire. I knew one day it would be a problem."

There was compassion in her eyes.

"I've come to care for him." The words were out before Kate could swallow them back.

Realization crossed Louise's gaze. "Oh, Kate ...," she whispered.

"We didn't expect to see you, *Sallie,*" Lottie said, causing Kate to jump as the woman rushed up beside her.

Kate's heartbeat pounded in her chest, and she clasped her sherry glass with both hands to hide the slight tremble in her body. "I'll bet you didn't," she said, refusing to be cowed by the woman.

Lottie's attention shifted to Louise. "A partner?" she asked, raising an eyebrow.

"This is my friend, Mary Saunders," Kate lied.

"And where are you from, *Mary*?" Lottie emphasized Louise's alias, obviously not buying it.

"Why I'm from the big state of Texas, where law presides." Louise smiled coolly.

"The law should step carefully," Lottie said. "It doesn't always know what it's doing."

"I beg to differ," Louise said quietly. "I think it does."

Lottie shifted back to Kate. "And where is your dear Gilbert? We *were* expecting him."

Along with the gold.

"He'll be here shortly," Kate lied again.

Arthur materialized from the crowd, his tall frame commanding the room, and unease twisted Kate's stomach.

"Don't even think about getting help from law enforcement in town," he said. "They're very loyal to me."

Kate's confidence wavered. Was the arrest warrant in Louise's possession useless? Had it been a mistake to come here, just two women? Perhaps they should've insisted that Henry and Ian accompany them.

"I think you overestimate yourself," Louise cut in, her voice calm, almost breezy, as if they were making idle chitchat.

Arthur stepped closer. "I'm intrigued by you women .... Female Pinkerton agents. An error in my mind. Women don't have the fortitude for this kind of work."

"And you would know this because ...," Louise countered, holding her ground.

"Kate Ryan?" A woman's voice rang out from the crowd.

None other than Mrs. Estelle Marsh, her grandmother's acquaintance, rushed forward. She wore a tiara atop her tight curls and a pink taffeta gown.

Shocked, Kate frantically sought for a way out, but all she had was, "I think you're mistaken."

The condescending cast of Lottie's gaze wasn't hard to miss. "Estelle, do you know Mrs. Holmes?"

"I do." She reached out to Kate and squeezed her forearm, craning her head up with a delighted smile. "It's a pleasure to see you, dear. Your grandmother never said you'd be here. Did you get married?"

"I'm sorry. I think you have me confused with someone else." Kate stepped back, away from the woman's grasp.

The bewildered look on the older woman's face tugged at Kate's conscience. Before it could go any further, George abruptly joined them, his appearance ragged and weary.

Kate immediately took his arm to keep him upright. "George, what are you doing here? You should be resting."

"I need to speak with you," he said to her.

"All right."

Arthur's gaze landed on George, sharp with warning. "You need to leave."

"What will you do to me?" George countered.

"Please don't make a scene," Lottie hissed.

George shook his head. "I've been doing this too long. It's time to end it."

"End what?" Mrs. Marsh asked.

"Just remember your promise to Minnie." Lottie's voice was low, her lips barely moving.

"I'm beginning to think she'd be better off in California. I'll convince her. I'm done with the forgeries."

"What forgeries?" Mrs. Marsh exclaimed.

"It's nothing," Lottie said, batting away his words with a hurried hand. "George is an Indian with no homeland. He likes nothing more than making trouble."

The Wingate butler signaled Lottie from across the room, and with visible frustration she stepped away.

At Arthur's nod, two of the waiters came to either side of George, pushing Kate from him.

As he struggled, he turned back to Kate. "Where is it?"

"What?" she asked.

"The gold. I had it, and now it's gone. Henry took it. I know it was him."

The crowd quieted as Lottie rang a small bell. "May I have everyone's attention," she said, her voice ringing out across the room. "We have a special surprise this evening. As many of you know, we've long enjoyed a special relationship with the painter extraordinaire, J. Montgomery. We're privileged to present to you a brand new, never-before-seen work. Now," she held up a hand, "please note that this piece is already spoken for, so it's not for sale. But you all are so special to us that we wanted you to be a part of the unveiling."

She nodded toward a man on her staff. He pulled the cloth free, and the audience gasped.

It was the piece Kate had found at Minnie's house. With the excited tittering of the crowd and the better lighting, it was even more exceptional than she'd remembered.

A Comanche warrior atop a horse, both in full regalia, faced the audience. The detail was intricate, and the man's presence was palpable, leaping from the canvas with an immediacy that was breathtaking.

George's masterpiece.

And he deserved the recognition for it.

"George," Kate said to him around the men who were holding on to him. "It's extraordinary."

Mrs. Marsh watched them. "Is *he* the artist?"

"Yes," Kate said.

"That painting isn't for sale," George said. "I didn't give permission for it to be sold. The Wingates took it."

"I can assure you that J. Montgomery is the creator of this piece," Lottie continued, her cheeks blooming red. "And that we have a wonderful working relationship with him. This man," she nodded toward George, "is an imposter. He will be escorted from the premises. Please do not concern yourself with him." She took a steadying breath. "And now, I'm most pleased to introduce our buyer for this one-of-a-kind piece. I believe he's here, and all the way from Europe. Mr. Thomas? Would you step forward?"

A mature gentleman, clean-shaven with graying hair, emerged from the crowd, and when Lottie's gaze landed on him, her face blanched white as if she'd seen a ghost.

"What's going on?" Arthur muttered under his breath. He crossed the room to Lottie and said to the crowd, "Please enjoy yourself. There's plenty to drink and eat."

When his eyes landed on the buyer, a similar shock also registered on his face. When the man of their attention turned, a chill snaked down Kate's spine.

Hugh Maguire.

Gone was the scruff of Francis O'Malley, the hunched-over countenance of Dutch who had brought her to the Wingates two weeks ago. This man stood tall. This man was no longer hiding.

Henry and Ian's resemblance to him was starkly obvious.

Arthur and Lottie closed in as Hugh came before Kate, Louise, George, and Mrs. Marsh.

George stopped fighting against the men trying to escort him from the party. "How?" he said, his voice breaking.

Hugh swung his gaze around the circle. "Arthur. Lottie. George." He took in Kate and Louise with a nod.

Any uncertainty about O'Malley's identity was swept aside. Kate didn't know whether to be elated for Henry or heartbroken. Intuition told her he wouldn't take the news well.

"I'm sure you're all wondering how it is that I'm here. Let's just say that Walter Beckett wasn't very good at his job."

He'd been thankfully just as incompetent when he'd tried to hurt Kate.

"It was you," George accused. "Not Henry. You took my gold."

"It was never yours, George," Hugh said.

Lottie stepped forward, her voice an angry whisper. "It's not yours either."

Hugh swung his gaze to her, the malice in his eyes hard to miss. "Lottie, you overstep yourself. You always did."

"What is it you want?" Arthur asked Hugh.

"Just looking after my interests. And no, I don't have your gold."

Someone tugged on Kate's arm. She turned to see a frantic-looking Delia, wearing a blue day dress, her hair spilling from her bun. Why wasn't she dressed for the auction?

"It's Gilbert, or rather Henry. You have to come with me."

Henry? Delia knew their cover too?

"What are you talking about?" Kate asked, aware that everyone in their tight circle could hear her.

"Walter plans to kill him."

Kate locked eyes with Louise, who said, "Let's go."

Henry jolted awake. With the starry night above him, and the clip clop sound of horses, he deduced he was in the back of a wagon.

He tried to sit up, but both his hands and feet were bound tightly with rope. Craning his neck, he searched for the driver. With only the man's backside visible, it was difficult to tell, but then memories of the evening came rushing back.

He and Ian had been hiding in the Wells Fargo stage. When Clint and whomever he had recruited attacked, Henry had slipped from the stage to hide in the nearby underbrush for cover. Ian would remain with the stage and the money, and between the two of them they would catch Clint red-handed while also locating the subsequent hiding place. They believed that the previous theft would also be there, and it would clinch their case.

But then, suddenly, the world had gone black.

Someone had found Henry and his hiding spot, and if the tender spot on the back of his head was any indication, had struck him. Hard.

But who? The same person who'd attacked him near the spring before pushing him into the ravine?

Henry strained again, and he managed to catch a side view of the man's face.

Walter Beckett.

How had Beckett known about the stage? How had he known about Henry being on it?

And what about Ian? Was he hurt, or worse? Or was he still with Clint and his men, on his way to wherever they planned to stash their stolen Wingate counterfeit money?

Henry slid toward the foot of the wagon as it began an uphill climb. When it came to a halt, Henry suspected they were at the mine where he'd first met Beckett. The mine where Hugh Maguire had been killed.

Remembering Kate's actions the day before when Walter had assaulted her, Henry closed his eyes and pretended to be unconscious just as Beckett set the brake and jumped to the ground.

Footfalls sounded as he left the wagon and a padlock clicked, then a wooden door creaked open. Did it lead to where the equipment was stored, or to the mine itself?

A sense of foreboding settled over Henry. Beckett had killed his father all those years ago, and now he would kill Henry.

He tested the strength of the rope around his wrists. Tight. His ankles wouldn't move either. He would have to overpower Beckett while bound up, and for that the man would need to be close.

Beckett came to the end of the wagon and lowered the tailgate. He jumped into the bed and grabbed a hold of Henry, shaking him.

Henry brough his knees up and shoved Beckett in the abdomen while grabbing the man's shirt with both hands. He painfully turned his body and pushed Beckett onto the floor of the wagon, but the man was a lot stronger than Henry had expected. Beckett released a guttural yell and brought his hands around Henry's neck, squeezing.

Henry wheezed, trying to catch his breath, twisting Beckett's shirt with enough force to choke him. Beckett's grip loosened.

"What the hell are you doing?" Henry said.

"Taking care of loose ends. And stay the hell away from Delia."

"I was never interested in her."

Henry's muscles strained as he held Beckett mere inches from his face, but he was fast losing the small advantage he'd had from surprising the man. Beckett pressed into him so hard that Henry's head slammed into the wagon.

"Let him go!" a man's voice boomed.

Dutch?

Beckett was pulled from him. Henry awkwardly sat up, trying to focus his eyes in the dark. The man pushed Beckett onto his back and held him there. Henry blinked to clear his vision. It couldn't be....

"You're dead," Beckett wheezed, his voice straining through the chokehold of the other man. "I killed you."

"You were such a little troublemaker back then, Walter, and not a very smart one. You tried to drug me, but I knew. I pretended to be out and then I jumped you when you brought me here. Didn't you ever wonder about your blackout? About the lost time?"

"You're lying. There were footprints to the mine's edge, you were—"

"It was all faked."

"Why?" Henry finally got the word out, past the shock of seeing his father. Alive. Kate had been right all along.

Hugh Maguire shifted his gaze to Henry. "I'm sorry. I truly am.

It seemed the only way, and you and Ian were better off without me...."

Beckett took the opportunity to twist out of Hugh's grasp. From his boot he pulled a knife and plunged it into Hugh's shoulder. Henry lunged forward and flung his bound hands around Beckett's neck, pulling hard. Hugh fell back against the side of the wagon, precariously close to falling over the side.

Henry released Beckett, flinging his body across him to grab hold of his father's pant leg.

Beckett scrambled away and jumped out of the wagon as Henry held fast to Hugh and brought him to a sitting position.

"You'll be all right," Henry said, panic in his voice. "You'll survive."

Gunshots rang out in the night and Henry tried to shield his pa, but his hands and feet were still bound, making it difficult.

"It's all right, Henry," his father said. "It's Kate."

She appeared out of the darkness, wearing her fancy dress and holding a revolver in her right hand. "I got him," she said. "He won't be going far. Louise! Delia! We've got to help Hugh!"

Kate shoved her gun into a skirt pocket and hoisted herself into the wagon. She lifted her petticoats, showing a bit of leg, and retrieved a knife from a holder tied against her thigh. She made quick work of cutting the ropes from Henry. He immediately helped his father lie back.

"We need to get him to the doctor in town," Henry said.

"Delia will drive you," Kate said, concern etched on her face along with a determination he'd never seen. "Louise and I'll go after Beckett."

"No," Henry said, thinking it a terrible idea. Beckett was unhinged.

Delia was already in the driver's seat. Kate jumped to the ground and secured the tailgate.

"Where's Ian?" Henry asked.

"I don't know," Kate replied.

"Go, Henry," Louise said. "We can handle this."

"Did you serve the warrant to Wingate?"

"Unfortunately, no."

Delia got the horse moving and the wagon lurched forward. Kate and Louise dissolved into the night.

CHAPTER 31

Kate and Louise searched for Walter Beckett deep into the night, but now the sky was turning from black to gray as dawn beckoned.

Kate stopped to catch her breath. "I definitely shot him."

The two of them looked ridiculous running through the woods in their fancy dresses, the hems tattered and torn, and Kate's feet aching from the fancy buckle shoes she wore. She imagined Louise was in as much discomfort as she was.

Louise pushed loose hair behind an ear, a dirt smudge decorating her cheek. "But not a kill shot?"

"No, of course not. I clipped him in the shoulder." As she was trained to do.

Louise nodded.

A twig snap had them spinning around and aiming their guns. Ian Maguire approached, hands up although he also possessed a revolver in his right hand. They lowered their weapons.

"Have you seen Walter Beckett?" Louise asked.

"No."

Kate glanced around. "How did you find us?"

"I've been tracking you. How did you manage to lose his trail?"

Kate's shoulders sagged in exhaustion. "He's like a ghost. What happened to you?"

"I lost Henry when the stage was held up, but I assumed he would manage. I followed Clint and his men. The money is hidden in barrels in Wingate's warehouse in town."

"Henry and I saw them when we broke into the building," Kate said.

"Did you arrest Wingate?"

Louise shook her head. "No. There was no time." She sighed. "We should do it now. He didn't know that you found his secret room," she said to Kate. "The evidence should still be there, and now we have the location of the stolen money." She turned to Ian. "Will you help in your capacity as a Deputy Marshal?"

"Yes," Ian said. "I've notified my boss. I've got full authority to finish this."

Kate stepped toward Ian. "Do you know about Dutch?"

"That he's my father?" Disbelief crossed Ian's face. "Yeah."

"How hurt is he?"

"He'll be fine. He was in surgery to repair damage to his shoulder and arm. I told Henry I'd find you both so that he could stay. I didn't realize how much guilt he was carrying over Pa ...." Ian released a dry laugh that had no humor to it. "But Hugh Maguire has much to answer for."

Something niggled the back of Kate's mind, about the gold and Hugh.

"Why did he come back?" Kate asked.

"For you and Henry?" Louise added.

"I don't know." Ian rubbed the back of his neck, the strain of the evening showing on his face. "If he did, I'd say it's eight years too late."

Then why did he return?

"Let's get to Wingates," Kate said, "and arrest Arthur and Lottie."

And then she needed to return to the Purcell cabin and see if her hunch was true.

It was late morning when Kate arrived at the doctor's office in town. Arthur and Lottie's arrest had been tempestuous at best. Ian had called in two local men he trusted to help and who were outside the influence of Wingate. As Louise had predicted, the counterfeiting equipment was in the secret room.

When Kate had opened the bookcase door to the hidden passageway, Lottie had gasped. "How did you know about that?"

"You didn't think I was really unconscious, did you?" Kate had asked, quite fed up with the whole lot of them. "While you and Walter all but spilled your guts."

That had shut the woman up.

"You'll hear from my lawyer," Arthur had boomed, but Kate had paid no mind.

She left Ian and Louise to clean up the details. Still dressed in her peach gown, she rode her horse to the cabin she'd been sharing with Henry. He wasn't there, of course, but for a moment she had thought maybe he was, and her stomach had tumbled with butterflies.

She went inside and quickly changed into a starched white blouse and dark skirt, similar to Louise's attire when she was in her professional mode. Because it was time for Kate to finish the job she'd begun.

She went to the barn and after a brief search she located a crowbar, then she went to the steps of the front porch and began inspecting cracks and crevices. That first night when Dutch had picked her up, she'd found him loitering around these steps. It had been slightly disquieting since for a brief moment she'd wondered if he were a peeping tom.

But now she suspected another reason.

She found an opening in the wood slats, so she levered the crowbar and removed part of the siding. Getting down on her hands and knees, she'd peered inside and although she'd deduced it was here, it still tripped her heartbeat into double time.

Gold bars. Stacks of them.

They'd been in front of her and Henry the entire time.

She replaced the panel she'd removed, climbed atop her horse, and rode into town, not stopping until she reached the doctor's office.

As she entered the waiting room she looked for Henry, but a young woman greeted her wearing a starched white nurse uniform.

"Are you here for Mr. Maguire?" she asked.

Kate wasn't certain to which Maguire she was referring—Hugh or Henry—but the answer was yes either way.

Kate nodded. "I'm Pinkerton Detective Kate Ryan. I need to speak with Hugh Maguire. Is he awake?" She showed her badge, stamped with Pinkerton National Detective Agency. Above it was the "all-seeing eye" and below it was the Pinkerton motto of "We Never Sleep."

"Yes," the nurse replied, while inspecting Kate's identification.

"Is Mr. Maguire's son here? Henry?"

"No. He left about thirty minutes ago."

Disappointment washed over Kate, but she knew it was for the best. She didn't need Henry present for this conversation.

The woman led Kate into a room in the back. Hugh was resting in a bed, his shoulder bandaged.

"Sallie Holmes," he murmured.

"Hello, Mr. Maguire," Kate said as she sat on a wooden stool beside his bed. "Or shall I continue to call you Dutch? And I'm sure you already know that my name is Kate Ryan."

"Henry's partner." He gave a wan smile. "You're here to interrogate me."

"Yes. It's my job." This was no time for sentiment, and yet she couldn't help but ask, "You've spoken to Henry?"

Hugh sighed. "I have."

"Why did you let him and Ian believe you were dead?"

He looked up to the ceiling, revealing dark circles beneath his eyes. "I've found honor to be a fleeting thing, and something I've struggled with, I suppose."

"We all struggle with it, sir. We can only hope that tomorrow we'll do better. Did you come here to make amends after all these years?"

"What? No."

Kate felt the sting of Hugh's refusal on Henry's behalf. She had to swallow back a terse retort.

"You never wondered how Henry and Ian were getting on?" she asked, her voice tight.

"Oh, of course I did. I kept tabs on them."

"From where?"

"Europe."

She hadn't really expected Hugh to be honest with her, although his honesty was casting him in the same vein as Arthur, Lottie, and Walter Beckett. She wanted to believe that Hugh possessed some measure of character that set him apart from the others.

"Then why did you come back?" she asked.

His blue eyes flashed at her, reminding her of Henry, and her heart twisted from the resemblance.

"You heard about the gold bar that was found a few months ago," she said, answering for him. "You came for the gold."

"You have no proof of that."

"Please tell me one thing then. If you had found the Confederate gold bars that went missing from Arthur Wingate's home eight years ago, what would you do with them? Would you turn them into the authorities and have Arthur arrested?"

"Well, I've heard that Arthur was already arrested," Hugh said. "You managed to accomplish what I couldn't."

She considered him. "Except that I'm not so certain that arresting Arthur was ever your goal. You were always after the gold. You and Charlie Purcell."

"Charlie double-crossed me."

Hugh obviously didn't realize how the statement sounded, how incriminating it was.

Kate nodded. "Because the goal was for Charlie to get Arthur to trust him by telling him that you were about to arrive at his home with a search warrant based on information that Minnie Wingate's brother, George, had told you. Then Charlie would take the gold and disappear. But you two were actually partners."

"We *were* partners," Hugh said. "And Charlie did disappear."

"I'm guessing you hadn't planned for that. You and Charlie had a joint bank account, well-hidden I'll grant you. I'm going to surmise that you two had always been working together. You never planned to turn in the gold. You were going to keep it. The only question is why? You were a respected Secret Service agent, although I'm going to go out on a limb and say not a well-paid one." Kate paused, then said, "I know about your gambling troubles, at least from eight years ago." Louise had dug up that information. "It puts all the pieces together. You needed the gold to pay off your debt."

"It's a nice story, Kate," Hugh said, his expression showing no signs of his guilt. "But a little gambling problem isn't grounds for becoming a criminal."

"It wasn't a little gambling problem," she said quietly. He'd been indebted for large sums at six different casinos.

"Well, it doesn't matter now. As soon as I'm well, I'll be going back to Europe."

"I'm afraid not, Hugh."

His eyes met hers, filled with challenge. He was a formidable man, a man from whom Henry was cut, and she could see so many similarities, although maybe it was simply that she was now looking.

She had hoped this conversation would go differently, that maybe somehow Hugh Maguire would come clean, and then she could try to negotiate leniency when a judge heard his case. But then, what did she expect? This man had let his sons believe he'd been dead for the last eight years. Hugh Maguire's moral compass was no longer pointing true north if it ever had been.

Her heart broke for Henry.

"I'll tell you what I think happened," she said. "Eight years ago, you came here under the guise of investigating Arthur Wingate for counterfeiting, but what you were really after was the Confederate gold that you, he, and Clayton Beckett found during your time as spies for the North in the War. Arthur had it well-hidden and I'm guessing you may even have given up hope. But then there was George, and you two struck up a friendship. He was bitter because he'd made a deal with Arthur for his sister, Minnie, to keep her home after the death of her husband—Arthur's father. But to do it he had to sell his artistic soul and hide under a pseudonym for his amazing work, as well as paint forgeries that helped Arthur and Lottie to launder money. So George sought to help you and hurt Arthur.

"You and Charlie concocted a scheme whereby Arthur would trust him and allow him to move the gold. You two were supposed to run off with it together, but something happened, and Purcell disappeared. You thought he double-crossed you, but in reality, he most likely had a terrible accident. The gold was lost to the wilderness for eight years. But then a bar surfaced, and the hunt was on. George, however, had a head start on everyone.

"You and Clayton and George had one thing in common—you all knew of the cave near the spring. George found the gold and stored it there, believing no one else knew of the location. You and Clayton were dead, after all. But, disguised as Francis O'Malley, you moved it. Here's where I have to appreciate your sense of humor, because you put it where you and Charlie had planned to stash it, right? Under the porch of his cabin, right under Wingate's nose."

Hugh's face shifted from smug confidence to the dawning realization that his plan had been discovered.

"Yes, I've found it."

Kate took no joy from her discovery. In fact, she felt sick to her stomach.

"Hugh Maguire, you're under arrest."

CHAPTER 32

Henry found Ian in the waiting room at the doctor's office, slouched in a chair, his eyes closed.

"You son-of-a-bitch!" Henry bellowed.

Ian startled awake and bolted to his feet. "Henry," he said, his voice holding a warning. He shoved at Henry's chest as Henry closed the distance between them.

"I just saw the police chief. He told me Pa was under house arrest. How could you?"

Ian backed up as Henry pressed on his brother. When they had been boys, Ian always had the advantage during altercations, being older and bigger. And although they were roughly the same height now, Henry knew that if Ian wanted to put Henry in his place, he no doubt could. It only irritated Henry more that Ian wasn't fighting back.

"Henry! Goddammit, Henry! Stop!"

"We've only just got him back, and now you're going to send him to jail?"

"It's not that simple and you know it."

Ian spoke the truth, but all Henry knew was that the guilt he'd been carrying for the last eight years was suddenly absolved, and

Henry wanted a chance to make everything right. He wanted another chance with his pa, and he didn't even care that Hugh Maguire had obviously deep parental flaws. That the man's honesty was a slippery slope that would likely break Henry in half. None of it mattered in light of the fact that Hugh Maguire was alive.

Ian released a heavy sigh and took a step back. "It wasn't me." The reluctance in his voice was as thick as wool. "It was Kate."

HENRY FOUND her at the cabin, cleaning the kitchen with Louise. She met his gaze and froze, her cheeks flushed and so beautiful that it caused a physical ache in his chest. She'd donned the attire of a Starling, simple and professional in a blouse and dark skirt. Despite the anger he felt, his body responded to her, telling him he was about to make a terrible mistake.

But Kate Ryan had been a mistake from the beginning.

If he said it to himself enough then he was sure to believe it.

Louise came to him, a compassionate look in her eyes. "Follow your heart, Henry," she whispered. "The world won't end if you do." Then she stepped through the front door, shutting it behind her, leaving him alone with Kate.

"Henry," she began, "I have something to tell you."

"I already know what you did to my father."

She hesitated, and he vowed he wouldn't label the pained look on her face as regret.

"You didn't have to do it, you know," he added, not bothering to hide the anger from his tone. It was far better than allowing the hurt that pulsated below the surface free rein—that he was about to lose his father all over again, that Kate Ryan had never felt anything for him, that she had simply embraced their playacting so she could gain more information about the case. If he wasn't reeling from the betrayal of those he loved—God, did he love her?—he could almost admire her ambition and drive. She'd be a hell of an agent.

"Have you spoken to Hugh?" she asked. "Have you asked him about everything he's done?"

"And I suppose you have. Just because you found him before me doesn't make you an expert on the Maguire family." He wouldn't admit that his conversations with Hugh so far hadn't been very revelatory. He hadn't wanted them to be. And that made Henry an emotionally compromised agent, the very thing Louise had feared would happen. The very reason that Kate had been assigned to watch *him*.

Hell, of all the things he'd expected to find when he'd come here, the last was Hugh Maguire, alive and well. It was the one outcome that Henry hadn't accounted for.

Kate visibly sank back, her shoulders sagging and her face becoming impassive. She gave a nod. "My assignment is finished. I'll be returning to Chicago to file my report." She paused, and cleared her throat, looking almost as if she might cry. "It's been a privilege to work with you, Henry. I wish you only the best in the future."

She walked past him, briefly filling his senses with everything Kate Ryan—her flowery scent, the soft skin of her cheeks, the curves imprinted in his memory from their time in the ravine. He almost reached for her and said the hell with it, but there was no future for them. She'd taken on her role as his wife like a consummate actress—what she felt for him hardly matched what he felt in return.

He closed his eyes.

He'd fallen for her. Hard.

He reminded himself that she'd taken a second chance with his father from him.

He would request never to work with her again.

She picked up a valise near the door. "I'm sending someone for the trunk," she said from behind him.

The door clicked shut, and she was gone.

CHAPTER 33

Chicago
Pinkerton Main Office
Three weeks later

Henry sat across from his boss, Edgar Jones, in the modest office he occupied in the Pinkerton Building. Jonesy was ten years older than Henry with bushy brows and dark sideburns that put Henry in mind of a pirate. Jones kept the main office in line. He was smart, fair, and calm under pressure, which only made Henry conclude that Jonesy was wasted pushing paperwork—he needed to be in the field.

"It's good to see you, Henry."

"Sorry it's taken me this long to get back."

Jonesy stacked some papers. "I understand. How's your father?"

"Recovered. Ian and I got him a lawyer and he'll remain in Trinidad until the local judge can hear his case. That should be in a few weeks. Then his trial will likely be moved to the federal level."

"For what it's worth, I've got contacts in Washington," Jonesy said. "I think we can push for leniency in his sentence."

Henry was grateful for Edgar's assistance, but the truth was Hugh Maguire hadn't been an upstanding Secret Service agent. Eight years ago, he had fully intended to steal the gold from Arthur, and that had been his intention recently as well. He had large gambling debt. He'd faked his death and escaped to Europe.

Henry had read Kate's report.

She'd done him a favor in arresting Hugh. Henry never could've followed through with it, and a night filled with more than one glass of bourbon had Ian admitting the same thing. The knowledge had left them both questioning their livelihoods.

"What's the word on the Wingates?" Henry asked.

"Lottie Wingate has confessed," Jonesy said, sitting back in his stuffed chair. "I suppose she's hoping it will lessen her sentence. Maybe. Turns out she was a grifter from a young age, having learned it from her mother. It would seem she was always seeking the woman's approval, even in death, which is why she started the séances. But she also saw a way to gather intimate information from others and use it for blackmail. After Arthur lost the gold to Charlie Purcell eight years ago, Lottie was the one who pushed the counterfeiting. They'd been doing it before then, but it had been small time. The operation became much larger when Arthur gained access to printing presses through his business dealings.

"Lottie was the one who instructed Walter Beckett to kill your father, worried that he knew too much about their criminal activities. Beckett was to drug Hugh and then dispose of his body, but somehow Hugh knew and faked being unconscious. He overpowered Beckett and knocked him out, then staged his death. Lottie said Beckett never told them he'd been knocked out, instead he'd insisted that the job had been done. I suppose he was too embarrassed to admit that he might've failed."

Henry nodded. His father had told him as much during the

many conversations they'd had. Hugh had expressed his regret over everything, and while Henry knew it would never be enough to erase the last eight years, it was at least something.

Jonesy took a deep breath and continued. "According to Jean Beckett, her husband, Clayton, had struck a deal with Arthur for a portion of the gold, but Arthur reneged on it. So when she learned of the gold bar that had been found recently, she felt well within her rights to claim the rest of it for herself. She and Arthur knew about you and Ian. It turns out Arthur was aware of your identity all along, and for that I'm sorry. You and Kate were at more risk than expected.

"You and Ian were brought in because both sides presumed that Hugh might've told either of you where he'd hidden the gold, or at least some of it. While Arthur had all along assumed that Purcell had run off with it—he'd even sent Walter Beckett to look for him, for three years no less—once that bar was found this year the assumption was back on that Hugh had somehow been involved. Both Arthur and Jean were hedging their bets that you or Ian would lead them to it."

"I did have something that belonged to my father," Henry said, coming clean. "A map that I'd found a few months ago among his belongings."

"Why didn't you tell me?"

"I honestly didn't know what it was. It was only once I was there that it became clear it was tied up with the gold bars. I was going to report it."

"Right." Jonesy's tone conveyed his skepticism.

Henry ran a hand through his hair. "Probably."

"I gave you a lot of leeway with this one, Henry. I don't condone that Louise went behind my back when she instructed Kate to watch you, but in retrospect, I'm glad she did. You were in over your head with this one."

"Probably," Henry repeated. His father's resurrection had

blindsided him. And Kate ... hell, he was loath to admit that his feelings for her might have permanently knocked him off his game. "What about George Ortes?" he asked, trying to shift the conversation back to more neutral ground.

"He's been charged with the forgeries, of course. Wallace Wingate was also picked up in San Francisco, but it was once again Lottie behind all of it. They bought and sold art as a way to launder the counterfeit money, and the forgeries gave them more reach. But George was manipulated as J. Montgomery, and that should help during his sentencing. I don't think he'll go to prison for long."

"And Minnie?"

"George had the good sense to get the deed to her land put in her name per his deal with Arthur, so she'll be allowed to remain. The Wingate property will be sold to pay off Arthur's debts, which are more substantial the deeper the authorities dig."

"I'm glad to hear she can stay."

"Jean Beckett will be staying too. Nothing she did was of the criminal sort. Now, as for her son ...."

"Has he turned up?"

"No. But I've heard through channels that Ian has gone looking for him."

"He mentioned something about it," Henry said. He would've helped except for the fact that Hugh wasn't dead after all. If there was any justice, then with hope, Beckett had died in the woods after the wound Kate had given him festered. Ian pursuing him seemed a waste of time in Henry's mind.

"I'm going to send Louise to help him. I think he's missing a key piece of evidence."

"What's that?"

"Delia Wingate."

After the dust had settled, Delia had come for Henry one evening at the boardinghouse in Trinidad where he'd been staying while Hugh recovered from his wound. Although subdued and more than a little bewildered at how fast her life had been turned upside down, she'd made another romantic overture, believing the biggest obstacle between them—Kate Ryan—had been removed.

But to Henry's growing frustration, Kate Ryan's presence was still front and center in his life, a barrier that Delia Wingate would never overcome.

"She appears to have known nothing of the illegal activity happening under her nose, and she certainly tried to help when she learned that Beckett had you," Jonesy continued.

Henry owed his life to her. The night of the art auction, she'd gone to the warehouse to retrieve a ledger that was kept in her father's office that Lottie had needed. While there, she'd overheard two of Walter's buddies speak of Henry's blown cover and how Walter planned to deal with it. She'd immediately gone to the party and alerted Kate, risking the wrath of her aunt and uncle.

"Now that she's destitute, she's taken herself to San Francisco to clean up the mess her father has left behind. Walter Beckett was obsessed with her. Louise is convinced that's where Beckett will go, if he's still alive."

"Ian won't appreciate the help," Henry said.

"You Maguires seem to be the same."

Jones stood, walked over to a side table, and poured two snifters of brandy. He brought the glasses back to Henry and handed one to him.

Jones lifted his drink. "We've been friends these past three years. You're my best agent, Henry, with an impeccable record."

Henry suppressed a grimace. "But ...."

"Tell me about your work with Kate Ryan."

"I submitted my recommendation. I think that says it all."

"Yes," Jonesy said. "You gave her a glowing review, along with a note never to work with her again. Tell me what really happened."

Henry downed his drink in one swallow, letting the liquor burn his throat. "Why are you asking me this?"

"She's taken a break and gone home to Texas. She's not sure she wants to remain an agent."

"What?"

"She's got good instincts, sharp reflexes, and an intelligence to match. Louise has done nothing but sing her praises. But after one assignment with you and she's ready to throw it all away. Why?"

Henry didn't know how to respond. Was it his fault?

"I don't know," he answered truthfully.

"Do you need to pay a visit to Texas?" Jonesy's gaze didn't waver as he watched Henry.

As if caught in a current, Henry felt himself rushing toward something. He stood and set his empty glass down on a side table.

"I think so."

CHAPTER 34

North Texas
Rocking Wren Ranch
One week later

Kate rode alongside the herd of longhorns with her pa and her older brother, Eli. Tugging her hat forward to keep the sun from her eyes, she pulled the bandana tied at her neck over her mouth and nose as the wind stirred a dust devil.

Checking on the cattle that were out to pasture north of the Rocking Wren was a balm to her soul, reminding her of happier times from her youth when wearing trousers and braiding her long hair were par for the day, when she could lie down at night and sleep soundly from a hard day's work.

And thoughts of Henry were pushed from her mind, along with the uncertainty of whether she should continue to be a Pinkerton agent.

But still, a part of her didn't quite fit here anymore. She'd been excited to go to Chicago nearly six months ago, but her experiences since then had changed her, had somehow expanded her. Knowing Henry had fundamentally changed something in her, and she knew with a sinking feeling that she would never be able to go back to the girl she had been, no matter how many times she joined her pa and Eli under the bright Texas sun.

Eli reined his horse in beside hers. "Why do you look lost, Kate?" he asked. He was only twenty-one but had already been married for a year, with a young son with his wife, Cassie. Kate adored little Samuel, doing her best to ignore the pangs of longing for a baby of her own. For Henry's baby. So much for the platitudes she'd given Henry about being an independent woman who only wanted a lover and nothing more.

"I'm not lost," she replied. "Why would you say that?"

"Ever since you arrived five days ago, you've not been yourself. You only do paperwork at the Pinkerton Agency. Surely they can survive without you for a few weeks."

She hadn't told her family that she'd been promoted to field agent, although it had been only one job so far. She felt guilty about lying but she hadn't really wanted to talk about the case, or about Henry, just yet. She'd done the right thing turning in Hugh for his role in trying to steal Confederate gold, and she knew her pa would praise her for her level head and moral rightness, but that didn't mean she didn't feel ambivalent about it. Or that she didn't at times second-guess her actions. That in her darkest moments, she questioned whether she really had what it took to be an agent, because her first job had shaken her.

It's just because of Henry, her heart and her mind reminded her. She should simply request a transfer to a different office, so that it wouldn't be possible for them to work together again.

She'd confided her doubts to Edgar Jones during her debrief with him, because Louise hadn't returned from Colorado, having remained to tie up loose ends, and Kate had needed someone to talk to. He'd suggested she take a few weeks off to think about it, and when he'd told her to go somewhere that would make her happy, that would ground her again after an intense undercover case, there had been only one destination that would do—home.

"Eli," she said. "I'm not a secretary. Well, maybe I was at first, but not anymore. I'm an undercover agent."

Her brother stared at her. "Are you serious? Why didn't you tell us? Ma and Pa will be so worried."

"That's why." She worried her lower lip. "I'll tell them tonight."

"Have you been on an assignment?"

"Yes. One."

She proceeded to tell him the details of the insurance fraud, counterfeit money, art forgeries and true identity of J. Montgomery. She included the outrageous outcome of Hugh Maguire's return from the dead, and she even mentioned that she'd been pretending to be another agent's wife.

"That's incredible," Eli said, his face telegraphing his shock.

It filled her with pride, with a desire to return to her job.

"Somebody's not earning their keep."

Kate jumped at the sound of her pa's voice.

Her father, Matt Ryan, still cut an imposing figure, with his hair only slightly graying at the temples. He was well-respected by the other ranchers, and while there had been more than one push for him to consider an entry into local politics, he had always resisted. He protected nothing more closely than his family, and his wife, Molly, most of all. He'd always said a political career would dredge up a history that was better left private. Kate knew he was referring to her mother's past as a Comanche captive, and the murder of Molly's parents, Kate's grandparents, whom she had never known.

"We're almost finished," her pa said. "And then the two of you can gab like a couple of hens."

"Yes, sir," Kate replied.

Eli moved his mare close to hers and said in a low voice, "Tell him." Then he rode away.

Kate took in the wide blue sky and the bright sunshine, and she reveled in being home. Except that a piece of her now belonged somewhere else.

"Can I talk to you, Pa?"

"Always, Katie."

As they continued to check on the herd, she told her father everything, including her feelings for Henry.

"Mrs. Marsh, I don't know what to say," Kate said.

Just before supper, Estelle Marsh had appeared at the ranch, a man accompanying her. He'd retrieved a large rectangular box from the back of the buggy she'd arrived in and carried it inside.

Kate, her sister, Josie, and her mother, Molly Hart Ryan, stood beside the woman, admiring the painting she had brought. It was the Comanche Warrior by J. Montgomery, or rather, George Ortes.

"I spoke with Susanna," Mrs. Marsh said, referring to Kate's paternal grandmother. "I'd been trying to purchase the painting for her, but we agreed that you should have it."

"Me?" Kate asked with a frown.

"Well, no," Mrs. Marsh replied. "Not you, but your mother." She smiled at Molly.

Kate's ma nodded in acknowledgement, unable to take her eyes from the piece. "It's an extraordinary rendering. How can I ever thank you?"

"No need," Mrs. Marsh said. "Susanna paid for it."

After Kate had confessed her current role as a Pinkerton detective to her pa, she'd returned to the main house and confided in her mother. She was surprised at how well the two of them had taken the confession, and even more by the fact that they had praised her in her handling of Hugh Maguire. Both had remarked that it couldn't have been easy. As for Kate falling for Henry ... her pa had urged her to keep her options open—"there are other men out there, don't give it all up for the first one to come along"—while her ma counseled Kate to give the relationship space to breathe. "You might be surprised what comes back to you when you least expect it," she had said.

So Kate didn't need to hide the fact that Mrs. Marsh had been with her in Trinidad.

Kate turned to the woman. "I've been wanting to ask you," she said. "Why did you come to the cabin that day? The Purcell cabin where I was living with Henry, or rather my husband 'Gilbert'?"

"Oh yes, I'd overheard that 'Gilbert's' wife had arrived." Mrs. Marsh pressed her lips together. "I also was aware of the overtures that Delia Wingate was making toward him. I wanted to meet you myself and give you fair warning."

Kate couldn't help but laugh, warmed by the gesture. "That's very kind of you. I hope you understand why I avoided you."

"I do, but you could've told me." Mrs. Marsh patted Kate's arm. "I would've kept your secret, I can assure you."

"I'll remember that for next time," Kate teased. "Now tell me how you got the painting after Arthur and Lottie were arrested? The art auction must've been shut down."

"It was, but once everything died down, I asked the authorities directly," Mrs. Marsh said. "And George, too. I know he's being detained for the forgeries, so I suggested that the money for the portrait could be given to Minnie. Everyone agreed, including George."

"That was very thoughtful of you."

"She plans to use it to hire a lawyer for him. I think it's a grand idea. From what I learned, George was a pawn in all of this."

Kate couldn't disagree. Before she'd left Trinidad, she had stopped at Minnie's home to say goodbye to her and Nell, and to discuss options for George. She'd also spent time with Bandito, even offering to take the dog since it was unknown what George's fate would be, but Minnie was determined to care for the animal, optimistic that George would eventually return to them. Kate understood although she would always harbor a great affection for the mutt.

Mrs. Marsh soon departed. After supper, Kate sat in the sitting room with Josie and their mother, admiring the J. Montgomery artwork that now belonged to Molly Ryan.

Eli's wife, Cassie, came from the foyer and announced that a rider had just arrived, her two-month-old son holding a fist of her dark curls and trying to put them in his mouth.

"Who is it?" Molly asked.

Cassie shrugged, untangling her hair from Samuel's chubby hand. "I don't know. I don't recognize him." Her attention was soon diverted when Marley and Jeb came running by, their tongues out and their tails wagging. Cassie deftly sidestepped them.

Matt and Eli appeared from the kitchen. "We'll take care of it," her pa said.

Josie stood and followed, obviously too curious to stay behind. A knock on the door fired up the dogs, who scurried back and began barking loudly. The sound of a door opening and muffled male voices filtered back to them.

Josie leaned around the door to the sitting room, her dark hair cascading around her shoulders. The sleeve of her dress slipped to her elbow and revealed the scars, faded to white now, from the mountain lion attack.

"It's for you," she said to Kate.

"What's for me?" Kate asked.

"The man. He's come to see you. His name is Henry."

Kate's stomach dropped. "He's here?"

Josie nodded. "He's your partner, right?" Kate had also shared everything with her sister, although she'd glossed over her true feelings for her coworker.

"He must really want to see you to have come all this way," her ma said.

"Wait," Josie said, stepping in front of Kate. She tucked stray strands of hair into place and straightened the shoulders of Kate's blouse. "You look unkempt," she said under her breath, then she stepped aside.

Since when did Josie care what a man might think?

But then Kate realized she was still wearing trousers from her day of riding, and her hair probably did look a fright. She wished she had time to undo the braid and pin it into a bun.

Kate's pa and Eli returned to the room, Henry behind them. Kate stopped fussing with her hair and simply enjoyed that he was here, looking better than she'd remembered.

He was less formal than he'd been while they'd been undercover, the sleeves of his shirt rolled to the elbow and a hat that had seen better days resting in his hand, reminding her of their time in the wilderness on Wingate property.

"Let me take that," Josie reached for Henry's hat, which he gave her. Then she reached out a palm. "I'm Josie. I'm Kate's sister."

"I'm pleased to meet you," he said, then released her hand. "You two look alike." Which earned him a smile from Josie.

Kate wished her heart would slow to a manageable pace. "What are you doing here?" she asked.

"I've come to see you." His gaze caught her, holding her in place.

Shaking herself free, she said, "Pardon my manners. This is my mother, Molly Ryan."

Henry gave a nod. "It's a pleasure, ma'am."

"And my sister-in-law, Cassie. And you've met my father and my brother."

"I have."

The men in Kate's family were imposing, almost larger than life, and as Henry stood beside them, he managed to fit right in. She reminded herself that Henry's presence in her life was fleeting.

"This is Henry Maguire," she said to everyone in the room. "A fellow Pinkerton agent."

"It's nice to meet you all," he said. "That's a beautiful baby," he said, nodding toward Cassie.

"Thank you. He's a typical Ryan, very stubborn." Everyone laughed.

"Please sit," Kate's ma said. "You've just missed supper, but can I pull together something for you?"

"No. I'm fine, thank you."

"I've got coffee brewing. I can at least offer you that." Molly left and went back to the kitchen.

"Have you come all the way from Chicago?" Eli asked Henry.

"I have."

Kate didn't miss the flash of amusement her brother sent her way. Clearly, they all thought Henry was here because he was smitten with her and couldn't stay away. Was it true? Kate tried to keep her hopes in check.

She tried hard not to stare but it was difficult. She had missed him more than she cared to admit. Seeing him only intensified her regard for him, but she had begun to fear, deep in her heart, that he didn't feel half as much for her as she did for him.

Nerves overtook her. Maybe he still didn't feel strongly for her. Perhaps it had just been the heat of the moment. Maybe he was here for an entirely different reason.

She sat in a nearby chair and sought to appear calm, resting her hands on her lap and refraining from blurting out the dozen questions that hung on her lips.

"Kate told us about your work with Arthur Wingate," her pa said. "It sounded a little dangerous."

"I can assure you, Mr. Ryan, that Kate was very much up to the task. Although it was my first time working with her, she was a professional and very competent. I was lucky to be partnered with her."

Her pa gave a nod but said nothing more. Kate sensed his wariness and supposed she couldn't fault her father for not welcoming Henry with open arms.

"Why did you come here, Henry?" she asked, inwardly wincing. She hadn't meant it to sound accusatory or so desperate.

There was hesitation in his eyes but before he could speak, her mother came in bearing a tray with a coffee pot and cups. Everyone became busy getting their beverage, adding sugar and cream, and snatching from the pile of cookies on a plate. Her ma sat down beside Henry with Cassie beside her, so there were now too many people between them for Kate to converse with Henry in any meaningful way.

His gaze fell on the painting. "How did you get it?" he asked, a hint of awe in his voice.

"Mrs. Marsh brought it," Kate replied. "I never told you, but she was at the Wingate party that first night I arrived. She knew my grandmother and I had to get creative to avoid her seeing me. She purchased it for my grandmother who then gave it to my ma."

"I'm glad it found a good home."

After another thirty minutes of idle chitchat, Molly said, "It's getting late. Henry, you can't ride back to town tonight, so you must stay here. We have a spare room."

"I wouldn't want to impose but thank you."

"And I imagine you would like to speak with Kate alone."

Kate's pa started to interrupt, but her mother stood, effectively silencing him. She soon had everyone saying goodnight and ushered them out. Commotion from the foyer could be heard as Eli and Cassie prepared to leave for their modest ranch house only a mile to the east. Samuel had started to wail.

The last to leave, Josie turned to Henry. "What's it like being an undercover detective?"

"Frankly, it's a lot of work and takes a lot of concentration."

"That doesn't sound very fun."

Henry laughed. "No, I suppose not. I guess that's why not everyone is cut out for this type of work."

Josie looked at Kate. "He's just like you." And with that her sister said goodnight and left, closing the door behind her.

Kate was now alone with Henry.

"How did you know where I live?" she asked.

"Jonesy."

"Henry, I never got the chance to apologize," she said in a rush.

"For what? Doing your job?"

"I never wanted to separate you from Hugh so soon after finding him. He left me no choice."

"I know." His face conveyed the sincerity of his words. "You followed through. You have the makings of a good agent, but Jonesy told me that you might quit."

She went silent.

"Don't do it on my account," he added.

He was right, of course. But it was her heart that had taken over since she'd left Trinidad, and it had been more broken than she'd realized. Sitting across from Henry was soundly driving that point home.

"I've needed time to think," she said.

Henry scooted to the end of the sofa so that he was closer to her. "I have to admit," he said, leaning forward and resting his elbows on his knees. "My pride was bruised when I learned that you'd been instructed to babysit me. That maybe what had unfolded between us had been an act."

"Do you really think I would jeopardize my first assignment by falling for my partner?"

Henry's gaze retracted somewhat, and Kate realized how misleading her words were.

"What I mean to say is," she amended, "despite my best intentions, I fell for my partner."

The light came back to his blue eyes. "I'm glad to hear it.

Because it would seem I've broken my professional rules and fallen for my partner as well."

Her pulse quickened. "Not Louise?"

He smiled, broad and relaxed, and it transformed his quietly handsome features to something more compelling than Kate had ever imagined. And her imagination had been quite thorough when it had come to him.

"Not Louise."

He reached for her, and she took his hand, feeling immense relief to touch him, as if she'd been only half alive these past few weeks. Is this what it was like to have a person imprint on your soul?

"I like you this way," he said, indicating her hair and her attire.

"A cowgirl?"

"Yeah. You look happy."

She sobered. "You make me happy, Henry."

He brought a palm to her cheek, his hand warm, and his lips gently met hers. She sank into him, the knot in her stomach that had been there since the day she'd left him at the cabin finally loosening.

She slanted her mouth across his, deepening the kiss, and he met her with the same longing, his lips consuming hers. She moved off her chair and he tugged her onto his lap, wrapping his arms around her, the kiss becoming hungry with need.

He pulled back, and Kate struggled to catch her breath, to remember where she was.

"Now that I've met your father," he said, "I've no doubt he would string me up if I don't do right by you."

Kate was going to refute his statement, but he was right.

"Are you still against marriage?" he asked.

"Generally speaking, yes. But it would seem being married to you has changed my mind."

"You're my first wife, Kate. I'd like you to be my last."

"What about our work?"

"I'm not asking you to quit."

"That's good, because I've decided to remain an agent."

He grinned, his mouth a few inches from hers. "Then we'll tell Jonesy about us, and I'll beg him to let me work with you on assignments."

"So long as you follow my lead."

He leaned forward and kissed her neck just below her ear. "I can do that."

His lips and his breath on her skin were sending tantalizing shivers through her body.

"How long can you stay?" she whispered.

"Long enough to take you back to Chicago."

"All right. I'm sure my pa and brother, as well as my uncles, would be happy to put you to work."

"A test, I take it."

"Didn't I have to earn your trust as your partner?"

He leaned back and looked her in the eye. "Yes. I suppose you did. I'll admit I was determined to keep you at arm's length. But you never backed down. I suppose that's how I knew you're the one for me. So how long?"

"How long what?" she asked, burying her fingers into his hair.

"How long will I have to court you?"

She shrugged and gave him a wicked smile. "However long it takes."

READ IAN and Louise's adventure in the short story *The Starling and the Fox,* included in THE WEST: A ROMANCE COLLECTION.

kmccaffrey.com/the-west/

U.S. Deputy Marshal Ian Maguire doesn't need help on his current case, but there's no getting around Pinkerton agent Louise Foster. Locating his fugitive is the least of his problems.

DON'T MISS the introduction of Kate Ryan and her cousins in the novella THE SONGBIRD.

kmccaffrey.com/the-songbird/

SIGN up for Kristy's newsletter for exclusive content and book news.

kmccaffrey.com/subscribe/

The Canary
Wings of the West Book 9

Paleontologist Jack Brenner enters a fake marriage with Sarah Ryan to protect her in the Arizona desert, but he never expects to fall for her ...

Read now
kmccaffrey.com/the-canary/

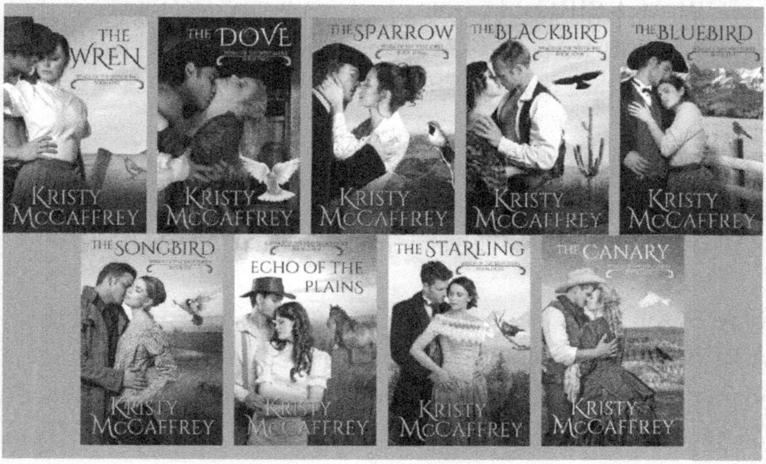

Don't miss the Wings of the West series

Honorable men and courageous women. Experience the grit, the hope, and the romance of the Old West.

"Ms. McCaffrey writes from the heart..." ~ The Romance Studio

THE WREN – Captured by Comanche as a child, Molly Hart was assumed dead. Ten years later, Texas Ranger Matt Ryan finds a woman with the same blue eyes.

THE DOVE – Reunited with Logan Ryan on the steps of the White Dove Saloon, Claire Waters hides under the guise of a fancy girl...and lets the ex-deputy believe the worst.

THE SPARROW – Within Grand Canyon, raging rapids and ancient spirits sweep Texas Ranger Nathan Blackmore and Emma Hart into a wild adventure.

THE BLACKBIRD – Haunted by a deadly attack, Tess Carlisle turns to bounty hunter Cale Walker to find her missing *padre*. But in the land of the Apache, can he free her heart?

THE BLUEBIRD – Molly Rose Simms arrives in Colorado to meet her brother, but instead finds herself searching for the mythical Bluebird mining claim with a man known as The Jackal.

THE SONGBIRD – In this novella set fifteen years after THE WREN, Matt and Molly are attending a fair in Denton, Texas, when they uncover a connection to Molly's past with the Kwahadi Comanche. You'll also meet their daughters—Katie and Josie Ryan.

ECHO OF THE PLAINS (a short story) – Seventeen-year-old Eli Ryan, Matt and Molly's son, plans to capture the renegade stallion known as Echo but Cassie Callahan stands in his way.

THE STARLING – Pinkerton Henry Maguire is about to gain an unwanted "wife" in the form of new agent Kate Ryan (Matt and Molly's daughter).

THE CANARY – Sarah Ryan (Logan and Claire's daughter) and paleontologist Jack Brenner search for an elusive dinosaur fossil in the Painted Desert.

THE NIGHTHAWK – U.S. Deputy Marshal Benton McKay is undercover tracking the notorious train robbing Weaver gang when he's forced to work with reporter Sophie Ryan (Logan and Claire's daughter).

Learn more about each book at Kristy's website
kmccaffrey.com/books/

Into The Land Of Shadows

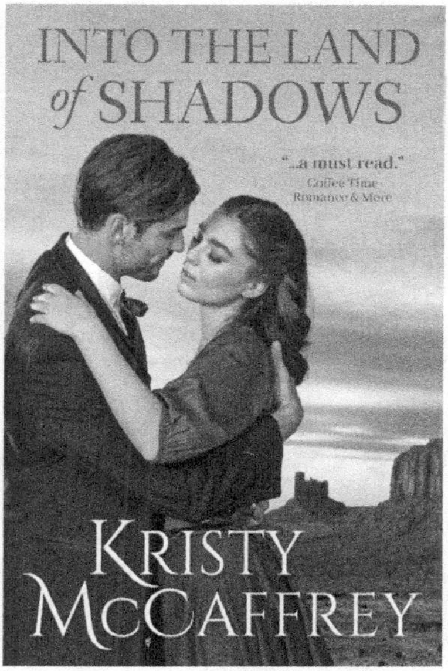

A Stand-Alone Novel

This book was previously published in 2013 under the same title. While the text and cover have been updated, the story remains the same.

It's been five years since a woman came between Ethan Barstow and his brother, Charley, and it's high time they buried the hatchet. When Ethan travels to Arizona Territory to make amends, he learns that Charley has abruptly disappeared after breaking more than one heart in town. And an indignant fiancée is hot on his trail.

When Charley Barstow abandons a local girl after getting her pregnant, Kate Kinsella pursues him without a second thought.

She's determined he set things right, and even more determined to end her own engagement to him, a sham from the beginning. But an ill-timed encounter with a group of ruffians lands her in the company of Charley's brother, Ethan, who suggests they search together.

As Ethan and Kate move deeper INTO THE LAND OF SHADOWS, family tensions and past tragedies threaten to destroy a love neither of them expected.

kmccaffrey.com/into-the-land-of-shadows/

Don't miss this collection of short stories filled with chills and romance.

It's Hallowtide in the Old West. Join three bounty hunters fighting dark magic and the women destined to love them.

The Crow and The Coyote
Among the red-rock canyons of the Navajo, bounty hunter Jack Boggs—known as The Crow—aids Hannah Dobbin in a quest to save her pa's soul during Hallowtide.

The Crow and The Bear
When no one will help Jennie Livingstone enter a haunted ravine to find her papa, she must accept the aid of enigmatic bounty hunter Callum Boggs, sometimes called The Crow.

A Murder of Crows

Eliza McCulloch is determined to reclaim her family book of spells and her only hope is Kester Boggs, a manhunter named The Crow.

These stories were previously published separately.

"A suspenseful ride into the supernatural with a western twist." ~ Devon McKay, author of *Lead Me Into Temptation*, Gold Dust Bride Series

"With just the right amount of mystic and adventure..." ~ Michelle Reed, Sunshine Lake Reviews

kmccaffrey.com/the-crow-and-the-coyote/

ABOUT THE AUTHOR

Kristy McCaffrey has been writing since she was very young, but it wasn't until she was a stay-at-home mom that she considered becoming published. A fascination with science led her to earn two mechanical engineering degrees—she did her undergraduate work at Arizona State University and her graduate studies at the University of Pittsburgh—but storytelling has always been her passion. She writes both contemporary tales and award-winning historical western romances.

An Arizona native, Kristy and her husband reside in the desert where they frequently remove (rescue) rattlesnakes from their property, go for runs among the cactus, and plan trips to far-off places like the Orkney Islands or Machu Picchu. But mostly, she works 12-hour days and enjoys at-home date nights with her sweetheart, which usually include Will Ferrell movies and sci-fi flicks. Her four children have flown the nest, so she lavishes her maternal instincts on Jeb, an American bulldog her family adopted in 2021. She recently lost her beloved chocolate Labrador, Lily, after 15 years.

Connect with Kristy

Website: kmccaffrey.com
Newsletter: kmccaffrey.com/subscribe/
Facebook: facebook.com/AuthorKristyMcCaffrey
Instagram: instagram.com/kristymccaffreybooks/
BookBub: bookbub.com/authors/kristy-mccaffrey
TikTok: tiktok.com/@kristymccaffrey

Made in the USA
Las Vegas, NV
20 July 2026

51335473R00177